**Her gaze was making him distinctly uneasy. Somehow, it was as though she had the upper hand.**

The only way to win back control was to return to his sarcastically amused self. "So. Now that's been decided. Join me for tea in a few moments in the library."

"No thank you, Mr. Holmes. I know my place. I shall retire to my room and ring for tea when I am ready for it." She gave another brief curtsy that signaled—more clearly than speech—that he was being summarily dismissed.

Should he press on? Make her come down to tea? After all, he had wanted to speak with her about Juliet's upbringing. He glanced at the set of her jaw and the fire in her eyes. No. Better to leave while he still had some modicum of authority.

He'd give her time to cool off, and then they would speak sensibly. Becky Siddons was supposed to solve his problems and make life easier for him. But already she was causing more trouble than he'd eve

**Books by Lily George**

Love Inspired Historical

*Captain of Her Heart*
*The Temporary Betrothal*
*Healing the Soldier's Heart*
*A Rumored Engagement*
*The Nanny Arrangement*

## *LILY GEORGE*

Growing up in a small town in Texas, Lily George spent her summers devouring the books in her mother's Christian bookstore. She still counts Grace Livingston Hill, Janette Oke and L. M. Montgomery among her favorite authors. Lily has a B.A. in history from Southwestern University and uses her training as a historian to research her historical inspirational romance novels. She has published one nonfiction book and produced one documentary, and is in production on a second film; all of these projects reflect her love for old movies and jazz and blues music. Lily lives in the Dallas area with her husband, daughter and menagerie of animals.

# The Nanny Arrangement

## LILY GEORGE

**HARLEQUIN**® LOVE INSPIRED® HISTORICAL

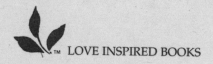 LOVE INSPIRED BOOKS

Recycling programs for this product may not exist in your area.

ISBN-13: 978-0-373-28285-2

THE NANNY ARRANGEMENT

Copyright © 2014 by Sarah Baker

www.Harlequin.com

**Printed in U.S.A.**

I am the vine, you are the branches.
He who abides in Me, and I in him,
bears much fruit; for without Me you can do nothing.
— *John* 15:5

For Olivia and Taylor,
whose two-year-old antics inspired Juliet.

For Maddie and every child battling cancer.
#fightformaddie

# Chapter One

*Tansley Village, Derbyshire*
*Spring 1811*

The letter from the penny post gave a nervous crackle as Rebecca Siddons, commonly known to family and villagers alike as Becky, withdrew it from the willow basket she used for her weekly marketing. Her heart thumped solidly against her rib cage as she glanced over the fine, meticulous handwriting on the envelope. Yes, it was from Lieutenant Walker. She hadn't heard from him in ever so long. One would expect a letter sooner from a young man who was, hopefully, soon to be one's fiancé.

She'd lain awake night after night since the lieutenant's regiment left the village, praying for his safety. And when no word came—well, it was difficult indeed not to imagine the worst. But at long last, he'd sent a painfully thin missive. Perhaps his duties at his new post kept him too busy to compose any letter of great length.

Becky turned off the well-beaten path along the storefronts of the tiny village and struck out into the open. One couldn't read a letter like this in the confines of the prim and proper millinery shop she kept with her younger sister, Nan. She certainly couldn't bear to dawdle along, snatching glimpses of her letter while making polite conversation with passersby.

No. For this letter, she craved the wild freedom of the moor.

Becky dashed across the meadow, the long grass catching at her skirts as she ran, her bonnet wrenching free of its hold and dangling down her back like a useless sack. Her long mahogany curls tossed breezily in the wind. Yes. One could breathe up here. One could dream romantic, impossible dreams without being dragged down to earth by a practical little sister or a bossy older one.

She flung her basket aside and with shaky fingers broke the seal of the letter. Would he ask her to join him in Liverpool? Had he finally kept the unspoken promise between them? At last she would be wed to a dashing military hero, have a home of her own, to be a mistress of that house…everything her elder sister Susannah had, and which Becky secretly envied.

*My dear Miss Siddons—*

Rather formal, but perhaps he had fears of their secret romance becoming too quickly public?

*I must tell you that I have met and married the sweetest girl here in Liverpool. I know you will rejoice in our happiness, as kind and generous as you are. Her name is Rachel—*

A faint buzzing sounded in her ears. Becky gave a quick, decisive shake of her head. Either her eyes were playing tricks on her, or this was some sort of cruel joke. Surely Lieutenant Walker felt about her as she felt about him. With an achy heart, she grasped one of her curls and wound it about her finger, a gesture that brought comfort to her since childhood. The smiles they'd shared, the lingering glances, the brief touch on her arm as he bade her goodbye...

She opened her eyes wide and forced herself to read each word deliberately and slowly, until she reached the end of the letter. This Rachel was her lieutenant's new bride. When she, Becky, had been so certain that she would, in a matter of months, bear that title.

The weight of dawning realization pushed down her shoulders, forcing her to her knees in the grass. The letter fluttered away and caught on a twig. Hot tears pooled in Becky's eyes and she pursed her trembling lips. No wedding was hers, with redolent orange blossoms. No home of her own waited patiently for its mistress. She must continue to toil away in her millinery shop with Nan and her blunt, practical ways, her constant criticisms and complaints draining the very artistry from Becky's days. She was both a spinster and a fool.

Becky dropped her head in her hands and allowed the tears to fall, deep, wrenching sobs that convulsed her as she knelt in the rough, scrubby stalks. Her heart thumped in her chest, the sound growing louder as she continued to weep.

She must inhale. Otherwise, she might faint. She

took a hitching, jolting breath. Her heart was pounding heavily.

No. She raised her head, forcing her streaming eyes open.

No—not her heart. Hoof beats.

"Ho there!" the rider called in a deep bass voice, reining in sharply. His mount, a magnificent sorrel, made a jagged turn to the right, showering Becky with stinging little blades of grass as he skidded to a halt. Becky froze, her sobs quelled as she watched the precision and control with which the rider managed his horse. He dismounted in one easy, fluid movement and tossed the reins over the saddle.

"Really, miss," he scolded. "What on earth are you playing at, hiding out here in the moor? I could have run you over." He strolled over, tucking his riding crop under one arm, and removed his hat.

As he looked down, Becky gave an inward groan. How perfectly perfect, as her sister would say. Here she was sobbing out here on the moor over her lost dreams and hopes, and along came Paul Holmes, her brother-in-law's teasing and jesting friend.

"Becky—what on earth? Are you quite all right?" He held out his hand and she took it, allowing him to pull her up from her hovel in the grass. "Whatever has happened?"

"I—uh." She couldn't brazen this one out. She must look a sight. Her nose must be swollen, her eyes must be the color of a tomato, and tear tracks must certainly have trailed down her cheeks. And yet, one couldn't let Paul in on the most private, secret dashed hopes of her girlhood. Paul was so intimidating, really. He was handsome, with dark brown eyes and sandy, wavy hair that always looked rather tousled. And he was wealthy. But what made him most nerve-racking was his teasing manner, coupled with his high-handed attitude. If she spoke the truth, he'd laugh. Or lecture. And she didn't particularly relish hearing either right now. "I received a letter with some distressing news."

"I am sorry to hear it." He fumbled in his jacket pocket and withdrew a fine linen handkerchief. "Here, blow your nose. There's a good gal." He held the crisp linen square to her nose as if she were a mere five years old.

"I can handle it by myself, thank you," she responded in her haughtiest tone, and took the handkerchief with as much dignity as she could muster. After being jilted by one man, she was having a difficult time being civil to another, especially one who treated her as a child.

She gave her nose a hearty blow—not a romantic sound, but then who could think of romance now? She flicked a glance over at Paul. His sandy hair blew untidily in the wind, and his brown eyes held a distinct gleam of mockery. He was tall and powerfully built, but for all the handsome figure he cut, one couldn't get past the feeling that he was laughing at everything in general and her predicament in particular. She must compose herself before going back to the millinery shop, and how could she do it now, with Paul standing like a comical sentry before her?

"I really should be going back," she managed, folding the handkerchief into a dainty square. "Thank you for the use of this. I shall launder it and return it to you."

"No need, no need." He brushed aside his handkerchief the way some men might brush aside a scrap of paper. And it was fine Irish linen, too, quite dear. The kind of material they sometimes received in their shop for the use of the gentry. "And I wouldn't dream of you going back by yourself. Not in this condition. I could never look Susannah or Daniel in the eyes again if I left you weeping all alone on this dreadful moor."

"My sister and brother-in-law don't have to know about this." The words tumbled out before she could check them. No, indeed. No one need ever find out if only Paul could leave well enough alone. "I was crying over a private matter, and now I feel better."

"But you look miserable." Paul strolled over to his horse and gathered the reins.

"Thank you." She could not check the sarcastic tone. What was coming over her? Usually Susannah was the sharp one and Nan the biting one. She'd hardly ever uttered an acerbic comment in her life.

Her tone must have shocked Paul, for his grin faded and he cocked one eyebrow at her. "I didn't mean that in an insulting way. I just mean that, whatever your news was, it must have been quite shocking. I've never seen you behave in such a manner." He led his horse over to her, pausing to scoop up her basket and the letter still tangled against a twig. "Here. Jump up. I'll lead you. I am sure you'll feel better once you go home and see Nan, and start work on a new bonnet."

"You sound like Susannah. Work is not my panacea.

And Nan is so…difficult." She folded her arms across her chest. "I'd like to stay here a bit longer." She couldn't face the prosaic reality of her life once more. She had to stay out in the moor just a few moments more and lick her wounds in private. If only he would just go away and leave her in peace.

"Nan has always been trying, hasn't she?" Paul leaned against his mount, fixing her with his mildly amused gaze. "What makes her company so unendurable today?"

"Because…" Becky paused. How much should she say? She couldn't tell Paul that her marriage prospects were now completely obliterated and she'd be living under her little sister's thumb for all eternity. "Susannah was the heart behind our business. And now she is married and committed to managing Goodwin Hall. Nan is the brains behind the business." She couldn't tell him the whole truth. 'Twould sound too selfish and childish to admit that she was stuck in the middle, not allowed to make any business decisions, her designs often hampered because they were too expensive or too fancy or too delicate for rural wear. She wasn't consulted as an artist, and her opinion was often simply passed over.

"And as for you…you've no real place." He nodded. How funny. 'Twas as though he understood her thoughts precisely and yet didn't think her quite a ninny for feeling them. "Have you ever thought about something else? Do you have to work in the shop, Becky?"

"I thought my circumstances might soon change, but they won't, so I might as well face facts." She looked at him squarely, though it was terribly difficult to do so. It wasn't that she was afraid of Paul—he wasn't a scary sort of person. He just made her nervous with his joking ways.

His expression shifted, and the vague sympathetic moment they'd shared vanished like ice melting in the sun. "I think the reason you're out here sobbing is in this letter I found." He cast a crooked grin her way and tapped Lieutenant Walker's letter against his chin with a mockingly thoughtful gesture. "Shall I read it and find out?"

That was a mistake. Paul had pushed the teasing too far, just as he had with his own younger sisters. Becky's fine, dark brows drew together as she made an impetuous grasp for the letter.

"Give it back to me," she pleaded, her violet-blue eyes sparkling with fresh, unshed tears. "You have no right to take my private property." She extended her small, trembling hand out, palm up.

He swallowed, giving himself an inward kick. Here he was, making matters worse when she had finally begun to calm down. He pressed the epistle back into her hand, taking a quick glance down as his did so. Bold, decisive script—definitely the handwriting of a man. Likely she had been jilted in some form or fashion by some ridiculous blackguard. And that was the reason she was out here crying—she'd lost her chance that marriage would end her servitude at the shop.

"You're right, I don't." He shrugged and handed her back the basket she'd dropped. "Forgive me. It's the privilege of being the eldest brother, you see. I always teased my younger siblings in a merciless fashion."

"I'd love to have a fraction of your license," Becky admitted, the ghost of a smile hovering around her pretty lips.

She looked a little like his younger sister Juliana, though Becky's features were softer, more feminine. Juliana, too, had had her heart broken by an undeserving male.

"I had no idea you had so many brothers and sisters to lord over."

"Oh yes, Juliana is close to your age." *Or was.* One short week was hardly enough time to adjust to the fact that his beautiful young sister was—but no. This wasn't the time or place for such thoughts. He stifled a cough and continued with a happier memory. "But she always got her revenge. Once, Juliana put pepper in my snuffbox. You can only imagine how long it took me to recover."

Becky laughed, a dimple touching her left cheek as she smiled. "Jolly good for her." Then her laughter ceased, and the dark shadow fell over her face once more. The change was disappointing, for Becky was a pretty little thing. With her dimpled cheek and that dark waterfall of hair, she could certainly become a diamond of the first water, had her family been able to give her a season. Funny, he'd always thought of her as just the middle daughter of an extraordinary family... but she was coming into her own now. Not that it mattered to him, of course.

"I don't suppose I've convinced you to return to the

shop, then?" He gave the reins a tug, and Ciro stopped munching the moor-grass. He had business to attend to, and couldn't spare any more time talking to a girl, appealing though she might be.

Becky shook her head, the wind ruffling her curls. "No, thank you."

"Well, if you insist on staying out here, then I must ask you to at least stand upright." He swung into the saddle and settled in comfortably. "I could have run over you, buried as you were in the grass."

Becky's delicate features hardened and she turned her head aside. "I promise I won't do anything as silly as allow myself to be run over. You might be more careful yourself, you know."

He suppressed a grin at her haughty tone. She certainly hated being told what to do. No small wonder, being squeezed in between two termagants like Susannah and Nan. Just to be perverse, he leaned down over his saddle and fixed her with his best "lord of the manor" gaze. "If you aren't home by sundown, I shall tell Daniel and Susannah that you were wandering the moor like some lovesick heroine in a Romantic poem."

She turned, lifting her chin and fixing him with a glare that could have withered the moor-grass. "When I come home is entirely my own affair, Mr. Holmes. Your friendship with my family does not extend to playing the role of my keeper." Apparently he offended her so greatly that she chose to abandon her earlier plan of remaining on the moor. She tucked the willow basket and her letter under her arm and strolled off, her bonnet bobbing against the middle of her back as she wound her way back to the village.

He chuckled ruefully. Whatever had that lad who jilted Becky been thinking? The fellow couldn't be in his right mind. Paul gave Ciro his head and the beast responded with astonishing speed, carrying him over the moor and back toward home with grace and agility. He never really had to think when he was riding Ciro. The horse had such an uncanny sense of timing and pace. It gave a fellow time to think.

But what was there to think about? Becky Siddons wasn't the only one to receive a horrible letter lately. He, too, had received a terrible missive only a week ago, from Italy. Juliana was dead of a fever. She had died alone. The blighter who carried her away from her family and from England was dead, too, of the same fever. But a few years before they both died, Juliana had borne a child. A child who was now his responsibility.

Juliana was dead. He said the words in his mind but they made no sense. Juliana had a child. Her name was Juliet. And she was his ward. He crammed the rising grief and panic back down his throat and shut the door against his own anguish. 'Twould be one thing if a fellow believed in God or Heaven. There might be some comfort in thinking about Juliana then, if he could believe she was in a better place. But while he wasn't precisely an atheist, he'd taken no comfort from religion since Ruth Barclay, his fiancée, had passed away. After she died, the cold trickle of doubt had entered his soul.

So there it was. It was never good to dwell on pain. In fact, a fellow shouldn't even feel any kind of sorrow.

He must remain in control, master of all situations. He was the head of his family now. This was his duty. He must attend to anything that required his attention, and later he might have his reward—perhaps a trip to London would be in order. Duty first, then pleasure.

He turned his mind back to the problem at hand. Juliana was dead, and her daughter would be at Kellridge Hall in a matter of days. He had no time or resources to care for a child. His niece was being attended to by a servant, but who knew what kind of servant Juliana had hired abroad? No, she must have a proper English nursemaid. No one at Kellridge could assume that role easily; each servant's duties were clearly delineated and none of them had time for children.

He could try to hire someone from the village, but that might incite gossip about Juliana and the circumstances of her daughter's birth and her own demise.

Ciro gathered speed and strength as he tore through the open gate; yes, he knew what he was about. Those gates meant the barn was nearby. Paul quirked the corner of his mouth. Ciro understood his motto, too. Duty first, then pleasure.

The situation warranted someone who had a proper upbringing, who would raise a girl in a suitable manner until she was of age to be sent to school. Someone who wouldn't gossip, who could be trusted to handle this with poise and tact.

Poise and tact. Just like any genteel young woman should possess.

A young woman like Rebecca Siddons.

Why not? She was aching to get away from the millinery shop. She could be Juliet's nursemaid and later her governess. Their families were so close; Becky could be trusted not to gossip. And even if she had no experience with children of her own, raising a baby just came naturally to women. It was instinct, pure and simple. She was a romantic, dreamy little thing, but surely she would take to raising a baby as a duck took to water.

That was the answer. He would call upon her tomorrow and ask her.

## Chapter Two

"Oh, Becky, whatever have you done with the bonnet Mrs. Parker ordered?" Nan poked her head into the sitting room where Becky made use of the early morning sunlight streaming through the window. Such fine stitches needed a lot of good light, and this room was best lit at dawn. "I thought I told you—we cannot afford to use that fine muslin for the brim. We cannot turn a profit if you keep using such expensive materials. Why didn't you use the cotton I ordered from town?"

Heated words bubbled to Becky's lips and her fingers trembled as she laid another fine stitch in the fabric. She took a deep, calming breath. If she were to do this for the rest of her life, she must maintain control of her temper. "The cotton is too rough and slubby for a dress bonnet," she argued. "I only used a small bit of the muslin, and with the ruching I added, I conserved quite a bit of fabric." There, she showed that she had given cost some thought. That cotton was just so terribly ugly. Why Nan ever bought it was a mystery.

"But I specifically told you to use the cotton, Becky." Nan strode into the sitting room and cast herself down on the settee. "Honestly, the profit we'll see on that bonnet is quite slim. The more money we earn on each sale, the more secure our finances. Surely you see that."

"I do understand," Becky replied in an even tone. "But the more alluring our bonnets, the more clients we should attract. If we use inferior materials, then we will lose the kind of genteel clientele that will spend a fortune on our creations season after season."

"Yes, but if our bonnets are affordable and well-made, we will garner loyalty from the villagers—the women who cannot afford something grand, perhaps, but may require a bonnet that is sturdy and hard-wearing. Those women are the bread and butter of our shop." Nan leaned forward, her mild blue eyes wide and cajoling. "Come, now. Susannah left the shop to our care when she married Daniel. Isn't it up to the pair of us to see to it that it becomes a successful venture?"

Well, when Nan put things that way…Becky was hard-pressed indeed to think of a retort. To buy some time, she concentrated on another stitch, pursing her lips tightly together as she did so. Of course she didn't want to see the shop fail. But what was the harm in offering lovely bonnets as well as serviceable ones? "If we restrict ourselves to one kind of trade, surely we chance losing a portion of our customers," she admonished in as gentle a tone as she could manage. "After all, it was the commissions of three gentlewomen who gave us our start, if you will recall."

"I know." Nan leaped from her position on the settee

and began pacing, a nervous habit that wore on Becky's nerves. "But honestly, a simpler style of bonnet is more easily made, and I can train our other helpers to make them quickly. The finer stuff must be left to the two of us, and already we're stretched thin as it is. The profits we make are higher, and they sell more quickly. And the villagers pay more quickly than gentry. I really do feel most strongly that we should stop making fancy creations and concentrate on the plain and sensible."

Becky heaved a deep sigh. Plain and sensible. There was little room for imagination and artistry in the plain and sensible, particularly if Nan kept buying such dreadful fabric. She would be chained, for the rest of her life, to stretching scratchy cotton across buckram frames. A vista of ugly, cheap bonnets unfolded before her, and her heart gave a lurch of revolt. True, she was stuck. A spinster forevermore with no hope of marriage to Lieutenant Walker. But did that mean she needed to relinquish any sense of beauty in her life?

"I'm going to see Susannah," she declared, casting the bonnet to one side and rising from her chair. "She founded the shop. I'll put my case to her."

"I shall go too," Nan rejoined. "After all, I have been seeing to it that the shop is a gainful venture since I took over."

"Since *you* took over?" Anger surged into Becky's being, leaving her trembling in its wake. "The shop was given to both of us when Susannah married. We are equal partners, Nan."

"We would be, if you had a practical bone in your body! But honestly, how are we to make any money at all if you squander our resources? It's been up to me to make sure that the shop stays profitable."

"If you say that word once more, I shall scream." Becky took her own bonnet from the peg near the front door and clamped it on her head, rebellion singing through her veins. "Since the store is so beholden to you, you can stay here to manage it while I talk to our sister."

She flounced out of the shop and slammed the door shut behind her. Whatever had taken hold of her? Even if she wasn't the practical one in the family, she had always gotten along well enough with her sisters. Why was she letting Nan needle her so? And why was she getting angry over each little thing?

"Because they're not little things any longer." She spoke the words aloud as she scuffed the grass with the toe of her boot. For once, the distance to Goodwin Hall was worthwhile. She needed time to compose her thoughts. If she couldn't put her argument to Susannah sensibly, then her elder sister would simply say that her emotions were running too high. That would discredit her argument before she'd even begun.

"If I can't have beauty and purpose in my life, Lord, everything seems hopeless." The moor didn't care if she prayed aloud. Saying the words was strangely calming. If she couldn't be married and have a home of her own, she would have to find fulfillment in work. If the methods of her work were being proscribed, well, then it felt as though the walls were closing in on her.

She continued to mull over those thoughts, and breathed lungful after lungful of fresh air. Already the blond stone walls of Goodwin Hall loomed on the horizon. Goodwin meant Susannah, and Susannah meant wise counsel.

Yes, Susannah would surely see her side of the matter. Why had she taken this long to see her sister? She'd pinned all her hopes on a proposal from Lieutenant Walker, that's why. No need to raise a fuss when she had been so certain that she would marry and leave the shop. Well, that wasn't happening, and she needed to make the best of her situation. The blank horror of the lieutenant's desertion still held her in its grasp.

In time she would grieve over her dead romance. Now she must think of her future. If she wasn't to be anyone's bride, she should at least be allowed a say in her own business.

She gathered her skirts and mounted the wide, gracious steps of the hall. No sooner had she set foot on the second step than the door opened, and Baxter stood, waiting with a patient and solemn air.

"Miss Rebecca. No one told me you were coming." The butler, no doubt accustomed now to the clockwork precision Susannah had imposed on the manor house, frowned. "But you are welcome all the same. Mrs. Hale is in the library."

"Don't fret, Baxter," she reassured him as she strolled into the vestibule. "This is an impromptu call." She removed her bonnet, intending to hang it on a peg; but with consummate skill, Baxter slipped it out of her grasp and placed it on the nearby mahogany table.

"Yes, Miss Rebecca. Mr. Holmes is visiting as well. They are having tea. I'll bring another setting for you."

With a wave of his hand, Baxter shooed her down the hallway toward the library.

Paul Holmes? Becky slowed to a halt before the library door. If Paul was here, had he told them about meeting her on the moor yesterday? How was she supposed to speak with Susannah about the shop if they had company? Oh, this was just like her, to meet him here again. She grasped a tendril of hair that slipped loose from her chignon and twirled it.

Where was the courage that stiffened her spine yesterday? She'd had no qualms about defending herself to Paul then. Circumstances were different, though. Confronting Paul, Susannah and Daniel all at once was, well, akin to bearding a lion in its den.

Becky took a deep, steadying breath and deftly unwound her finger from her hair. Then she pushed open the door.

Daniel and Paul rose as she entered the room, and Susannah turned in her chair. "Becky, my dear, we weren't expecting you. Not that you aren't welcome, of course." Susannah kissed her cheek as Becky leaned down, and then Susannah glanced over her shoulder. "Where's Nan?"

"At the shop." Becky settled across from her sister, nodding her hellos to Daniel and Paul. Paul caught her glance and held it so long that heat began rising in her cheeks. She averted her gaze and turned a fraction to the right in her chair so he could only see her in profile. There. It was altogether uncomfortable to be stared at. He needn't be so fresh.

Susannah glanced over at Becky, her gray-green eyes

keen and perceptive. "Whatever is the matter?" Then she turned to Daniel. "Would you ring the bell? I'll have Baxter bring more tea things so Becky may join us."

"Baxter already said he would." If only she could somehow, wordlessly communicate the need for privacy with Susannah. She lifted her eyebrows and widened her eyes, silently pleading for Susannah to understand.

"Something is wrong. Out with it," Susannah commanded in that familiar, eldest sister tone of voice. The morning sunlight gilded her auburn hair, touching it with gold. "Have you two been quarreling again? Honestly," she turned to her husband, "sometimes I think I should have kept the shop. But Becky and Nan got on so well when we were all together. Now that I am not there, they fight. If I weren't so busy with Goodwin…"

How provoking to be talked about like she was just a child, squabbling with Nan over a toy. "She has no artistic spirit at all, Susannah," Becky burst out. "All she cares about is how much money we can make. She runs roughshod over my designs, and insists I work with inferior materials."

Susannah shook her head. "Becky, do calm yourself. Remember, you can always count ten."

Becky rolled her eyes. Count ten indeed. That was Susannah's remedy for her truly awe-inspiring temper.

"You two must learn to work together. What Nan proposes is sound. We cannot expect only genteel clientele. Now that we are thoroughly entrenched in Tansley Village, we must include the kinds of goods that everyone can afford." Susannah spoke as though she were reasoning with a toddler.

Becky opened her mouth to protest, but Daniel cut her short, a reassuring smile hovering around his lips. "Shall we give you two some privacy?"

"Actually, I have a solution I think could benefit us all." Paul's voice, rumbling from his corner, jerked Becky to attention. "If it's amenable to the lady, I'd like to hire Becky."

Three pairs of eyes turned toward Paul—Susannah's startled gray-green gaze, Daniel's bemused green eyes, and a pair of violet-blue, decidedly defiant ones that belonged to Becky. Well, at least he had her attention, even if she did seem a little affronted by his presence.

"I haven't told anyone this, but my youngest sister, Juliana, passed away." As he spoke, Becky's mouth opened slightly, and the rebellious light in her eyes dimmed. He glanced away. Susannah made a murmur of apology, but he cut her short with a wave of his hand. If anyone showed him sympathy now, he might break down and that would not be acceptable. Better to stick to the facts of the matter at hand. "She died of a fever in Italy, where she had been living for some time. She left behind a daughter who is now my ward."

"I am sorry to hear that Juliana died, old fellow." Daniel shook his head and sighed. "I know she was your favorite sister."

"Yes, well. She's gone." His tone was brusque, even to his own ears, and he covered the moment by clearing his throat. "The point of the matter is that her daughter, Juliet, is coming to live with me. She's only about two years old. I've no idea if Juliana employed anyone suitable for her care—" lovable, impractical Juliana; how ridiculous to think of her employing servants, much less caring for a child! "—and at any rate, I want a proper English girl to bring her up. At least until I can place her in school." He clenched his jaw, wrestling back any traces of grief. "Becky, I would like it if you cared for Juliet until she is of age."

"But Becky has no experience as a governess." Susannah's brows drew together. "She also has her duties at the shop to consider. Surely there is someone among your tenants or ours that could do? At least until a nursemaid can be hired from London?"

Paul raised his head and fixed Becky with a searching look. If she didn't appear interested, then he would have no choice but to agree with Susannah. But Becky sat back in her chair, twirling a lock of her brown hair around one finger, an absorbed expression drifting across her features. "I've thought of that, too," he admitted. "But the circumstances of Juliet's birth, and of Juliana's stay in Italy, might be cause for gossip among people who don't know my family well. I can't raise my niece under a cloud of disgrace. I feel I can trust your family with decorum. Moreover, Becky bears a passing resemblance to my sister. That could make the adjustment easier for Juliet."

"The child's comfort and welfare must be considered above all else," Daniel agreed. "If you feel that Becky is the right person for the job, then it remains only to see how the shop can fare without her there, and whether or not she feels equal to the task."

Paul shifted his regard back over to her, and Becky

raised her eyes to his. There was no defiance, no rebellion, no anger or annoyance in her gaze any longer.

"I feel equal to the task." Though the words were spoken quietly, there was strength to her tone that was intensely heartening. "In truth, I am glad of the opportunity."

"But Becky, what of your duties at the shop? Of course, I am gratified for Paul's trust in our family—" Susannah gave him a brisk nod "—but you cannot care for a child and continue to work as a milliner. The shop was our dream, don't you remember? You can't simply give up on it and allow your sister to carry the weight alone."

"The shop was your dream, not mine." While Becky didn't mince words, her tone remained gentle and strong. "When we worked together, it was fun. I love designing bonnets, Susannah. And I love all the handiwork that goes with it. But since you left, it's not enjoyable any longer. Nan and I argue all the time. I feel stifled now, as though I don't have a say in anything that happens."

Susannah sat back against her chair, flinging her hands in the air. "You two never argued before. I was envious of your closeness, in fact, before I wed Daniel. And now?" She shook her head as though exasperated by her sister.

"Before you left the shop, you hired Bets and Rose. They help Nan with much of the work. Most of my designs are discarded or greatly altered before Nan will allow them onto the shop floor. I don't do much for the business any longer, Susannah. It's ruining my friendship with Nan. You're right—we used to get on much better than we do now. We fight. I want the chance to stay close to her, even if we don't agree." Becky turned to Paul. "When will Juliet arrive?"

Paul shrugged. "I was informed of Juliana's death only recently. Daniel, you recall my younger brother, George, the sea captain? He made arrangements so that my niece could travel to England in one of our yachts. So I expect she should arrive within a week. I am sending a servant to meet the boat." That would be the best way to handle it. No personal connection that way. Nothing to upset or disturb his routine. Perhaps he could even arrange to be away when she arrived. That way, he wouldn't be reminded of Juliana or her lonely death.

"No, indeed. We shall travel there together. Poor child, she will be so frightened and confused—" Becky broke off as a discreet knock sounded on the door, and Baxter entered with another setting for tea. "Thank you, Baxter. I am famished."

The butler gave a courtly nod and excused himself. Paul allowed Becky's comment to fade. He was her employer and he would decide when and even if they were going to meet Juliet's boat or not. But he still needed to win Becky fully to his side. The time for setting out the rules would be later.

Susannah turned to Daniel. "She's already made up her mind, and I appear to have no say in this. Consider my throne well and truly abdicated."

Daniel threw back his head and laughed. "I don't know that it's such a bad idea. What Becky says is true.

The shop seems to be harming her relationship with Nan. Why not allow her to try something new? As long as the shop is well staffed and Nan isn't too burdened. Paul needs someone whom he can trust to be discreet. This opportunity could work out for the best for everyone involved."

Susannah sighed and shook her head, turning to Paul. "My only wish is that we do all this on a trial basis. Becky has no experience with raising children. If she doesn't like the job or doesn't perform well with it, I think we should ask you to find a replacement. Does that meet with everyone's approval?"

"I am sure Becky will do fine. Like all females, I am sure she has a mother's instinct," Paul rejoined in a hearty tone of voice—one that, hopefully, masked his relief. He'd not given much thought to how difficult it would be to talk of Juliana's death aloud. "But if she's not happy within three months, I'll make inquiries of an agency in London." He took a deep breath and steeled himself for the most difficult part of their discussion. "There must be some living arrangements, too. Juliet is so young—she will need care at all times of the day and night. I can either make arrangements for Becky to live in the east wing of Kellridge or I will need to provide her with a horse and carriage so that she can be reached at any time."

The color in Becky's cheeks rose and she gave her sister an uncertain glance as she sipped her tea. "I hadn't thought of that. Juliet will need to have someone about at all times."

Susannah straightened her posture and fixed Paul

with a pointed gaze. Susannah's expression could be truly formidable at times. "Paul has said he trusts our family. Therefore, I must return that trust in equal measure. If Paul can make the east wing your living quarters, and control any gossip so that no one will think anything untoward about your presence there, then I will agree. Provided you are comfortable with the arrangement."

Paul's heart began to beat hard against his rib cage. If only Becky would agree to the plan. He wouldn't have to see Juliet at all, then. He could trust she was being well cared for, and he could make plans to be away from home as much as possible. He'd have little contact with the child. Then he would not have to suffer any painful reminders that Juliana was gone.

"I have to agree with my wife," Daniel rumbled from his chair. "As long as everything is quite honorably handled, I would consent to Becky becoming a live-in nursemaid. I know it will, for you've already said you don't want to incite gossip."

Paul nodded. According to plan, this new development in his life would be handled to a nicety. The east wing would become Juliet's nursery, and Becky would be there to care for her at all times. There you go. Every emotion, every detail, neatly tucked into its own compartment. He would never have to feel pain or anguish. He could continue living his life as he enjoyed, knowing that he upheld his duty in caring for Juliet. "Everything will be taken care of. As long as Becky accepts the position and these arrangements. At least for three months, so that we may see how it fares." He turned to Becky, fixing her with the same look of authority he wielded with his servants. "Well, Becky? Will you be Juliet's nursemaid?"

Becky drew herself up with a prideful gesture and placed her teacup to one side. Then she gave a regal nod. "I will."

# Chapter Three

"I still don't see why you have to move away." Nan's voice verged on the quarrelsome. "After all, Kellridge is only a quarter of an hour from here. Why can't you just stay there during the day?"

Becky folded another gown and tucked it into her valise with a deft hand. Now that the process of moving to Kellridge had begun, it was all rather exhilarating. In fact, she was hard-pressed to remain steady and calm when the desire to give in to giddiness was so great. "But Juliet is still quite young. I need to be with her at all times, even when she awakens at night."

"That's quite enough of being pettish, Nan." Susannah glanced up from the small pile of nightgowns she was folding. "We've already had this discussion. This arrangement is beneficial to all parties. I won't have my sisters fighting. We shan't become estranged from one another. We've been through too much. If this will salvage your relationship, then 'tis well worth it." She frowned and smoothed the bodice of one nightgown before handing it to Becky. "I can't believe you two have argued this much. 'Tis troubling indeed."

"But—" Nan caught Becky's gaze and her blue eyes filled with tears "—I'll miss you."

Becky's heart lurched in her chest. With one impulsive gesture, she gathered her little sister into her arms. Nan might be practical and efficient to a fault, but she would always be so dear. She patted Nan's back with a soothing gesture. "Don't cry. This is a good thing, I promise. You'll have room to grow the shop as you wish. I can try to find work that suits me better. I want to be there for Juliet. She has so little in this world. I won't be far, and I shall visit you often. I promise."

Nan circled her arms around Becky's waist and they stood, embracing, for a moment. How long had it been since she felt this close to Nan? Months, at least. Well before Susannah's marriage. They had been such chums back then. When Susannah left, the steadying influence had drifted out of their daily lives and they'd squabbled over so many things, both big and small. Distance really was the best way to mend the fences between them.

Lieutenant Walker's marriage still stung her deeply. In fact, it rather left her breathless to think how quickly he'd forgotten about her. The only way to overcome the humiliation was to prove herself worthy and useful to someone, even if she wasn't a bride.

"That's enough, you two." Susannah's gentle yet commanding voice broke into Becky's thoughts. "Nan, go downstairs and brew some tea. I want to talk to Becky alone for a moment."

Nan wiped her eyes with the corner of her apron and,

giving Becky a watery smile, quit the room. Funny, Nan would never take orders from Becky that way. Only Susannah could boss them both around in that manner. Becky turned to face her sister, steeling herself for the lecture on deportment and decorum that was sure to come. Susannah was so particular about manners.

"When I was packing your vanity table, I came across this." Susannah held up Lieutenant Walker's letter. Becky gulped. Now the depths of her humiliation would be known.

Susannah sat on the bed, the mattress giving a mournful squeak as she did so. "What is the meaning of this? Why are you receiving letters from a man?"

Becky cast about for something—anything—intelligent to say. She should have packed the contents of her vanity table herself. Not that she had anything to hide—but still—trying to explain this was going to be an utterly mortifying experience. She shook her head, sending a silent plea that Susannah would drop the matter entirely.

"How did you meet him?" Susannah placed the envelope in Becky's lap.

Of course not.

"His regiment was quartered in Tansley. We met by chance at the bakery one day." A beautiful, sunny day, when the world was full of promise…

"A soldier? How often did you meet him? Has he proposed? Does Nan know?" Susannah was losing her temper, and if she did, then nothing could be done. She must confess the awful truth of her humiliation.

"Not much happened." Funny. Looking back on it

now, their friendship seemed so thin and insubstantial. Yet, at the time, it had meant the world. "We met a few times out on the moor and went for walks. I am sure it was nothing more than a pleasant diversion for him, for he wrote to tell me he has been wed. I'm such a fool, Susannah. I was so certain he was going to propose to me. I thought we both felt such a spark." Her lips trembled violently and she pursed them for a moment to gather her wits. When it was safe to proceed, she continued. "I stayed with Nan and with the shop—even with things as bad as they had grown—because I was so sure I would soon be married. Then, when I received that letter, I found I just couldn't bear it anymore."

"Oh, Becky." Susannah took her hands in her own and squeezed them. "You were always such a romantic little thing."

"Well, I'm not any longer." She straightened her spine and willed herself to stop shuddering and simpering like a ninny. "When Paul offered me the chance to be Juliet's nursemaid, he opened my prison door. I can strike out on my own. I won't have to be under Nan's thumb anymore. I can learn to lead my own life."

"Don't give up being who you are. Your dreaminess and passionate views about life make you the Becky we know and love." Susannah gazed at her with eyes that had turned a stormy-gray. "When I needed to be released from caring about the shop and being mother to the two of you, you set me free. Do you remember that night?"

Becky nodded, smiling a little at the memory. "Yes. Nan slept through our whole conversation."

Susannah laughed. "Yes, she did. A placid soul, our Nan. But you gave me the freedom to love and to create a life of my own. So I now return the favor. Becky, if this is what you want, then go ahead. Don't worry about the shop or about Nan. All will be well."

"Thank you." She would give up on love and romance. They nipped too deeply into her soul. From now on, despite Susannah's well-meant warning, she would give them up and try to be useful. "I want to learn a trade. Now that I know I shan't marry, I will become a nursemaid and a governess. When Juliet no longer needs me, I can find a job in another house."

Susannah shook her head, her mouth quirking gently. "Don't let one man ruin your hopes and dreams. You may yet find love with someone else, you know. You're so young."

"No, indeed." Becky gave a defiant toss of her head. "I shall be an independent woman from now on." And she would, too. She must prove—if to no one but herself— that she was of some value in this world. She was done with passion, tenderness and romance. No more walks on the moor for her. No more windswept moments with her long curls streaming behind her. There must be a reason for all of this. Perhaps this was God's way of telling her that she needed a firmer foundation.

If that were so, then from now on, she would be as practical as…as…as that willow basket in the corner. She seized the letter, unfolded it, and tore it across three times.

Susannah watched her destruction of the missive,

disapproval written plain across her pretty face. "If that's what you wish."

Becky continued her massacre of the missive, tearing it into little bits, heaping the pieces into a pile on her lap. Each rip brought both pain and relief, like removing a bandage from a wound. "This is precisely what I want. I cannot wait to start my life anew."

Paul walked to the library window and flicked the curtains aside for the fifteenth time, peering out onto the lawn as rain streamed down from the sky. He'd sent the carriage for Becky over a quarter of an hour ago. Even with this spring shower causing a slight delay, she should be here by now. If only she'd hurry and get here, he could get her settled.

Then he could indulge in his baser habit, that of drink. He drank alone now that Daniel had disavowed liquor. Drinking helped dull the pain of an engagement that never came to fruition, of a marriage that never was, and of a partnership that was abruptly broken off, never to continue. And now, a drink would dull the pain of his failures as a brother, his complete inability to save Juliana from her willful, harmful path. But even when imbibing alone, he had a strict ritual. First, he must attend to business. Then, when his duties as master had been attended to, he could give himself some leeway.

This interminable waiting strained his nerves. If only he could be done and shut the door on this particular responsibility.

His brother, George, had helped arrange Juliet's safe passage home, and now that Juliet's itinerary was well planned, he needed to get Becky set up as governess. Then and only then, he could take himself off to London for a few months of self-indulgence.

At last his carriage flashed into view, tracing an undulating path over the sodden gravel and drawing to a halt before the front steps. Paul bounded out of the library and down the hall. His butler was wrenching the front door open when Paul hastened into the vestibule.

In fact, Wadsworth had already retrieved an umbrella and was preparing to shelter Miss Siddons with it. Perfect, just like clockwork. If he continued rushing about breathlessly, he'd seem ridiculously out of place in such a well-run household. He grabbed hold of his dignity and assumed the mask of cynical good humor that had served him so well for the past decade or so.

"Miss Siddons." He bowed as she scurried inside. "Where are your sisters? I had thought Susannah would be with you."

"No." She gave him a brisk smile and allowed Wadsworth to take her wrap. "I come on my own, as you see."

Interesting. Was this his first glimpse of Becky's independence? Yet, he couldn't make too much of it, not with his butler standing right there. "Wadsworth, see to it that the library is set for tea. I shall show Miss Siddons her quarters and then we will meet in the library to discuss my niece's schedule."

"Very good, sir." His butler gave a respectful bow and headed off for the kitchen.

"I thought your housekeeper would show me about," Becky interjected as he led her toward the stairs. "This seems rather unusual."

"Mrs. Clairbourne will of course meet you later, but I always show my new help over the house. I like things to be well under my control, and I find it is communicated more easily by myself, at least the first time." He looked down at her as they climbed the last step. Her brow was furrowed as though his words confused her. Bother. He had to explain it better, so he didn't sound such a tyrant. "You see, Kellridge has been under my care for at least six years. More, if you count the decisions I made when I was a lad. It runs with precision and timing. This is how I keep the pendulum swaying, if that makes sense."

She nodded. "Of course. I understand."

He motioned for her to follow him to the east wing. It really was a nice part of the house. Mrs. Clairbourne had done amazing things with it since Juliet's arrival was announced. The walls were painted a pretty shade of pale yellow, and the dour family portraits had been removed. Now a few gilded mirrors reflected their profiles as he took Becky to her new quarters.

"This is your room." He opened the door, freshly painted with a glossy coat of white. "You can see the connecting door there. That will lead you to Juliet's room."

"Oh, it's beautiful." Becky stepped into the room and looked about her, her hands clasped over her chest. What was different about her today? She seemed... tamer. Perhaps it was her hair. Instead of streaming down her back in bouncy curls, it was tucked up high on her head. Shame that pretty hair wasn't being shown in its full glory, but she did have a graceful neck all the same.

He abruptly switched off his thoughts. He might be a connoisseur of female beauty, but it was hardly appropriate to think of Becky as anything but his help in his time of need. In fact, he would leave her alone now, for if he continued to show her about the house, he might continue to dwell upon her loveliness, and that simply would not do.

"Well, I shall leave you to explore for a few moments. The bellpull is here—" he waved at a cord by the door "—and in the mornings, you can ring for your breakfast to be brought to your room. You can poke about in Juliet's room, too. If there's anything you require, make a list. I shall try to see to it before I go to London."

"When are you leaving for town?" Becky turned to him, her firmly compressed lips registering frank disapproval.

"In the next day or so." Surely she wasn't going to start that nonsense about meeting the boat again.

"Paul, I really do feel most strongly that you should stay. Juliet will be so confused and so frightened. You must let her know that she is welcome in your home and that you will take care of her." Becky removed her bonnet and her gloves, casting them onto her dressing table. "How far is the ship docking from Kellridge?"

"The ship should be arriving in Cleethorpes, a mere half day from here. Not that it matters." He was torn. Should he try to tease her out of this ridiculous notion? Or should he simply play his role as lord of the manor?

"I need to be in London, and so I shall go. You'll be on hand to welcome her. That should be enough."

"But Paul—you must want to see her. She's your niece, after all. As her uncle, surely you owe her something more. She is your responsibility."

Her words broke a dam within his soul. He could not let those feelings out. Feeling anything—rage, grief, pain—was a terrifying experience. He felt that dam burst once six years ago when Ruth had died. She was going to be his helpmeet. She was someone on whom he could depend. When she died, a black hole of despair had swallowed him, and he had cried. No more. Never again.

"While you are in my house and while you are in my employ, I must make a few things quite clear to you, Miss Siddons. Though I am a friend of your family, I am still in control. My word here at Kellridge is final." He cleared his throat. "I have great respect for my responsibilities, and I take care of them as a man should. I am doing what I can to make Juliet's life comfortable and pleasant. I don't need any reminders from you about what I should and should not do. Do I make myself quite clear?"

She took a step back, her delicate features hardening. "Perfectly clear, Mr. Holmes." She bobbed a brief curtsy. "As your newly employed governess, I feel it my responsibility to do what is best for Juliet's care. As such, with all the dreadful traveling the child has endured, only to arrive in a foreign land where she may not even know the language, I simply cannot allow her to arrive unwelcomed. Someone must be there to embrace her and assure her everything will be fine. There-fore," Becky folded her hands before her and gave him a frank stare, "I will require a carriage to take me to Cleethorpes on the appointed day of Juliet's arrival." Becky folded her hands before her and gave him a frank stare.

His sardonic humor began to creep back, triggered by her calmly defiant manner. "Is that an order, Miss Siddons?"

"It is a reasonable request, Mr. Holmes." Her voice had lost all its sweet charm, and her lovely eyes burned—with anger or with disappointment? No mat-ter. He had his plan all laid out, no matter what she said.

"When word arrives, I shall make sure that Wad-sworth knows you are to have a carriage at your dis-posal, and a servant to ride along." Her gaze was making him distinctly uneasy. Somehow, it was as though she had the upper hand. The only way to win back control was to return to his sarcastically amused self. "So. Now that's been decided. Join me for tea in a few moments in the library."

"I must refuse your invitation, Mr. Holmes. I shall retire to my room and ring for tea when I am ready for it." She gave another brief curtsy that signaled—more clearly than speech—that he was being summarily dis-missed.

Should he press on? Make her come down to tea? After all, he had wanted to speak with her about Ju-liet's upbringing. She was in his employ. He glanced at the set of her jaw and the fire in her eyes. No. Better to leave while he still had some modicum of authority.

He'd give her time to cool off, and then they would speak sensibly. Becky Siddons was supposed to solve his problems and make life easier for him. But already she was causing more trouble than he'd ever dreamed.

## Chapter Four

The dress was hers, all right. Becky gave herself a brisk mental shake to clear her mind and held her arms up in the air as the servant—Kate, her name was Kate—draped the fabric over her shoulders and tied the tapes in place. But it was the only familiar thing in this room. Kellridge was not her home yet, not after just one night here.

How very odd that someone besides her sister was helping her dress. In the mornings, Nan would come to her aid and then she would help Nan turn about. She'd shiver from the early morning drafts blowing in from the opened window, and Nan would be scolding her for lollygagging. Then they'd rush downstairs to eat a hurried breakfast before opening the shop.

But in her new room at Kellridge, a fire crackled in the grate, warding off the morning chill. Kate, with deft fingers, worked quickly to help her dress without badgering her one bit. Soon she would be enjoying a delicious breakfast, brought up to her on a tray, no less.

She should be happy. What luxury this new position was bringing to her workaday life. What refinement.

And no nagging, scolding sisters.

Sudden tears stung her eyes and she bit back a sob. If only she could go home to Nan. Prosaic and practical as she was, at least she was familiar. There was quite a difference between dreaming up a new life for oneself and living it out. Paul had been so horrid, so high-handed and lord-of-the-manor-ish. Of course she'd only seen his carefree and joking side when he came to Goodwin. Now that she knew how stern he could be, she couldn't escape it by simply ducking out of the room when he came to call. She was not only living in his home, she was his employee. If she was going to succeed in this new life, she had to become comfortable with the unfamiliar and learn to bear Paul's domineering ways.

Kate fluffed out the skirt of her gown and took a step backward.

"You look very nice, miss. You wear white quite well. It's such a good contrast to your dark hair and eyes." Kate clasped her hands behind her back and beamed. "Did you do that embroidery yourself?"

"Yes." Becky smiled. It was always so nice to have others appreciate her efforts with the needle. "Thank you for noticing."

"Well, I did hear that you and your sisters have a millinery shop, so I figured you must design your own clothes." Kate tilted her head to one side and surveyed the hem of Becky's skirt with a critical eye. "My ma was a nimble hand at drawn thread work, and she taught me to appreciate it. Never could do it well myself, though."

"Was your mother in service here at Kellridge?" Perhaps by reaching out to Kate, she could begin to navigate this new world she'd cast herself into.

"Yes, she worked for Mr. Holmes—not my master, but his father. And of course, Mrs. Holmes, who died three years after Miss Juliana was born. I grew up with Miss Juliana and worked as her maid, so my family has been part of Kellridge for many years. In fact, my sister works in his home in London." Kate flicked a bit of dust off Becky's sleeve and gave a brisk smile. "Shall I bring your breakfast up?"

"Certainly. Thank you for your help." Becky watched as Kate quit the room, closing the door gently behind her. The frost had melted just a little when Kate spoke kindly and familiarly to her and all at once, this journey didn't seem so insurmountable. In fact, she was charged with a renewed vigor to see this new adventure through to the end. A little kindness and compassion worked wonders in life.

Becky glanced at her reflection in the looking glass. She was a nursemaid now, and she had someone that she must care for. She tucked and coiled her hair up on top of her head and stabbed it into place with a dozen hairpins. If even a little touch of friendliness made this much of a difference in her outlook, how much of a change would it make in the life of a child? Why, it could mean the world to a scared little girl who'd just lost her mother.

That settled it. Whether he felt it necessary or no, she must convince Paul to come with her to meet Juliet at the docks. A personal plea, one from the heart.

Surely if he heard how much it would mean to Juliet, he would relent. She must tell him, face-to-face, this morning. That meant tracking him down to tell him so, without delay.

How long would it take a servant to bring her breakfast? And where would the master of the house be at this hour of the morning?

She had no idea. But she was Juliet's voice in this house, and hers was a voice that must be heard.

She gathered her skirts and quit the room. Kellridge was a puzzle to her still, even after Paul's brief tour the day before. She couldn't very well go knocking on every door looking for Paul, but she could at least rule out the east wing. He had made it quite clear that that part of the house was for the nursery only.

The best course of action would be to go downstairs and into the west wing of the house. She rushed down the stairs, brushing her hand against the satin-smooth walnut banister. Then she crossed through the vestibule, the thick Aubusson carpet muffling the sound of her slippers. Funny, for a home so thoroughly staffed, not one servant passed by as she made her way to the west wing. And the silence in the house was deafening. Not even the ticking of a clock marred the absolute quiet of the hallway.

The rooms—how perfect and still they were. Each one had its door flung open to the world, and admitted a view of balance and precision. The music room fairly glowed with instruments polished to a high gleam, yet those very instruments sat mute, crying out to be played. A billiard room, handsomely masculine yet vacant. A small sitting room, pretty and elegant but as blank as a canvas awaiting an artist's touch.

She paused in the doorway of the library, a room redolent of aged leather and paper, and breathed deeply. Shelves lined the room from floor to ceiling, and on those shelves rested books. Books that marched up and down the shelves in perfectly ordered precision, grouped by binding color as well as by size. The over-all effect, in contrast with the sweet and musty smell she breathed in, jarred her nerves. The contents of this room were surely well-loved, judging by the age of some of the volumes on the shelves. Order was an affront to its dignity. An old beloved library should be cozy, or at the very least, some disorder should mar its sterile perfection.

She stepped into the room and crossed over to a large, round mahogany table that commanded her attention. A massive arrangement of roses and chrysan-themums rested on its smooth, gleaming surface. She plucked a slightly wilted leaf from a rose stem and cast it onto the floor. She took a step backward and surveyed the result. Better, but not enough. She tugged another leaf from the arrangement and cast it onto the surface of the table.

There. A small act of defiance, but a necessary one. She wouldn't openly rebel against Paul's fastidious stan-dards, but a few stabs at insubordination might do Kell-ridge a world of good.

She backed out of the room, her heart pounding in her chest at her temerity, and continued her progress down the hall. One door stood resolutely closed to the outside world, in direct contrast to the others that had been flung open.

Likely this was his study. Perhaps he was in there?

She couldn't very well fling the door open. She wasn't brazen enough for that. She knocked twice, rapping her knuckles against the glossy painted wood.

"Enter."

Becky paused a moment. What should she say? She'd come here so certain of her purpose that she hadn't given a moment's thought as to how to communicate that purpose.

"Parker, is that you? I said enter."

She gathered her skirts along with her courage and opened the door.

Paul didn't bother to glance up as he perused his ledger book. "What took you so long, Parker? I must finish these accounts before I leave for London."

"That is precisely what I wish to talk to you about. Your departure." A soft feminine voice, utterly unlike his estate manager's, spoke. Startled, he glanced up.

"I thought we had come to an agreement about this yesterday." He tilted back in his chair and clasped his hands together, drawing them upward and cradling his head in them. If he affected an air of breezy unconcern, perhaps she would drop the matter entirely. Or at least, not become so overwrought about it. Her trembling, fluttering manner was forcing that uncomfortable sensation to the surface, like something crawling against his skin.

Too much emotion. With Becky, every sentiment

bubbled right to her surface. How downright fatiguing it all was.

"Imagine how she must feel—a little girl journeying to a faraway land. How lonely she shall be! You should meet her at the docks and make her feel welcome."

He forced himself to stare at the ceiling, avoiding any glance at Becky. Her voice was still soft, but she was commanding him. This was not a plea, but an edict. He must—for the sake of the child, of course—expose himself to the raw wounds of Juliana's death, his own failings as her brother, his disgust at how poorly things had been managed, as well as all the chaos and upheaval of Juliana's rushed marriage.

Becky Siddons definitely did not understand what she was asking. He brought his hands down upon the desk and looked her in the eyes.

"If you are accusing me of shirking my duty, Miss Siddons, let me remind you that I brought you on board here solely to act as Juliet's caregiver." He used the same clipped tone of voice he reserved for negotiating contracts and setting terms in his business dealings. "I've converted an entire wing of my home to serve as her nursery and your living quarters. Moreover, I am leaving a carriage at your full disposal so that you may personally meet her upon her arrival. Juliet is being very well cared for. I haven't neglected my duty at all."

"I am not saying that you are," Becky argued. "But think of how nice it would be for her to see her uncle's face."

Did Juliet even comprehend she had family in England? No telling what his sister had said about her relatives. No doubt that blackguard she'd married had a thing or two to say about the Holmes family. Paul had never seen a portrait of Juliet. Did she look like her mother? Or perhaps she favored her father.

A sharp pain stabbed through his being at the thought of little Juliet's face—probably so like her mother's, with a dimple in her chin—and he winced, closing his eyes against the anguish. He breathed in deeply, allowing the icy frost of disinterest to creep over his soul. He must remove himself entirely from all passion and sensation.

He grew so cold that when he opened his eyes, 'twas strange indeed to see sunlight streaming in through the windowpane. Surely when one was chilled to the bone, there should be a storm raging outside.

"I have given you my answer about this matter." He met Becky's disapproving gaze. "Never ask me again, Miss Siddons."

She recoiled as though he'd slapped her. "Very well. I shan't." Though she spoke little, her rigid pose and heightened color spoke volumes. Becky was quite offended, but she would soon get past it. As with everyone else at Kellridge, she would simply have to learn that in some matters, he was both right and unyielding.

He unclasped his hands and sat forward. At least she showed genuine concern for Juliet's welfare. In that way, she was the perfect person to be his niece's caregiver. She was willing to defy him and to press her point to make sure her charge's needs were at the forefront of every discussion. 'Twas admirable, in a way. But she had overstepped a boundary, and she should never be allowed to cross that line again.

He cleared his throat. "So, now that we understand each other, I will let you know that I am leaving for London on the morrow and shan't be back for some time." Why had he said on the morrow? He had been planning it for two days' time from now. That uncomfortable tension must be broken, and the only way to do so was to run away. He was just running sooner rather than later.

Becky nodded, her features frozen and impassive. "Very well, sir. When may we expect your return?"

"Not until after the season ends." He had planned to come home sooner, but why not stay the length of summer? 'Twould give plenty of time for Juliet to become acclimated, and then he would be home—after that, he could leave to go hunting in Scotland during the autumn months.

She cast her glance down toward the floor. "I hope that you have a good stay."

"I am sure I shall. And of course, if you should need anything, you may send a servant into town. I have runners that often traverse the distance between Kellridge and London. I like to be kept informed of matters here, and shall continue to attend to Juliet's needs even when I am not in residence." There. That showed that he was keeping his niece in his thoughts at all times. Not all men had such a system, but for his needs, having runners allowed him to keep the tight rein on his household that Kellridge required. It would work well for attending to his ward.

"You are most generous." Her eyes remained stub-

bornly fixed on the floor, but that same spirited temper—
the one that had flared when he'd met her out on the
moor—was beginning to show. The quirk of her mouth
alone spoke to her burgeoning sarcasm.

He wasn't behaving in a monstrous fashion—not if
she understood his side of the matter. He just couldn't
bear heightened emotions, or passion, or anything that
reminded him of his own failings. What he felt before
still held true—Becky must learn her place at Kellridge
and in his life. Even so, for some inexplicable reason,
he couldn't bear for Becky to think ill of him.

Whenever the road got bumpy at Kellridge, he could
always smooth the path with gifts. Perhaps she would
think kindly on him if he offered something, anything.

"Is your room to your liking? You can change it
around, you know. If the green doesn't suit you, I could
have the room redone."

"No, it's lovely." She rose, her bearing reminding
him of what Lady Jane Grey must have looked like on
the way to the scaffold—an affronted, yet subdued,
sovereign. "You are very kind, Mr. Holmes. My room
here is a palace compared to my usual accommodations.
May I have your permission to withdraw?"

"Of course." He rose. Better to make one last stab at
peace. "Anything you need from London, for yourself
or for the child, please do let me know. Send a runner,
if you wish."

Becky nodded, her head held high. "I am sure we
will want for nothing, but you are good to think of us.
I wish you a safe journey." She bobbed a slight curtsy,
and with a swish of creamy skirts, she was gone.

Paul sat back at his desk, rubbing his thumb meditatively over the smooth pages of his ledger book. He might have the running of things at Kellridge for now. However, this little milliner with her charming dimple was likely to sorely challenge his long-held and unopposed reign.

## Chapter Five

Anger surged through Becky as she marched back down the hallway with as much dignity as she could muster. She couldn't even think of strong enough terms to adequately express her outrage. Her hands shook and she grasped them together to still their trembling.

Paul Holmes and his autocratic, domineering ways.

His lack of concern for others.

The clockwork precision and cold, emotionless way he lived his life and ran Kellridge.

Thinking that a few trinkets would make everything better.

'Twas rather like applying a mustard plaster to a broken heart.

Becky paused in the doorway of the library. Her leaves—the leaves she had scattered not moments ago—were already gone. Picked up by some silent servant, no doubt.

For a brief moment, she simply stared. How could they already have vanished? The mechanical preciseness with which Kellridge was run was truly astonishing. She hadn't seen the servants cleaning as she passed by before. No, someone must routinely make the rounds to ensure that every room was exactly as it should be, not a speck of dust marring a polished surface, not a single leaf disgracing a thick, plush carpet.

She might fling back her head and howl at the absurdity of it. Why was Paul so afraid—aye, that's what it was, genuine fear—of disorder, of disarray, of basic human emotion? In the brief moments before he shut her out completely, she had glimpsed the stark terror in his dark eyes.

Well, it didn't signify why Paul was afraid. Not really. He wouldn't change in that, not while he was lord of the manor. He was too used to everyone obeying his every command and anticipating his needs. She must either accept it, or leave.

Becky leaned her head against the satin wood of the doorframe and closed her eyes, willing herself to calm down. God must have sent her here for a reason, and for His sake, she could not waver. She could not leave. Leaving meant failure. Leaving meant forsaking His purpose for her life. Or at the very least, what she thought His purpose might be. By giving up now, she would be admitting she wasn't good at anything. She wasn't a milliner, and she wasn't a nursemaid. She certainly wasn't any man's bride. For the rest of her life, she would be a failure at everything, and that would be intolerable.

Besides, she must be here for Juliet. No child should grow up in a home devoid of all feeling and emotion.

She must remain as long as she could for Juliet's sake. She would make their corner of Kellridge a pleasant and cheerful place. What if God had called her here just for this reason? Did He promise it would be easy or effortless?

"I must learn to choose my battles with Paul," she murmured under her breath. Somehow, saying the words aloud gave them strength. "I cannot change him, but I can always try to act in Juliet's best interest."

"Excuse me, my dear," an unfamiliar voice piped up behind her.

Becky gasped and whirled around. An older woman smiled gently at her, the late-morning sun reflected in prisms of light in her spectacles. Her graying hair was bound in braids around her head and she was gowned in a simple dress of cinnamon moiré. There was something more than just practicality and elegance in her bearing. In the brown eyes behind the spectacles, Becky glimpsed warmth and good humor.

"I must admit I heard someone speaking, and I wondered if perhaps there was something amiss." She gave a slight bow of her head. "Are you by any chance Miss Siddons, our new nursemaid?"

"I am." Becky grasped after her manners and bobbed a slight curtsy.

"I am Mrs. Clairbourne, the housekeeper. I do apologize for not meeting you yesterday and showing you about the house myself. Mr. Holmes prefers to meet new employees and introduce them to Kellridge personally." She gave a slight tilt of her head, and the corners of her mouth turned downward with something like mirth.

"So, I let him do as he wishes, though I always want to do my own introductions afterward."

Becky nodded. "I understand." Perhaps Mrs. Clairbourne was choosing her battles, as well. "Kellridge certainly is well run. I imagine nothing slips by Mr. Holmes's notice."

"Well, he did come into the running of this house very young." Mrs. Clairbourne motioned for Becky to follow her. "He was only eighteen when the elder Mr. Holmes passed away. Still at an age when most young men are trying to learn their places in the world, and so many siblings to care for! All of them determined to follow their own paths—'twas rather like trying to keep kittens in one basket. I imagine that discipline is how he managed to take control and run the estate so well." Mrs. Clairbourne paused as they entered the vestibule leading to the other wings of the house. "Would you like to join me for a little tea? I usually have a few moments to myself in the morning before we begin worrying about dinner."

"I'd like that very much." How nice not to have to retire and sit by oneself in the east wing. She really had nothing to occupy herself with until Juliet's arrival, and that was not for another three days' time. She could visit her sisters, of course, but if she left now, she might struggle with coming back. Even though she was beginning to think she had been called here, it would be mighty hard indeed not to crumple and fold when she saw Nan's practical little face, or embraced fiery Susannah.

"Follow me, then. I have a little sitting room all my

own." Mrs. Clairbourne led the way through the back of the house, the part Becky had only glimpsed in passing when Paul had escorted her to her room the previous day. What a vast, rambling building this was. Becky craned her neck backward and peered all around her like a goose—after all, she was trailing behind the housekeeper, and no one would notice if she gawked. She would never find her way back to the east wing of the house on her own. She certainly would never find Mrs. Clairbourne's sitting room again, not without a map and a compass.

The housekeeper ushered her into a small, tucked-away room under one of the back staircases. How marvelous—it might have been a large closet at one time, but now it saw use as a lovely sitting room. Two deep wing-back chairs flanked an arched window with leaded panes. A vase of the very same chrysanthemums that had graced the library held cheerful court on a mahogany table. An orange tabby cat slept on one of the chairs, curled into a striped ball.

"I would never have guessed such a room even existed." Becky smiled, clasping her hands before her. "How different it is from everything else at Kellridge. So—alive."

"Do sit. Tabs, move out of the way." Mrs. Clairbourne shooed the cat out of the chair and patted the cushions down. "I've a tea tray right here. Cream or sugar?"

Becky settled into her chair and stretched out her slippered foot to scratch Tabs's back. The cat arched in appreciation and flopped onto the floor as if she were a rag doll. "Sugar, please."

"Here." The housekeeper handed over a delicate china cup. "Be careful, it's rather hot."

Becky blew on her tea and, as Mrs. Clairbourne busied herself with her cup, absorbed the atmosphere of this jovial little nook. "I rather think you'd need a place like this in Kellridge," she admitted as Mrs. Clairbourne sank into her chair. "It's so lively and warm. The rest of the house is so sterile."

"Sterile?" The housekeeper drew her eyebrows together over her spectacles. "I don't know about that. I do know that the master likes everything to be in place. He's a good man, and the house keeps me hopping."

"Oh, I don't mean to offend." Here she was, bungling her first chance at companionship at Kellridge. "The house is lovely. I've just never lived anywhere so precise. I rather wonder at bringing a two-year-old here."

"Well, that's why you are here." Mrs. Clairbourne took a careful sip of her tea. "Mr. Holmes anticipated that young Miss Juliet would be a handful. He knew we have too much to do as it is. So, with his usual foresight, he brought you on board to see that things run smoothly." She gave a little smile as she stirred her tea. "I must admit to a little mother's pride where he is concerned. I've watched him since he was just a wee baby himself, and he did his family credit when he took over. You'll never see an estate so well run as Kellridge, not in the whole of Derbyshire."

Becky tasted her tea. Lovely—just the bracing kind of thing she needed after her disappointing morning.

She'd have to tread carefully—Mrs. Clairbourne was clearly proud of Paul and, because of that pride, would hasten to defend him from any perceived criticism. If she were to preserve this connection, she must be more subtle. "I agree. The house is quite beautiful. You've done wonders with the east wing. I know Juliet will appreciate it. I certainly do."

"Good, I am so glad." The housekeeper fairly beamed under Becky's praise. "Anything you want, you know you may have it. Mr. Holmes is never stingy or mean. Do you need anything? Anything I've forgotten?"

Becky set her teacup aside and considered the matter. If she were in charge of Juliet and all her wants and needs, then she must keep her occupied. The suite they shared was delightful in every way, but was rather kitted out like a guest room for lords and ladies, not as a home for a child. "Toys," she admitted finally. "We don't have any toys, and I am sure that Juliet will want to play."

"Of course. Why on earth did I neglect such an important detail?" The housekeeper sat up straight in her chair. "I am sure Mr. Holmes can send things from London, but they won't arrive before Juliet is here." She shook her head and made a tsking sound. "Whatever am I going to do? The shops in the village only have a few things. Nothing too entertaining for a child, I fear. I suppose we shall have to make something."

If Paul knew she had just commissioned a lot of toys from his already overburdened staff, he would be furious. She had nothing to do for the foreseeable future. This task could keep her busy, and keep her from brooding until she was able to go and meet the child. "Perhaps there is a box of old things I could go through? Since Mr. Holmes had so many siblings, it may well be I could find some of their toys—clean them up and make them do until we can get more from London."

"Excellent idea." The housekeeper put her teacup aside with a brisk gesture. "In the attics, I am certain of it. We put trunks of Miss Juliana's things away after she left for Italy." She rose. "In fact, I believe you'll find several things up there you can use," she continued, punctuating each word with a wag of her forefinger. "Let me get the keys for you." She rummaged through the string of keys about her waist, procuring a skeleton key with a filigree handle. "Here it is. Now, I could spare a footman…"

"No, indeed." She could hunt for treasure all afternoon. A house as vast and rambling as Kellridge, with what had to be a storied past, would have all sorts of interesting things tucked away beneath its eaves. 'Twas the perfect scenario. She could enjoy looking through all the articles of Kellridge's past, imagining the stories behind each item. She would be out of everyone's way, and most importantly, she would be doing something nice for her charge. "I couldn't ask you to add to anyone's duties, and I have nothing with which to occupy myself as it is."

"Well…" The housekeeper trailed off, as though considering the matter. "I hate for you to do all that lifting alone, without help."

"If I need assistance, I promise I shall come down and ask for it." Sudden gladness rushed through Becky. Mrs. Clairbourne was such a dear. If she could but cultivate her friendship with the housekeeper, Kellridge could be livable. The prospect of having something to do for the next few days was heartening. "How do I find the attic?"

"You'll want to take the back staircase all the way to the third floor." The housekeeper opened the door and ushered Becky into the hallway. "When you reach the top of the stairs, the attic door will be to your left. Are you quite certain you will be all right? I do feel guilty about asking you to grub around among those dusty trunks."

"You didn't ask—I volunteered." Becky gave the housekeeper a bright smile and accepted the key. "I am very glad to do my part to make Juliet welcome here."

She began the long trek up the back staircase. Each step was as though she were marking her new path, starting out on her journey, and she prayed silently for strength and wisdom as she ascended. At the top of the stairs, she might find toys for Juliet. In some small way, she was also going to find a place for herself at Kellridge.

Paul cast his quill aside and stretched as Wadsworth bustled into his study with the afternoon tea. "I'm leaving tomorrow, Wadsworth, instead of in two days' time." Though he laced the words with masterful nonchalance, each syllable grated on his nerves. His plan had always been to leave two days hence. Changing that plan now went against the grain.

The butler stiffened as he laid out the tea tray. He,

too, hated change and the disorder it brought. "Indeed, sir?"

"Yes. I've decided there's no use lolling about. I'll strike out on the morrow. Business is waiting. Everything's been packed, hasn't it?"

"Well, yes, all is ready for your journey." Wadsworth tucked a serviette under one of the saucers with his usual efficiency, and handed it across the desk to Paul. "Except for your carriage. Jim is seeing to the wheels, making sure they are in prime condition for traversing all the roads. He was planning on being ready in two days' time, not tomorrow."

Paul clenched his jaw and shook his head slowly. This was what came of changing the established order of things. "Hadn't thought of that. I suppose I could take the landau instead."

"I had rather thought the landau was for Miss Siddons's use, when she was called to fetch Miss Juliet." The butler gave a courteous little cough. "Opening it up and allowing fresh air might be very nice indeed for traveling from the coast, especially since Miss Juliet will have been cooped up for so long."

"Yes, yes. You are right." Paul raked his hands through his hair. What an irritating problem. "I can't use the other carriages—the gig and the curricle are far too light and unsuitable. You'll just have to tell Jim to hurry up and have as much done on the town coach as can be done before tomorrow. I am certain it will be fine."

"I'll go at once." The butler prepared to take his leave but paused on the threshold. "There is one other matter I think you should be aware of. Mrs. Clairbourne gave

Miss Siddons the key to the attic. She is up there now, and has been for some hours."

Paul pushed his chair away from the desk and rose. "Attic? Whatever for?" No one ever went up into the attics. There was never any need. The attic held nothing more than the relics of the past—there was no use for them now.

"I believe she wanted to find some toys and playthings for Miss Juliet. I told Mrs. Clairbourne that she should have asked permission of you first, sir, but she did insist that it was all perfectly harmless." The slight edge to his tone spoke volumes of his feelings on the matter. Wadsworth and Mrs. Clairbourne had long ago declared an uneasy peace when it came to the running and management of Kellridge, yet every now and again, that competitive spirit showed through once more. Paul suppressed the urge to roll his eyes. It did no good to stoke the fire.

"I'll go and have a look. Do hurry and tell Jim about the town coach. I want to leave at dawn." Paul followed the butler out of his study and hastened—without breaking into a run, which might give more weight to the situation and thus more fuel for Wadsworth's tiff with Mrs. Clairbourne. What sort of things did they have tucked away in the attic? There was no telling. He climbed the back staircase with a growing feeling of unease. The last time they had done any great shifting up there was after Juliana left for Italy.

The door to the left of the stairs stood open, so he ducked inside. Daylight streamed in from the dormer windows, and dust motes danced in the sparkling sunlight. Paul drew his forefinger along one of the trunks and noted the gray smear of dust. For an attic, it was rather clean. All the boxes and trunks lined the walls with military precision. He glanced across the room.

"Miss Siddons?" He spoke in a regular, measured tone of voice. No use in sounding belligerent or ruffled. That would only get Becky's hackles up again. "Where are you?"

"I am over here." A scuffling sound caught his ear, and he followed it over to the left rear corner of the attic. Becky was hunched over a trunk, her pretty white dress smudged with dust, and a long trail of dirt marking her cheek. Beside her rested a pile of ancient playthings—dolls, jumping jacks and blocks. His mouth quirked in ruthful recognition—even a puzzle he'd spent hours assembling when he was a boy.

She clicked the lid of the trunk shut and faced him squarely. "Please don't be angry. Mrs. Clairbourne gave me her permission."

She seemed almost afraid, and yet her eyebrows held that same defiant arch. His heart dropped a little as he took in her bedraggled dress and widened eyes. He didn't want Becky to fear him or to think ill of him. If only they could recapture those brief, fleeting moments on the moor when they were comfortable with each other. For some reason, which he did not care to examine, he found himself drawn toward Becky. Of course, he must always maintain his mastery of his household—but couldn't he do so while befriending Becky? Couldn't they reach a truce, as Wadsworth and Mrs. Clairbourne had?

"I'm not upset." He sank onto the floor beside her, heedless of the dirt. "Just…surprised." He picked up the puzzle and began rearranging the pieces. "You're in the right, you know. I had no thought in my mind of playthings. I made her room up as I would for an adult guest. 'Twas a sore mistake."

"Well, no harm done, and I am happy to have plenty to do." She cast a shy smile his way and reached for a doll. "I shall clean everything up and have it ready for her once she comes."

"Good plan." A sudden urge to tell her everything about Juliana struck him. What if he told her the whole sordid tale and unburdened himself to her about his own failings? It might be a relief to share the painful past with someone.

He tamped the urge back. That was weakness. That was folly. He was master of Kellridge and of his own feelings and emotions. His past transgressions were his own to bear, and he must do so alone.

The cold frost that served him so well settled back over him as he clicked another piece of the puzzle in place. "I leave tomorrow. As I said before, do let me know if there is more that I can do. I'll send some proper toys from London. Not these worn, cast-off old things." He chuckled dryly and rose, dusting off his trousers. "Be sure to lock everything back up when you leave."

"I will." She gazed at him with an inscrutable look in her eyes. "Godspeed, Mr. Holmes."

He gave a brief nod and walked back out of the attic. He was doing the right thing. He was doing the only thing he could. His duty was done, and now he would fling himself back into London and the season and all its dubious delights as his reward.

Each step echoed through the quiet, still house as he descended.

There was emptiness in his life that only a strategic retreat to London could fill.

Funny how deep and vast that emptiness had grown in just the past few days.

## Chapter Six

The weather was nothing short of abominable. One of those late spring showers that soaked a man to the bone and made mud of the most navigable roads. Rain ran in rivulets down Paul's hat as he waited for the carriage to be pulled round, and he drew his overcoat closer to drive out the damp. The sooner they were started, the better. Perhaps they could make it as far as Derby before changing horses. The carriage plodded into view, its slow pace causing his pulse to quicken.

"Don't spare the whip," he remarked curtly to his driver as he placed his foot on the board. "We want to get ahead of this weather if at all possible. The roads aren't a sea of mud yet. Give the horses their heads." He gave a brief nod to the grooms, who had taken advantage of the rain to move up front onto the box, as he climbed into carriage.

"Aye, sir," the coachman replied. His tone sounded doubtful, though.

Well, that was simply too bad. Even if his driver

had some misgivings about his orders, he was bound to obey them.

The coachman's whip cracked through the air and the carriage leaped forward. Paul removed his overcoat and cast his hat aside. Then he settled against the squabs and watched Kellridge retreat into the distance. Who knew when he would see it again? 'Twould be months at least.

Guilt gnawed at his insides. He shouldn't leave. He could turn the horses around now, and no one would say anything. Well, that wasn't true. The gossip in the servants' halls would natter on endlessly, for the master never changed his plans, and already he had dithered over the day of his departure. His uniform and practical way of living had been severely thrown since Becky's arrival, and he simply had to gain mastery over his own life again.

Kellridge would get on just fine. That was why he ran things the way he did. Besides, he had business in London. Selling Father's shipping shares would grant him a tidy profit and dispose of a responsibility that he had grown too mired within. Everything would be attended to in his absence. The greatest reward lay in knowing he could run with the most decadent crowd in London, and no matter how dissipated his company or his time spent, Kellridge would be waiting for him when it came time for all revelry to cease.

The carriage bounced and jerked along the roads. Was it the high rate of speed that caused such a well-sprung carriage to jostle about? He usually traveled at an alarming pace, so surely that wasn't it. Perhaps the rain was already making a mess of the roads. Oh, well, nothing to do but endure it. Once they reached Derby, he'd enjoy a fine dinner and perhaps play cards with the innkeeper. He always was a good chap, up for a game at a moment's notice.

Paul wedged himself into a corner, which eased some of the discomfort of his travel. He could prop his head against one of the cushions and get a good nap in. 'Twas better to do so now, when en route to London. Once he reached his townhome, he'd get precious little sleep.

The carriage gave a violent jounce and skidded down a length of the road. His horses whinnied, his coachman cursed, and through the mixed and jumbled noise of chaos, he discerned the sickening and undeniable sound of splintering wood. He braced himself against the side of the carriage but was thrown like a rag doll. His head bashed against the window, which was odd because now the window was where the floor should be, and hundreds of drops of water splashed his face. No—they cut his face. 'Twas not water, 'twas broken glass.

As the carriage's mad flight ground to a halt, Paul put tentative fingers to his cheeks and discerned a warm, sticky trail of blood.

"Are you all right, sir?" the coachman cried out from above him—far above him, and not through the window, but through the carriage door, which was now where the ceiling had been. The coachman whistled softly. "You look as though you lost the fight."

"Thank you for that." Paul sat up gingerly, withdrawing his handkerchief from his jacket pocket and holding it to his face. "What on earth happened?"

"Has to be a broken axle." The coachman heaved

himself on top of the door and extended his hand down to Paul. "I know Jim was worried about that right front wheel. The grooms are taking a look at the damage now."

Paul allowed himself to be pulled upright, and then heaved himself through the door and onto the curiously slanting side of the coach. He slid down and sank onto the muddy road, pressing the handkerchief to his face to stop the bleeding. "This is what comes of changing plans," he muttered.

The rain picked up in earnest, and thunder boomed in the distance.

"Aye, it's a broken axle," one of the grooms shouted. "Can't repair it here."

Paul struggled to his feet, his cheek throbbing. "We need to get back to Kellridge. From there we can get enough hands out to set the carriage right, and bring it back for repairs." He turned to his coachman. "How far are we from home?"

"Riding at our usual pace, I'd say we're only half an hour away," the coachman replied. "Walking, I'd say about an hour."

"Right." Paul struggled to speak loudly over the din of the rain and the pulsing of his cheek, which made every movement a fresh agony. "We'll have to set out for it then. Each of us can walk one of the horses back." He tucked his bloodied handkerchief back into his pocket. "Let's at least try to set off the main road."

The horses, still skittish from the accident, tossed their heads and shuddered as the men unhitched them and led them to the side of the road. Paul worked as swiftly as his clumsy, wet fingers would allow to rig a tow line to the carriage. Together, men and horses struggled to clear the wreck from the roadway. Shards of glass tinkled, falling inside the carriage, as it slipped and bumped through the mud.

What an awful mess. Paul narrowed his eyes as he surveyed the damage. The axle was broken, all right—smashed clean to bits. The windows of the carriage yawned open and black, pierced now and again by jagged teeth of broken glass. His horses had been terrified but appeared uninjured. If they hadn't come out of it so well, he would be kicking himself right sharp. After all, a man could easily replace a carriage, but Kellridge had some of the finest horses in Derbyshire. Had a green lad taken off at such a fresh pace and caused as much damage, Paul would have been the first to take him to task for recklessness. As it was, he was now dealing with his own stupid folly.

'Twas both humbling and demeaning to find himself in such a position. And who knew what his face looked like. The shock of the incident was receding, and in its wake, his cheek stung and pulsed. In truth, his entire body ached, and his knuckles smarted where he'd scraped them as he pulled himself out of the carriage.

His hat and overcoat were still somewhere in the remnants of the carriage. It didn't signify anyway, for he was wet now, through and through. He had no desire to revisit the carriage and endure a new round of cuts and bruises. He untethered the horses and handed one off to each man. They turned and headed north up the road back to Kellridge, cloaked in exhausted silence.

As they plodded down the slime-covered road, Paul roamed through the incident in his mind. Whenever faced with tragedy, a fellow must learn all he could from it. Only then would the experience hold meaning. Before understanding and accepting the lessons learned from this disaster, he would have to first castigate himself for his part in it. He shouldn't have rushed away from Kellridge before the carriage was ready. Shouldn't have struck forth in such dreadful weather. Shouldn't have asked them to travel at such a pace. All of these mistakes had been made in the name of one thing only—avoiding his niece's impending arrival.

Had he been calm and measured in his response, he could have remembered that he was, after all, master of Kellridge. If he didn't wish to see his niece upon her arrival, then there was no need for him to do so. He could stay in his part of the house, and she in hers. He would have been under the same roof with her for no more than a day before striking out for London as he should—with a well-maintained carriage, better weather (one could hope) and a less pressing need for great speed.

If one were to be completely honest, he wasn't merely avoiding his niece. He was avoiding Becky Siddons, as well. She was too pretty by half, and he found himself thinking about her far more than was proper. He was avoiding not just her attractive form, but the disappointment that darkened her eyes when he'd refused to meet Juliet at the docks. Her anger when they spoke about it again in the study. Her fear when he'd spied her in the attic. Becky was a whirlwind of emotion, and he had run the risk of injuring perfectly good horses, killing or maiming excellent servants, and had completely destroyed a carriage in his haste to extricate himself from her chaos.

Whether he acknowledged it at the time or not, he'd allowed emotion to cloud his judgment. Because of his own fear of his feelings, he had run headlong into catastrophe.

Paul wrapped the leather straps of the horse's bridle once more around his hand, to help calm the deep ache in his head. When he got back to Kellridge, he would first change out of these wet, bloodied clothes and have a hot bath. Then, he would discuss with Jim how quickly repairs could be made on the broken carriage.

He would strike forth for London again when all was ready in good time, for he was not about to let fear or feeling dictate his journey ever again.


Becky turned the china doll over in her hands. Yes, a bit of mending on the dress and this toy would be as good as new. In fact, if she could ask Nan for a few bits of remnants from the shop, she could make some new dresses or even an entire wardrobe for the doll. She took her needle from her sewing basket and pulled out a skein of thread.

Beside her, Tabs purred blissfully. Rain pattered on the arched window in Mrs. Clairbourne's sitting room. In no time at all, that good lady would return with afternoon tea for the two of them. 'Twas a lovely way to spend a damp, ungenial day.

Loud cries erupted from the hallway and, above the din, Mrs. Clairbourne's voice rose, issuing some kind of orders. Becky cast the doll and needle aside and stood, straining her ears. No one ever shouted at Kellridge. In fact, noise of any kind seemed rather profane.

"The master had an accident..."

Becky stood with one hand on the door latch. Her heart hammered painfully in her chest. What kind of accident? Was he all right?

She opened the sitting-room door. Mrs. Clairbourne was in the hall, sending servants scattering in all directions. When the older woman spied Becky watching, she gave a tight smile. "I am afraid I'll have to postpone our afternoon tea," she apologized between orders. "The master's been in a carriage accident. One of the grooms saw them in the lower field, walking back home."

If he could walk, then at least he was not dreadfully injured. Even so...

"What can I do?" She had to have some occupation. Remaining in the sitting room would be intolerable. Surely she could help in some way.

"Oh..." The housekeeper shrugged. "Run along and grab a few hot bricks from the kitchen. Wrap them in flannel and take them up to the master's room. If his valet is in there, give them to him. If not, then tuck the bricks in the foot of his bed. The master will be chilled to the bone in this weather, and he'll need to get warm in a hurry if he's to keep from taking ill."

She had very little idea where the kitchens were, or where Paul's room was in the labyrinthine corridors of Kellridge. She couldn't very well stop and ask for more directions, not when everyone was so harried. She followed one surge of servants and, carried along on their current, managed to find the kitchens. Once she was there, she grasped a scullery maid by the arms. "I need some hot bricks for the master's room."

"O' course." The maid trotted over to the hearth and, using a poker, pulled out two bricks. Becky glanced around the kitchen—yes, there were the flannel cloths, in a basket by the hearth. She knelt and, with the maid's help, swathed the bricks in the cloth.

"Where is the master's bedchamber?" 'Twas rather bold to inquire, but otherwise, she would wander around the house forever. The maid nodded and tucked the bricks into a cloth-lined bucket.

"Follow the main staircase to the top of the second floor, then turn to your left. The master's chambers are in the west wing. Try the third door in the corridor."

Becky nodded and accepted the heavy pail with gratitude. There would likely be no gossip if she headed up to the master's chambers now. Everyone was too busy, too concerned with Paul's welfare, to worry about propriety.

She took the stairs as quickly as the weight of the pail would allow and made it down the corridor. She set the pail down before the third door and knocked briefly. If the valet was there, she would merely leave the bricks and go find some other way to help.

No one answered. She pushed the door open gingerly and stuck her head inside. The room was dim, lit only by the floor-to-ceiling windows. The curtains had been opened, and rain streaked against the panes.

Well, there was nothing to do but leave the bricks and then rush back downstairs. No need to be nervous.

No one was here, and she was doing Paul a kindness. She grasped the pail and hurried over to the large four-poster bed that must be his.

She flicked back the bedclothes and hastily stuffed the bricks down at the foot of the bed. Then she drew the heavy damask fabric back up and over, smoothing it down so that it looked almost as tidy as it had before. As she plumped the pillows back into place, she looked down at the small table beside Paul's bed. Two miniatures rested on its surface, framed in gold. Both were of young women.

Becky placed the pail beside her and peered closer. One of the young women bore a passing resemblance to Paul, but her hair was black, where his was sandy, and her eyes were a startling shade of blue. Her lips were curled into a challenging smile. As though she were a little amused at everyone. Could this possibly be Juliet's mother, the saucy Juliana?

The other woman was completely unfamiliar. The artist had captured her elegant, almost regal air. Her almond-shaped eyes were the color of toffee, and her wealth of copper-colored hair was massed around her noble head. Who was this? And who was she to Paul that her portrait sat right beside his bed? She didn't favor Paul in the least, so it wasn't likely that she was a relation. Her clothing marked her as a contemporary of theirs—not a woman from the past. Well, whoever she was and whatever Paul felt about her was certainly no business of hers. So what if this woman meant enough to be the first thing Paul saw when he woke each morning, or the last before he slept each night? She snapped her mind off.

In years past, she might have gone all dreamy and reminisced about some romantic love affair Paul had conducted with this woman, something beautiful and tragic and worthy of epic poetry. Never again. She was a nursemaid and a spinster, and she had left all those things behind. She would simply assume that the woman in the portrait was a family friend that was so close she was like an aunt to him. Aunt Hildegard, or some such. There. That put an end to all musing.

She better hurry back. There must be something else she could do to help. She picked up the pail and quit the room.

She closed the door with a gentle click, then turned... to find Paul standing before her.

She gasped and dropped the pail, which clattered to the floor, unheeded. "Mr. Holmes—oh, Paul, you look terrible." His cheek was horribly cut and bruised, and spatters of mud and blood marked his otherwise elegant attire. "Are you quite all right?"

What a stupid question. Of course he wasn't all right. He looked like he'd had a near brush with death.

He tried to give his usual ruthful smile, but paused and winced. "Hurts too much," he muttered out the corner of his mouth.

"Come in." She opened the door and grasped his arm, tugging him into the room. "I just put hot bricks in your bed," she chattered on, trying to cover her shock at his appearance. "I hope you don't mind. I wanted to help."

He shook his head from side to side, and then closed his eyes. "Fine."

"Where is Wadsworth? Or your valet? Surely they should be up here assisting you." She helped him sit in the easy chair before his hearth and knelt on the floor before him, tugging at his boots. "You're soaking wet. You'll catch your death if you don't dry off and warm up."

"Downstairs." He submitted to her tugging and the muddy Hessians finally slid free, knocking her backward a pace or two. He closed his eyes. "On their way."

"Good." She grabbed a blanket from the foot of his bed and wrapped it around him, then busied herself kindling a small fire from the hearth. That was the good of never having servants—you learned to do simple tasks on your own. The fire caught and blazed up, bathing the room in an orange glow.

"I'm going to send for the doctor. Your face—it's quite awful, Paul." His pallid appearance and weary submission to her ministrations pinched at her conscience. She must be kind and friendly and helpful to Paul now—as though she were still a milliner and he just a jolly friend of the family.

She drew closer and scrutinized his cheek. The bleeding had long since stopped, but the gashes were quite raw. "Yes, you do need a doctor. And I shall go for him now, unless one of the others already has. A tincture of arnica might help. If you don't have any at Kellridge, I know Susannah has some at Goodwin."

Paul opened his eyes. The usual light of mischief had been quenched from their depths; even the cold, businesslike stare with which he'd regarded her during their few disagreements had melted. He was in pain, and he was wretched.

"Paul, I am going to go now. I am going to find your valet and Wadsworth and make sure they are here right away to help you. And I am going to make sure a doctor has been called. I'll find the arnica as well." She patted his arm with a reassuring gesture. "Sit here and rest. Help is on the way. I'll see to it."

Paul grasped her hand with surprising strength and squeezed. He closed his eyes once more, his face turning a shade whiter as he lolled his head back against the cushion.

His cracked lips parted. "Thank you."

'Twas the first time Paul had ever shown deference or humility. Tears stung the back of Becky's eyes.

She squeezed his hand in return and quit the room.

## Chapter Seven

What an extraordinary few days it had been. Becky stared out the carriage window as raindrops streaked against the pane. Paul had been injured, but the doctor said he would recover in a matter of weeks. The gash on his cheek needed time to heal, as did the many bumps and bruises he'd sustained in the accident. So even though he was now home for Juliet's arrival, he wasn't able to travel with Becky to Cleethorpes. That was just as well. Juliet might very well be afraid of her uncle, what with that horrible wounded cheek.

Becky settled back against the seat cushions and tucked her book inside her reticule. She never was any good at reading on long trips. 'Twas much nicer to sit and watch the countryside roll by, imagining how her life might be if she lived in that farmhouse as she passed by. She and Nan would often make a game of it, which they called "Storybook Lives." Nan was always so practical about it. She'd look at the romantic ruin of an old house and remark, "I wouldn't want to bear the cost of glazing *those* windows," or some such, thereby completely destroying the fun of the game.

Becky's eyes misted over at the memory. Better not to think too much of the past. Better to enjoy the sound of the rain trickling against the landau windows as they made their sluggish progress into Cleethorpes. The roads were a good deal muddier after the rains of the past few days, which made for slower going. Good thing she was always of an imaginative spirit. One was never bored when one could roam through the fields of fancy.

The carriage swayed sharply to the right, and the smell of salt cut through the air. They must be nearing the shore now. Becky tucked her reticule next to the doll she'd brought along for Juliet, and pressed her nose against the glass. Gray sky met lead-colored sea, where froths of waves roiled and tossed. At least the rain had lightened to a sprinkle.

Dozens of seagulls cackled and screamed as the carriage drew closer to the docks. Becky's heart quickened at the sound. 'Twasn't a pleasant noise at all, and something about it set her nerves on edge. She dropped back against the seat cushion and drew a long, steadying breath. She was a nursemaid now, not some silly girl who grew frightened at strange noises. She couldn't very well show up to gather her charge while cowering like a ninny. No, no matter how she felt inside, she must present a facade of calm good-natured cheer. No need to fret Juliet, especially after her long journey.

The carriage ground to a halt, its tread heavy as the wet sandy soil caught against the wheels. She was here.

At long last, her life's purpose was about to reveal itself, and she would finally live the kind of life she'd always wanted. Or, at least, had wanted and prepared for the past week. She fought the urge to gawk out the window, seeking her charge. Instead, she waited until the coachman came around and helped her out of the carriage. Even with his assistance, she floundered a bit on the damp sand.

She righted herself with her last shreds of dignity and drew her hood up over her neatly coiled hair. The cold, misty rain was already penetrating her garments. The sooner she was able to get Juliet and her nurse back to Kellridge, the better.

Paul's schooner was right before her, tethered to the dock, as men scrambled around tossing ropes and calling orders. Perhaps her charge was still aboard? After all, it was still raining and although they had been cooped up in a cabin for weeks, a little girl could catch her death in weather like this.

She turned to the coachman. "Foster, do you mind asking one of the sailors where we could find Miss Juliet and her nurse?"

The coachman shrugged. "I could, but I see them myself." He pointed his gloved finger down the length of the strand.

Becky glanced out over the beach. Yes, indeed, that must be her charge. Very few two-year-olds would be wandering about here at this time of day and in this weather. There was a woman beside her. So that must be her nurse. "Thank you," she replied with as much dignity as she could muster. "I'll go and collect them.

Will you make certain that her trunks are brought back to Kellridge? They must have more than we can handle in the landau."

Foster bowed and made his way to the ship. Becky paused for a moment after he left. Her heart still beat in her chest like a big bass drum. She must stop being silly, and she must stop being…not exactly frightened, but nervous. After all, God was calling her to take care of this child, wasn't He? And she mustn't fail, or allow her courage to wane.

With a mental apology to her kid boots, she balled her skirts up in one hand and gingerly stepped onto the sand. 'Twas wet indeed, and sucked at the heel of her boots like quicksand. How embarrassing it would be to get stuck, halfway between the carriage and her charge.

"Hello," she called out, waving her free hand. The older woman looked up and gave a languid wave of her hand. Juliet did not, but then, she mightn't be able to hear her over the crashing of the surf.

There was nothing to do but keep moving forward.

After a small eternity, she drew close enough to see the pair in a clearer manner. Juliet hunched down, the skirt of her cheap black sateen dress caked in wet sand. Her long black curls tangled down the length of her small back. She was so intent on whatever she was doing that she never looked up, or right or left. She was digging in the sand, using a shell as a scoop. As Becky drew close beside her, Juliet flicked a scoop full of sand over one shoulder, pelting Becky's bodice.

"Oh," Becky gasped.

Beside her, the nurse gave a short exclamation in

what must be Italian. Juliet shrugged and resumed her progress, never looking back.

"Forgive her," the nurse said, her English touched with a singsong quality. "It has been a long journey."

"Of course," Becky replied. She dusted the wet sand off her dress with as much grace as she could muster. No harm done, after all. "I am Becky Siddons, and I will be her nursemaid at Kellridge Hall. I've come to take you home."

"Yes." There were bags under the nurse's kind brown eyes, and her mouth was tightly drawn, like a string that had been pulled. "Home will be a relief to us all."

Becky knelt in the sand. Her dress was already a mess anyway. A little more filth wouldn't make that much of a difference. "Are you Juliet?"

Juliet spared her a brief glance and then continued digging. She had a small, heart-shaped face and a pointed chin. Her large brown eyes were the precise shade of almonds and ringed with purple half moons— likely the result of fatigue. She was skinny and tangled and dirty, rather like a boy with stringy long hair. Not at all the demure little flower she'd expected.

"Would you like to go home with me to Kellridge Hall? Your uncle Paul is there." She tried to inflect a note of cheerfulness into her voice, but 'twas difficult to manage. For one thing, Juliet never responded to a word. For another, there was the uncomfortable sensation that she would sink into the sand if she didn't balance her weight on the balls of her feet.

"Her English is very poor," her companion piped up in the same lilting tone. "Her mama and papa spoke to her only in Italian. I have tried to teach her a little of English, but mine is very poor as well."

Becky rummaged through her mind for any Italian phrases she might know. She and her sisters never learned it. They'd learned French at home, then promptly forgot all but a few smatterings when they moved to Uncle Arthur's home. And those smatterings dealt mostly with fashion. *Toilette. Déshabillé. Soie. Mousseline.* None of these phrases mattered a whit now, because even if Juliet knew French, the words she could recall were utterly useless.

She had to seize control of the situation. Even if she didn't know Italian, she must communicate with her charge. She straightened, facing the nurse squarely. "Her uncle will want her to learn and speak only English," she admitted. "For the purposes of this journey, you may continue to talk to her in her native language. When we get home, I am sure Mr. Holmes will instruct us on how to proceed, Miss—"

"Sophia." The nurse gave a brief nod, her forehead puckering. "I shall try, of course, but it will be difficult—"

A fusillade of wet sand pellets slapped Becky right in the face. She took a step backward, blinking rapidly. The urge to give way to ridiculous tears fought with the urge to scream and yell, just like she had when she and Nan would fight as children. She took a deep, shuddering breath and faced her new charge, who broke into a sunny smile when she beheld Becky's face.

Sophia spoke in rapid-fire Italian and grabbed Juliet by the arm, tossing the shell to one side. Juliet let forth a wail that startled the gulls circling overhead. They flew off, shrieking.

Becky shook her head. Already this was disastrous, and Sophia was not improving matters. How could she possibly take control of the situation? For it was her responsibility to right it, no matter what.

"No." She pronounced the word with a snap, and the sharp sound of it penetrated the struggle between Sophia and Juliet. "We'll have no more of this nonsense." She pointed to the carriage and looked over at Sophia. "Tell Juliet I have a doll waiting for her in the carriage. All her own. 'Twas her mama's. If she's going to be naughty, then I shall tuck that doll right back into the valise and she shan't have it until she learns to behave."

As Sophia repeated Becky's instructions, Juliet's eyes widened. She gave a short nod to her nurse, and grabbed Becky's hand, as though silently urging her into the carriage.

"Very well." Becky allowed Juliet to lead her to the carriage. The sand threatened to pull her kid boots off with each step. Her hem was now caked with filth. For want of a clever remark, but still needing to say something to fill the silence, Becky called out, "We won't be able to put the top down on the landau thanks to the weather. So, we'll have to find other ways to entertain Juliet as we journey home."

*"Dio dammi forza,"* the maid answered.

"I am not sure what you said." Becky staggered the last few steps up the beach, with Juliet's wet, sticky hand grasping hers.

But it sounded rather like a prayer, which, given the circumstances, she considered highly appropriate.

Paul looked up at the ceiling. He'd been lying here, in this precise same position on his bed, for two days. And the patterns he'd traced in the crown moulding caused his head to ache abominably.

He'd have to get up. Kellridge needed him. He was master here, and carriage accident or no carriage accident, he couldn't simply lay abed for two weeks. No matter what Dr. Talbot said.

He gave the bell an impatient pull and struggled to a sitting position. Wadsworth entered the room, a tea tray in his hands.

"You seem to have anticipated my bell." An unreasonable wave of irritation surged through Paul. After all, he was still master here. 'Twas his hand that rang the bell, 'twas his voice that ordered the servants about. For Wadsworth to anticipate him almost weakened his hold on the precise manner in which he ran the house.

"Not at all, sir." Wadsworth gave a polite cough. "It is almost teatime, and since Miss Siddons has returned from Cleethorpes—"

"She's back?" Paul rubbed his hand over his forehead, gingerly touching the jagged scar that began above his right eyebrow. "How long has she been here?"

"They've only just arrived. Mrs. Clairbourne is getting them settled in the east wing." Wadsworth set the tea tray beside the bed and began pouring the steaming brew into a china cup. "From what I gather, it was rather a difficult journey."

"Not a broken axle again?" Paul accepted the teacup from Wadsworth with a grateful, if somewhat cautious, nod. "Surely not. The landau's in fine shape."

"No, the carriage made it back in one piece." Wadsworth fussed with the biscuits until Paul shooed him away with a languid wave of his hand. "I believe the problem was with Miss Juliet. She is rather…high-spirited, shall we say."

Paul took a bite of chocolate biscuit. Just like her mother. Juliana had been a handful from the moment she entered the world. Loud, contrary, intent on having her way…he glanced outside the window. Rain streaked across the panes. The weather hadn't improved in two days, and that meant they made the journey back from Cleethorpes with the landau closed, and that would have made the trip feel like an eternity.

"That will be all, Wadsworth."

The butler, long used to Paul's abrupt manner, quit the room without further comment. Paul took another long draft of tea. A strange war of emotions was building within him.

If Juliet was a handful, as her mother had been, then she had the power to turn Kellridge upside down. If he didn't make his presence known and felt in the east wing, it could soon spin out of control, and that would spread to the rest of the house.

No matter how he felt about losing Juliana, he couldn't allow chaos to seep in. Not when he'd worked so hard to run Kellridge like a precisely wound clock.

He rose from the bed, slowly and stiffly, and dressed himself. No need to worry about a cravat; his hand was still too swollen and bruised to do any kind of elaborate knot. And no need to trouble his valet. He would handle this matter on his own, as was his custom.

He limped over to the door, pain singing through his body. He held on to the pain and accepted it with something like gratitude. Physical discomfort would help to drive out any ridiculous and overblown feelings of grief or sadness he might otherwise fall prey to when he beheld Juliana's child.

Kellridge was silent and still, just as it should be at this hour. The servants were likely on the first floor, beginning the dinner preparations and lighting fires in the hearths. He would encounter no one, now that Wadsworth had left him.

As he rounded the corner into the east wing, a child's shrill shrieking rent the air. There was a sound of something hitting the floor—a small table, perhaps?—and Becky's tired voice rising above the general commotion. "Honestly, Sophia. Was she like this at home? This is preposterous!"

"I couldn't agree more." Paul pushed open the nursery room door and took a few steps in. As he entered, a hush fell over the room. The little imp who was causing all the fuss simply fell down onto the floor, her bottom hitting the wood with a little slap as she stared up at him with round, brown eyes. "Hush," he commanded her, wagging his bruised finger in her direction. She gave a small hiccup and resumed her staring.

He turned to Becky. She looked as though she had been dragged through a pit. Her dress was fairly caked in wet sand, and her dark hair—normally so neatly and becomingly dressed, as would befit a milliner—straggled down her cheeks. Her extraordinary eyes—usually so full of spark and fire—were pools of fatigue and frustration. And yet, somehow, in the midst of this chaos and her weariness, she was still one of the prettiest girls of his acquaintance.

Paul shook his head slowly. Thinking of Becky in that manner would never do. He must stop thinking of her in any way except as his employee. As someone who had dealt with Juliana's fits and temper tantrums, he knew that look on Becky's face all too well. His heart surged as he looked at her, and he almost put out a hand to touch her shoulder reassuringly. Poor girl.

"I understand my niece was rather naughty on the way home." It hurt too much to quirk his eyebrow, as was his habit.

"She…well…" Becky made an exhausted gesture with her hands. "She's been cooped up on a ship for a long time, sir."

He turned to the tall woman beside Becky, who was regarding him with an impassive stare. "You must be Sophia. Were you my niece's caretaker in Italy?"

"Yes."

"Can you speak to my niece's attitude at home?"

"I don't understand." The nurse's English was good enough, but heavily accented.

He gestured at Becky's bedraggled appearance and the overturned table. "Was my niece allowed to behave in such a fantastic manner at home?"

"*Signora* did not like to reprimand her. Nor did she want for us to scold her…" The nurse trailed off, shaking her head.

"Well, she is in my house now. In my house, this will not be tolerated. Kellridge is a haven of quiet and peace. Do you understand?"

The maid gave a respectful nod. "I understand. Making Juliet understand is difficult."

"She shall have to." He steeled himself to look over at his niece again. She looked so much like Juliana. The same long, black hair, the same heart-shaped face. Her brown eyes must have come from her father, for Juliana's had been blue. But for those eyes, she could have been his sister. "No more being naughty," he scolded, frowning at her. "Behave yourself."

"She doesn't speak English," Becky piped up. "Sophia is translating for me."

"That will never do." Becky was Juliet's nursemaid and it was her job to raise Juliet as a proper English lady. Not that he held anything against Sophia, but she was too permissive, and had been made to be so by his sister. Until she was gone, Juliet would continue to look to Sophia for direction and would be allowed to continue slipping back into her old slovenly habits. "She is in England now, and the best way for her to learn English is to only hear and speak it until she finds her way."

"Yes, sir. I try. My English is rather poor." Sophia shrugged her shoulders.

"Tell me, you must have family you wish to return to—another job, perhaps?"

Becky gasped and opened her mouth to speak, but he quieted her with a wave of his hand. "Miss Siddons, we only expected Sophia to bring Juliet here. 'Twas my plan all along to have her return to Italy. Raising Juliet is your duty."

"I do have relatives who miss me and a new job with a different family." Sophia's face settled into a blank expression. Perhaps she wouldn't miss her old charge—or the job of raising her—that sorely. "I thought perhaps you would want me to stay for a while, but since Miss Siddons is here, I may leave when you see fit."

"I'll make the arrangements for you to leave tomorrow." The sooner 'twas done, the better. Becky would have to step up, and Juliet would have to begin learning English and behaving like a little lady. "The yacht will still be anchored at Cleethorpes. I'll have my man drive you there tomorrow."

He stooped gingerly and righted the little table. Becky knelt beside him, placing the ornaments back on its smooth surface. He bit back the sudden urge to promise her he knew what he was doing, that he was still in control. There was no need to say it. The results would manifest themselves in but a few days.

"No more." He gave Juliet the sternest look in his arsenal. "Be a good girl."

Then he strode out of the room, confidence rising within him. He'd made it through. He'd seen his niece without breaking down. Life wasn't so bad after all. Despite a carriage accident, troubled niece, and rainy weather, he was still the master of Kellridge.

And, whether he was dealing with a temperamental toddler or a captivating young nursemaid, he was still the master of his emotions.

# Chapter Eight

Whatever was she going to do with Juliet? Becky crossed her arms over her chest and considered the matter. The little mantel clock chimed ten o'clock in the morning, and the creature still slept. In fact, she slept with her rosy mouth hanging open, and her tiny bottom in the air, crouched atop the coverlet Mrs. Clairbourne had so hospitably chosen for her. The doll that Becky had restored to a semblance of her former glory had tumbled to the floor at some point in the wee hours of the night. Becky sighed and stooped to pick it up. No harm done. She smoothed the doll's rumpled curls and tucked her beside her new mistress.

Of course, was it really surprising that Juliet slept so late into the morning, without stirring an inch? She had stayed up well past eleven the night before, pattering into Becky's room every half hour or so. It was like she couldn't understand what had occurred in her brief little life. She would peep around Becky's door, her brown eyes big as saucers. And when Becky would get up, she'd scurry back into her room and dive under the covers. And so it had gone on, until the mite passed out from sheer exhaustion.

Small wonder Juliet was so confused and doubtful. How dreadful to be left alone and then moved about when really she was still a baby. Why, when Mama and Papa had died, Susannah had been there to shelter both Becky and Nan. Moving into Uncle Arthur's home was the most difficult change she endured, but her elder sister had cared for her and for Nan as tenderly as their mother would have. She didn't have to travel across an entire ocean and then be dumped unceremoniously into a new and entirely foreign land. And even Sophia had gone, escorted to the maids' quarters for the night, and then whisked back to Cleethorpes at dawn.

For Paul had laid down the law, and in no uncertain terms yesterday. Becky suppressed a shiver. His wounds looked so dreadful. And yet—on him, it could be considered romantic. After all, some men could wear scars well. Now, if that horrid cut on his face had been obtained in a more dashing manner—say, perhaps, as the result of a battle over a lady's honor, or in detaining a highwayman—he could be considered rather handsome.

Well, he hadn't gotten those wounds from the blade of a villain's sword. Instead, he had got them from driving at too fast a pace while running away from his rightful duties as an uncle.

She turned from Juliet's bed. At least he had come to the east wing last night to see Juliet and restore order. He'd made it quite clear that Juliet's care rested securely in her hands—and her hands alone.

She walked to the window and pushed the curtain aside with one hand. Sunlight streamed in for the first time in days. The roads would still be muddy, but they would begin to dry. Juliet might be more manageable if she had time to run and play outside. After all, she had been playing quite nicely on the beach before she began flicking sand all over everything, including her new nursemaid.

Becky sighed. If only Juliet were a quiet, docile child. She should know then how to handle her very well. She herself had been such a tame girl, so given to flights of fancy. How would she understand the workings of Juliet's mind? And she couldn't ask Paul for help. Even if Juliet was the spitting image of her mama, he had, in his usual unambiguous and decided manner, told her that she would be solely responsible for Juliet's welfare.

She had no idea how to handle someone so strong-willed and obstinate. Why, only Susannah could come close in terms of temperament, and no one ever controlled her eldest sister.

Susannah might just be able to help. She had, after all, practically raised Becky and Nan after their parents died. And her temper, when provoked, was truly awe-inspiring. If anyone could help her find a way to reach her new charge, Susannah could.

Behind her, a plaintive voice called out, "Mama? Sophia?"

Becky steeled herself. Today would be the hardest. After that, each successive day would have to grow easier.

Surely it would.

Wouldn't it?

"You're in my care now, chicken, at your uncle Paul's home." She turned and gave a bright smile as Juliet pulled herself into an upright position, blinking her wide brown eyes in the sunlight. "It's stopped raining, and I think the best thing for us is to go outside for a bit. Do you fancy a trip to Goodwin Hall?"

Becky ran her tongue over her parched lips. She'd been talking nonstop now for nearly an hour. Doing so was the only way she could think to immerse her charge in the English language. She'd repeated the names of objects over and over as they dressed and readied themselves for the brief trip to Goodwin. And it took all her powers of persuasion to coerce Juliet into the landau. Only by pretending her doll wanted to go for a ride— "Doll, doll. See Juliet? This is your doll."—did she manage to get Juliet to climb in. No doubt the journey across the ocean and then into England had made quite an impression on her two-year-old mind. She wanted no part of any further travel, and even a brief ride provoked her temper.

At least the weather was fine enough today for the top to be opened. And that meant she could distract her charge by pointing and naming everything in sight.

She would be ready for a bracing cup of tea when they reached the hall, though. Being a nursemaid was far more difficult than she had imagined.

As they rounded the bend into the drive that led to the main house, an instantly recognizable rider drew alongside the carriage. "Daniel," Becky called happily, waving her hand. How nice to see and know people after a week or so of being among unfamiliar faces. In fact, the rush of identification made her fairly giddy.

Foster slowed the landau to a halt and Daniel dismounted, coming over to grasp her hands in his.

"Becky! Susannah will be so pleased to see you." He looked over at Juliet and his smile wavered the tiniest fraction of a second. "Upon my word, she looks like her mother."

"Does she?" Becky gave Juliet a kind pat on the shoulder. "I never knew Juliana."

"Yes. Only her eyes are brown, where her mother's were blue. Small wonder Paul was in such a haste to take his leave. Juliana's death hit him hard, you know." Daniel leaned forward, his normally open countenance clouded. "Is he all right? We heard about the accident."

"He seems to be better. He was up and about yesterday." No need to elaborate on exactly why he'd been on his feet so soon after his accident. She was in no mood to regale her brother-in-law with tales of her ineptitude as a nursemaid. However, Daniel's comment did raise the very question that had bothered her since she took her post. Why was Paul so terribly upset about Juliana? Her passing must be a shock—that was understandable. Yet his stubborn refusal to be more than a mere fixture in his niece's life was incongruous with his need to maintain control over Kellridge. In short, his motive remained a mystery, but she couldn't ask Daniel why. Certainly not in front of Juliet. Even if she didn't speak

English yet and wouldn't understand their conversation, some things were just in poor taste.

"I am sure he will be leaving for London, then. As soon as the carriage is fixed." Daniel shrugged and turned back to his horse. "Are you looking for Susannah? She's up with the tenants. They're planning a sewing bee, you know."

"Will I disturb them if I head that way?" Becky cast an uneasy glance at her charge. So far, she was playing with her doll so intently, muttering to her in a language that sounded unlike Italian or English—a Juliet-language. What if she had another temper tantrum?

"Not at all. Susannah has been worried about you. She won't say so, of course, but I can see it in her eyes." Daniel swung himself into the saddle and waved. "I'm off to ride fences. Take care, Becky."

She gave the directions to the tenants' homes to Foster and settled back in her seat. As they rolled and bounced along the gravel roads that led to the hall, she mulled over the mystery that was Paul Holmes—so ordered and meticulous in some ways, so overblown in others. Why was he such a contradiction of so many extremes? If he were romantic, well, then it might be the result of a broken heart. Paul was no romantic. He had not the soul of a poet.

The landau pulled up and stopped at the tenants' village. Becky stood. There—she would recognize Susannah's bright auburn hair anywhere. She was, of course, handing out directions to a group of people, sending them running in all directions.

"Susannah!" Becky waved her arms.

"Becky." Susannah walked, with her usual brisk speed, over to the carriage. "I am so glad to see you. Nan and I have been worried."

"No need to worry." Becky indicated her charge with a wave of her hand. "I have come to ask your advice."

"Of course. What do you need?"

As her sister spoke, a group of tenant children began to cluster around the carriage. Some ran their fingers down the smooth sides of the wooden wheels, while others simply stared. Juliet tucked her doll more tightly to her chest and looked away.

"They're just impressed with the landau," Susannah explained, helping Becky to alight from the carriage. "Paul always has kept an excellent livery stable of his own. Don't worry, they won't damage anything."

As Becky hit the still muddy earth, she reached a hand up to Juliet. Juliet remained fixed in her seat, her eyes turned toward the carriage floor.

"Juliet, come." Becky injected as much lightness into her voice as she could. Juliet remained fixed in her seat.

"Run along, now, children." Susannah shooed them away with a flick of her hand. "Go tell the others that we will start the sewing bee in a moment."

As the children dispersed, the tension that seemed coiled within Juliet faded. She hugged her doll to her chest as Becky boosted her out of the seat. Then Juliet clutched tight to her skirts, hiding her face against Becky's leg.

"She only speaks Italian," Becky explained, after an unsuccessful attempt to break free of Juliet's viselike grip. "And stubborn as a mule. That's why I came to you."

"Well, I don't know whether to be flattered or annoyed at what you're insinuating." Susannah crouched down to Juliet's level and gave her a smile—the kind of smile that could persuade a hesitant customer to purchase a bonnet. "Why, she's a lovely little girl. You need to get her out of that cheap black sateen though. It's entirely unsuitable."

"Her entire wardrobe needs work," Becky admitted. Funny that Paul's niece's clothing was both lacking and unbefitting a child of her age when his family was so wealthy. Almost as though her parents sought to bedeck her as a miniature adult, rather than as someone her age should dress. "I shall start on that with help from some of the other servants, if I can persuade Paul to allow them to take on additional duties."

Susannah cast a wary eye at Foster, who had turned in his seat and was facing away from them to give a modicum of privacy, but could still probably hear every word. "Bring her into Ann's cottage. We can chat and have tea for a moment before I start supervising the sewing bee."

Walking with Juliet attached to her leg was akin to playing at a three-legged race. Becky stumbled and tripped her way into the tenant's cottage, which was cheerful and bright and empty of all humanity. That was good. No matter what happened, she would not give in to tears when telling Susannah of life at Kellridge. If she weakened, at least no one else would be hanging about to witness her feebleness.

"Not only does she not speak English," Becky gasped as she managed to make it to the kitchen table, "but her temper is formidable, and her will strong as iron. She won't eat a healthy amount of food, she sleeps outside her covers—which in and of itself is rare, for you cannot imagine how difficult it is to persuade her to have a lie-down at all. And Paul refuses to help, for he says it's all my responsibility."

Juliet plunked herself down on the dirt floor of the cottage, the corner of Becky's skirt still wadded tightly in her hand.

"And he's quite right, too. You accepted the position, and with it, all the difficulties as well as the freedom it gives you." Susannah took a kettle off the hearth and busied herself preparing tea. "I know this must be a challenge for you, but we've been through worse—much worse—before."

"Yes, but I feel so alone." That was the whole of the problem, right there. That was why Paul's insistence on staying clear of the matter stung so deeply. "Always when we faced trials or tribulations, we faced them together. I have no one to help me, and I am so overwhelmed. Juliet is different than I expected her to be. I wanted a calm and docile child."

"Don't deride her temperament." Susannah set a steaming, fragrant cup of tea before her. "A strong-willed child can be a blessing in disguise. After all, she will never be easily led—and that could prove valuable if she ever falls in with a fast crowd."

Becky took a cautious sip of her tea. Amazing how

a cozy cup with her sister always seemed to set matters right. "I suppose that is true."

"As for her temper—well, she will have to learn to control it. If you establish calm and order into her life, she may not give vent to her bad humor so often. Make sure she has appropriate play clothes. Establish her mealtimes and make her eat regular, wholesome meals. And beginning a proper bedtime is essential." Susannah rested her elbows on the table and blew gently on her tea. "Children crave schedules and practice. I didn't know Juliana at all, of course. From what I understand, given what Daniel has told me, I assume Juliet's life with her parents was pandemonium?"

Juliet rose from her position on the floor and pushed Becky back from the table. Her small sticky hands tugged and pulled at Becky until she launched herself into a comfortable position in Becky's lap.

Becky's heart leaped in her breast and she glanced over at her sister. "Dare I hope she is softening toward me?" She squeezed her charge lightly but if Juliet felt it, she showed no sign. She merely sat, one finger in her mouth, staring straight ahead.

"She might be. Give her time. There's been a great deal of upheaval in her life at such an impressionable age." Susannah gave her an encouraging smile, one that lit her gray-green eyes with hope. "And you should bring her to our morning Bible study this Sunday. You aren't in this alone. Daniel and I, and even Nan, want you to succeed. As you know, the tenants and their children come, and we worship together each Sabbath. I am certain that being around other children would be good for Juliet, and seeing family might be good for you. And if ever a child needed the Lord's teachings in her life, Juliet does."

"Absolutely not." Paul shoved himself away from his desk and stood, facing Becky. Once again, her eyes widened into pools of disappointment. Hadn't they already played this scene several times before? It felt all too familiar to be in this position, defending his stance on how things were run at Kellridge while Becky tried to interfere.

"It's a Bible study at my sister's home." Becky shrugged her shoulders. "You want me to bring up your niece as a proper young English girl. Well, I can tell you right now that no proper young lady grows up without some sort of religious education."

"We don't worship here at Kellridge." Well, that wasn't entirely accurate. Mrs. Clairbourne offered evening prayers in the servants' quarters, but that was done in a clandestine manner. He knew of it, of course, just like he knew of everything that occurred in his home. He didn't give it his full acknowledgment. "I don't worship," he amended.

"I simply cannot be asked to bring up Juliet without teaching her about the Lord. I don't know precisely why you choose to abstain from religion, but that shouldn't influence Juliet. You're an adult, after all. You are free to make your own decisions. You cannot make those kinds of choices on a child's behalf." Becky's words were bland enough, and must have been carefully chosen. Her expression told a different story—her pursed lips and aloof demeanor said, in no uncertain terms, that she thought his decisions were questionable at best.

Paul turned away and stared out the window at the rolling pastures. Sunlight streamed down, gilding the fields, and cows and sheep munched contentedly on the grass. A pastoral scene to be sure, calming in its utter peacefulness, and a welcome antidote to his roiling emotions. If he continued fighting with Becky, then all the order that Kellridge relied upon would be disrupted. And that could not happen, not if he could prevent it.

And, in truth, 'twas downright unpleasant to be forever bickering with Becky. Before she came to work at Kellridge, he'd enjoyed her company. He would often find her at Goodwin when he came to call on Daniel and Susannah, and she was always so pleasant and sweet—a good deal friendlier than her sister Nan. She was pretty to look upon, too. She had charming manners, an eloquent way of speaking, and those attributes, when paired with her dark hair, made a lovely combination. One that could turn a young man's head, but he wasn't a young man any longer. He felt every one of his twenty-four years, and then some. He missed the easy companionship Becky used to offer. And if he crossed her at every turn, he would not regain it.

And, of course, there was the sneaking suspicion that she was right. A genteel young girl had to be brought up as a Christian. If he continued to balk at this, she might enlist the help and support of Daniel and Susannah. And they would not only back her side of things, but possibly condemn him for his choices as well.

He sighed, running his hands through his hair. Part

of being an effective leader meant choosing one's battles well.

"I shall allow you to take Juliet to Bible study on one condition." He remained fixed in his position, unwilling to turn and face the triumph that must be reflected on her face. He hated giving in, but in this case, surrender was necessary.

"Yes. What is it?" If she was exulting in her success, her voice continued to sound strangely impassive.

"That you do not make me go." He must lighten the mood. Get back to his old, teasing ways with her. The serious nature of the past few days grated on his nerves. He was keenly attuned to his duty, and when it was done and time began to pall, he enjoyed play as much as any man. "After all, I am sure that if I crossed the threshold of a chapel, I should be struck by a lightning bolt for my hypocrisy."

"Well, you made it through my sister's wedding in that same chapel without being singed," she replied tartly. "And allow me to remind you that if you question His very existence, then you shouldn't even worry about divine retribution."

He couldn't suppress a chuckle at that. She had the right of it, of course.

"Have we reached an understanding, then?" He turned to face her, the spark set off by their teasing causing hope to surge through him. Perhaps things would finally settle at Kellridge, and he would no longer have to play the role of the heavy-handed villain.

"Yes, we have." She cast a beautiful smile his way, her eyes glowing like amethysts. She was such an appealing young gal when she was happy. As pretty as Ruth Barclay, in a way. Yet Ruth lacked that inner warmth Becky possessed. Ruth had been one of the most beautiful girls in the county, and the kindest, but she had always been remote—as remote as a star twinkling up in the sky.

Well, it would never do to remember Ruth. She was gone. He had faced his dread once this week. He had gone to see his niece and endured the ordeal without breaking down into hysterics like an overwrought female. That was more than enough in one week—or even one year.

He showed Becky out of his study and closed the door behind her. It was also poor form to be comparing his fiancée to his niece's nursemaid. Becky was there to care for Juliet, and not to entertain and enchant him. He scrubbed his hand over his face. He must be tired. That was the reason behind all of this. He was weary because of all he had endured this week. He had been courageous and triumphed, and therefore, there was no urgent need to return to London. Of course, he would go for the season. It was expected of him, and it would be pleasant to return. But there was no driving need to distance himself from Kellridge. He could recuperate in peace, and set about on his journey in a deliberate manner, as he should have from the very start.

Funny. Facing the one thing he'd feared most was actually bringing him freedom, rather than bringing him to his knees.

# Chapter Nine

Becky held tightly to Juliet's hand as they skirted Goodwin Hall, heading toward the little chapel that rested on the fringes of the estate grounds. The chapel had been built by Daniel's mother some time ago, and Daniel had lovingly restored it to its natural beauty as both a tribute to her memory and a gift to his new bride. Already, tenants and servants were milling around outside, preparing to join into worship together. They were late, and she hated being late. How could she help it? At the very last moment, her charge had balked at wearing shoes, kicking and flailing her little feet so that Becky had to well nigh wrestle her to make her give in.

Beside her, Juliet made a hiccupping sound, her eyes still red from crying. They must look a sight. Becky had had no time at all to attend to her own toilette this morning, since she spent all her time working on Juliet. Nothing had gone right. Not one task. Waking her up at a decent hour, forcing her to have a decent breakfast, giving her a new dress to wear, combing her hair and of course the shoes—from the crack of dawn 'til this moment, their morning had been one long argument.

How could she be exhausted already? 'Twas not even half past ten yet. And already, she wanted nothing more than to curl up into a ball on her bed and draw the coverlet over her head.

Two children, a good bit older than Juliet judging by their size, drew up alongside them. "Can she play with us?"

Juliet pressed herself to Becky's side. Well, even if she had fought against her nursemaid all morning, at least she still depended on her in times of duress. That was something. Wasn't it? "Aren't we late? Surely we don't have time to play."

"Children's Bible study is over there." The other child pointed a grubby finger at a clearing in the woods. An entire brood of children congregated under the walnut trees, playing games and shouting at each other. "We play for a while and then our teacher reads us a verse."

"Look at her! She looks like a little doll in her dress and bonnet." The first urchin proceeded to grasp Juliet around the waist and then she struggled to lift her. "What a big dolly!" She set Juliet down and panted, taking a step backward.

"She's so cute. Can she please come with us?"

The other child grasped Becky's free hand. "Come on, little one! Don't you want to play?" She crooned the words in a high-pitched voice, as though she were the adult and Juliet the baby.

Juliet tugged her hand free and frowned, her eyebrows drawing together. Then she clamped her free hand around Becky's skirts. "No."

Becky could not check the flicker of happiness that sprang to life within her. Her first English word! Of course, how fitting that the first thing out of Juliet's mouth would be a refusal.

"You two run along," Becky said with a smile. "We'll be there in a moment."

The children backed away, their mouths turned downward in disappointment. Then they flew off, booted feet skimming the path. "Miss Eugenia! We have a new student!"

Juliet held Becky in that same viselike grip, her strength almost uncanny in one so small and so skinny. Becky leaned down and patted her thin back. "You'll have so much fun at Bible study. What a welcome change! Finally, people your own age to play with." She resumed their progress down the path, as though Juliet weren't clinging for dear life to her skirt.

"No." The single word was clearer and even more deliberate than before.

"Well, you simply must go. All good little girls learn their Bible lessons." No need to make a truly compelling argument, since Juliet probably still didn't understand most of what she was saying.

"No." Louder now, and more insistent.

"Come now." Becky's nerves were worn to a thread. Why must everything be so difficult with Juliet? Why couldn't she just submit to the normal decencies of everyday life?

"No!" Juliet shrieked the word at the top of her lungs,

and then threw herself onto the dirt path, kicking her scrawny legs with each repetition. "No. No. NO!"

The flock of children beneath the walnut tree all turned, watching the tableau with keen interest. The chapel door opened and Nan stepped out, rushing toward them with her eyebrows raised to her hairline. "We can hear you all the way inside! What on earth is the matter?"

"She won't go to Bible study." Becky's voice choked and for a dangerous moment, she feared she would lose all control, too. She wanted nothing more than to throw herself on the dirt beside her charge, kicking and screaming until all the pain and frustration of the past few days finally ebbed.

"Well, you can't very well allow her to throw a fit out here." Nan crossed her arms over her chest and looked down at Juliet's kicking, thrashing form. "Can't you calm her down?"

"If I could, do you think I would be allowing her to run on like this?" Nan could be so provoking at times. Here they hadn't seen each other for a while, and yes, the circumstances were quite vexing, but rather than recognize the emotional exhaustion staring her straight in the face, Nan pointed out the obvious defects of the situation.

"Well, I suppose not." Nan shook her head. "Honestly, 'tis hard to put together a coherent thought with all that noise. What would we do whenever Susannah gave vent to her temper?"

"Once you dashed her with a pitcher full of water."

Despite her fatigue and aggravation, Becky smiled at the memory. "That was an effective antidote."

Nan gave a half-hearted smile. "It wouldn't work now. One simply cannot dash water on a small child. On a sixteen-year-old sister, such an action is permissible."

"Well, we would often walk away," Becky recalled. "If Susannah didn't have an audience, her temper often simmered down."

"That's true. Many times we just had a sudden desire to walk to the village or down the street a bit when she was in the throes of a tantrum." Nan reached out and grasped Becky's hand. "Shall we try it?"

Becky nodded. That brief, warm surge of sisterly affection heartened her a bit. "Should we walk toward or away from the source of the problem? She doesn't want to go to Bible study. She seems frightened of other children."

"I say, let's walk away from it. For today. Then next Sunday, you can try again." Nan spun them around and they began walking down the path. Juliet's screams quieted.

"How are things at the shop?" Keeping up conversation was difficult under these circumstances, and she had the desire to spin around and check on Juliet. She took a deep breath, reminding herself that they were strolling away at a deliberate pace, and she was not very far behind them.

"The shop is doing well, though I miss you." Nan gave her hand a squeeze. "I have no one to argue with. All my workers are too compliant."

Becky laughed, but it sounded bitter even to her own

ears. "Oh, I have had plenty of arguments in my new position. I am sure Paul wishes he'd hired someone more amenable."

"Oh, I don't know. I heard Susannah tell Daniel that it was good for someone to stand up to Paul. What you're doing is admirable." Nan halted her progress and they came to a standstill. The patter of little boots on the path echoed behind them. "See? Already she misses you."

Juliet drew up beside them, her fresh summer dress a wrinkled mess, streaked with dirt.

"Well, I hope you are ashamed of your behavior. I must confess, I am appalled." Becky brushed the grime off the bodice of Juliet's frock. Juliet, in one swift gesture, captured Becky's hand and held it to her cheek. "You see how she is, Nan? One moment, a defiant temper. The next, she is sweetness and light. I never know how or when her mood will change."

"This is all very new to her still." Nan, in her practical fashion, delineated the trying aspects of the case. "She's in a foreign country, she's being made to mind for the first time ever in her brief life, and she's a child anyway. Even if circumstances were absolutely perfect, she would still, as a baby, have difficulty maintaining her temper."

"I suppose so." They neared the gates of Goodwin Hall, where Foster sat waiting with the landau. "Thank you for your help. I get overwhelmed at times. And at Kellridge, I am completely on my own."

"Doesn't Paul help at all?" Nan gave her an awkward

pat on the back. She was never very good at physical displays of sisterly affection.

"No. Juliet's care is entirely my responsibility. I go to him whenever I have a question about the methods by which Juliet is being raised. Handling her temper and implementing a series of routines to regulate her life—well, that is my duty. If I go running to him every time I have a bad moment, then he will think me incapable of handling the job." She stroked the top of Juliet's head. Despite her recent tantrum, her curls remained relatively smooth. That was some progress, at least. It had taken a good hour to detangle her hair this morning.

"Don't feel you have to stay if the job's too hard. I mean—you can always come back to the shop." Nan gave one of her rare, encouraging smiles.

Becky paused a moment. It was good of Nan to offer, and yet, the manner in which she offered still spoke volumes. The shop was Nan's to share now, no longer theirs together. And nothing would ever change that. Juliet— well, Juliet's care belonged to Becky alone. Though 'twas daunting, at least it was her challenge to accept. It would be nice to share the burden with others, but wasn't God calling her to care for Juliet? At the same time, if He did choose her, why did He make the work so very difficult? Her head throbbed.

"Thank you," she said simply, and kissed Nan on the cheek. The sisterly bond that held them together for so many years had subtly changed over the past few weeks. Of course she loved Nan. She always would. Here, their paths diverged, and it wasn't sad. Why, this was a part of life. She now had her purpose and her meaning, and though she was afraid of failure, at least this was hers alone. Tears pricked the back of her eyes as she turned toward the landau. "I'll bring Juliet by for a new bonnet some time," she promised, handing her charge up to the seats.

"Only if you promise she won't tear the place apart," Nan warned. She could be joking, but the same serious vein that underlay all her conversations remained fixed in place. No, she was being honest. And that was so much like Nan that Becky had to bite the inside of her cheek to keep from bawling in earnest.

Foster started the horses and they turned a broad circle, heading away from Goodwin. Kellridge, so foreign to her just a few days ago, was now no longer a mere place of employment, a forbidding and impressive house on a hill. Yet it wasn't precisely home either. Kellridge was a new beginning for her—of finding her place in this world and starting down the path God had chosen for her. Juliet's head sagged against her shoulder as they rolled and jounced over the roads. Becky wrapped her arm around her charge's thin shoulders as her heart swelled. After years of living in the shadows of her sisters, a sense of purpose and belonging trickled into her soul.

The bothersome thing about Sunday mornings was that there was so precious little to do. Everyone was attending church or services of some sort, and his servants often took the morning off to attend to their own personal matters. Even if he didn't believe in a higher power, Paul permitted Sundays to be leisurely and rest-

ful for everyone at Kellridge, from its master to the low-
liest stable hand or scullery maid.

He cast aside the book he'd been trying to read for
the past quarter of an hour. If he was in London he could
take himself off to pursue more exciting matters, even
on the Sabbath. Unfortunately, out in the country, he
was quite on his own.

He could go walk around the estate. The weather
was fine after days of rain, and he didn't ache quite as
badly today as he had in days past. He strolled out of
the library and down the hallway, just as the front door
opened to admit a struggling Becky. Foster held the
door open for her, but she was carrying Juliet, who had
fallen soundly asleep, her mouth forming a little "o."

There was no way Becky could carry her charge to the
second floor without tripping over her own skirts in the
process. No use having two injured people in the Kellridge household. He made a shushing gesture with his
hand, then nodded to her and grasped hold of Juliet, cradling her to his chest. She was so thin and bony. What on
earth had his sister been feeding her? Knowing Juliana,
she'd probably allowed her entire household to subsist on
pâté de foie gras served on tiny toast squares. Juliet had,
in all likelihood, never tasted porridge in her brief life.

It wasn't so bad to be this close to his niece. He
wouldn't go all to pieces. He could just pretend she was
someone else's child, and turn away from the fact that
she looked so much like her mother. Or he could fixate
on the practical needs of her existence, such as how to
get her to eat more. And he could concentrate on the

matter at hand, which was tucking her back into her bed without awakening her.

As they neared her doorway, Becky hurried past him to open the door. Then she beckoned to Juliet's bedroom, where she turned down the bed. As he laid Juliet onto the counterpane, Becky swiftly removed her boots. Juliet stirred, then turned over on her stomach and pushed herself to a semikneeling position. That was an odd way to sleep—certainly it couldn't be comfortable. He made a movement to turn her over, but a flurry of hand-waving from Becky halted his progress.

She motioned him out of the bedroom and shut the door. "She sleeps like that. I cannot think it comfortable myself, but she seems to prefer it," she whispered.

"Oh. Well. My apologies," he muttered. Well, that was taken care of. He turned to go.

"Thank you for your help." She had pitched her voice to a stage whisper. "I had no idea how I was going to make it up the stairs, but I was jolly well going to give it a go. She needs all the rest she can get."

That was the first time Becky had genuinely expressed gratitude to him for anything, and for some ridiculous reason, it was heartening. "I was just going to go for a walk," he offered. "Would you like to accompany me?"

"Oh, that would be nice, but I should stay close to Juliet." She motioned toward Juliet's door with her head. "She may sleep three hours, or fifteen minutes. It's impossible to say. And it was such a difficult morning that I find myself in need of a break, too."

"I see." That was rather a letdown. It would be pleasant to spend some time in someone's company. And Becky could be a lovely companion when the mood struck her. "I understand. Sundays at Kellridge are so quiet, I often find myself bored, to own the truth." There was no need to explain himself or his feelings, but something was driving him to continue this conversation. He wasn't ready to face the rest of the day alone.

"I was going to work on a new play dress for Juliet, and I am so used to talking with my sisters as I sew. I find it a lonely business to stitch away on my own, with no pleasant chatter to soothe my nerves," she admitted. "I am sure that you have far more interesting things to do than sit with me as I work, though."

"I'd be happy to." He said it almost too fast. No need to look and sound desperate for social interaction. "This is supposed to be a day of rest. Why work?"

"I don't think of sewing as work." She gave a shy smile. "It's always been rather like…like artistic expression, I suppose. I like it."

"Well, if you enjoy it and wouldn't mind the company…" He trailed off. "Are you hungry?"

"A little. Why?" She opened the door to the small sitting-room that adjoined her bedroom.

"I don't like a heavy lunch on Sundays, so I usually have the cook leave something light for me in the kitchens while she has her rest. Perhaps I could bring it up here, and we could share?"

Becky settled into her chair, pulling a small heap of lavender cotton into her lap. "That would be quite a treat, actually."

Paul dashed down to the kitchens and found the light

luncheon that had been set out for him in a basket—
bread, cheese, cold meat, sliced apples. And a few slices
of a rich chocolate cake. Normally he would grab a bottle of wine to go along with such a repast, but somehow, that didn't seem right. So he took a bottle of spring
water and two glasses from the nearby cupboard.

When he returned to the sitting room, Becky was
hard at work, her dark head bent down over the lilac
fabric. Sunlight streamed in through the window, and
a clock ticked softly upon the mantelpiece. Everything
was calm, and quiet, and still. And yet—it filled his soul
with a sense of peace, rather than of tedium.

Any given afternoon in London he would be pursuing
risk, or excitement or enjoying a fast time. London was
his second home, and his respite from the responsibilities
of being master of Kellridge. This, for some reason, was
far more satisfying than any of those pursuits. He laid
the luncheon on a little table and drew it close to Becky,
so that she could help herself as she pleased.

"Thank you for sharing." She set a small stitch in
the bodice. "Do all the servants fend for themselves
on the Sabbath?"

"No, they share in a community meal, for I don't like
to make them put forth a tremendous amount of effort
on me, unless I have guests. Which isn't terribly often."
He pulled a velvet-covered chair closer to the table and
broke the bread. "Why are you making a new gown for
my niece? Did she not have plenty of frocks?"

"She does, but I don't find them entirely suitable."
She snipped a thread and paused, helping herself to
an apple slice. "The fabrics are stiff and cause her to

itch. And they aren't cut loosely enough. She's in heavy mourning now, but I am making clothes for her to wear for half-mourning in a few months."

"It's good of you to think of her comfort." In fact, it was rather heartwarming. In a period of a few days, Becky was showing more care and concern for Juliet than possibly anyone had in her entire life. "My sister was not sensible. I am certain she dressed Juliet for effect, not practicality. If that little lavender dress suits her, and makes her happier, then we can move her on to half-mourning early."

Becky glanced up, her delicate eyebrows arched. "Are you quite sure of that?"

"Why not? My sister would prefer her to be in elegant colors. Juliana once told me she had a horror of black. And besides, we're rather isolated out here in the country. No need to be a slave to decorum." He wasn't so much pushing through the usual period of grieving as he was ensuring that his niece was well cared for.

"The more I hear of Juliana, the more I like her—though it sounds like she could be trying." Becky smiled and resumed her stitching. "She sounds like she would have added spice to life."

"Spice—yes, I suppose that is the best way to describe her. A little goes a long way, and all that." He shrugged and opened the bottle of water, pouring it out evenly between the two glasses. "When my father died, Juliana was only thirteen, and I only five years her senior. When I came into the running of Kellridge, and all the estate had to offer, Juliana was by far the biggest challenge I faced." And the only one he had failed—utterly and completely.

"Because she was so headstrong? I see that in her daughter." Becky accepted her water with a brief nod of thanks.

"Headstrong, willful and beautiful. She loved so fiercely and lived so passionately. If only she'd found time to calm down, to enjoy the simplicities of life." Just as he and Becky were doing now. If only Juliana could rest, or calm herself, perhaps she wouldn't have burned herself out so soon. So much of his life had been spent trying to rein her in.

"Did she find peace when she moved to Italy? She settled there with her husband, did she not?"

It was an innocent question, the sort of small talk he had encouraged by bringing a meal here to share with Becky. Even so, he had to take a sharp step backward. "Yes. Her husband was Italian. They married there, and there she lived until they both died."

Paul could feel her gaze resting upon him, yet he wouldn't look up. He wouldn't elaborate. If he said one more word, the dam would break. He would spill everything—how he behaved most shamefully in the years following Ruth's death. How Juliana fell in love with her music teacher, the man he himself brought to Kellridge. How she became with child and was sent off in disgrace, to marry in Italy. How Juliana blithely brought shame and dishonor upon their family at the tender age of seventeen and then fell in love with the blackguard who disgraced her. Then bore his child, who now slumbered in the next room.

Had Paul been a good guardian and a decent master, one who stayed at home rather than cavorting about London, none of that would have happened.

## Chapter Ten

The rest certainly did her charge no good. Juliet wailed and kicked on the floor of the study. All Becky had tried to do was make Juliet change from playing with her blocks in the study to washing up for dinner. Juliet certainly hated change of any kind, even if it simply meant changing from one activity to another.

"Juliet, come now. Your uncle will hear you." He had allowed them the use of the library after Juliet awakened from her nap, and 'twas nice to have a change of scene. Just as it had been nice to have Paul's company in the nursery earlier that afternoon. If they made too much noise, he might regret softening toward Juliet. He might freeze up, when he had just begun to thaw. And having Paul be pleasant to her was ever so much better than when he played the distant, forbidding lord of the manor, or the joking, teasing bounder.

Juliet gave another loud wail, and thumped against the table. A bottle of ink, jounced by the force of her tiny foot against the table leg, rolled off the surface and fell onto the thick Aubusson carpet. The stopper slipped out, and the rich black liquid seeped into its deep nap.

Becky stifled a scream of horror and gazed at the spreading pool. That rug was priceless. Just judging by the vivid colors and luxurious texture, it likely cost a small fortune. She fell to her knees and turned the bottle of ink upright, placing the stopper back. Behind her, Juliet ceased her frantic flailing and came to sit beside her.

"Oh no." Juliet stuck two of her fingers in her mouth, her eyes wide.

"Oh no, indeed." Becky placed the ink on the table. How on earth would she get that horrid stain out? Paul would be furious. Everything in Kellridge was supposed to be kept just so. And here he had allowed her to use this room, his first true concession to allowing Juliet in his life. And within just an hour, they had completely destroyed its furnishings.

She pressed her trembling hands to her forehead. Perhaps she could run and get Mrs. Clairbourne to assist. Surely the housekeeper would know how best to treat the stain. She stood, grasping Juliet's hand. "We need to go to the kitchens to get help." She turned to go, but was stopped by Paul.

He lounged against the doorframe, an inscrutable look hovering in his brown eyes. "I came to see what all the fussing was about."

"Well, we had a small accident…." Becky began. Had he seen the stain already?

"So I see." Again, that wry humor. Was he really angry? Or was he teasing her? Her heart hammered in her chest and she squeezed tightly to Juliet's hand.

He strolled into the room and gave the bell rope a pull. "I'll have Mrs. Clairbourne come see what can be done. Go ahead and take Juliet to her room."

"If it's just the same to you, I'll stay and clean." Better to own responsibility for the accident from the start. "I want to help. I know that rug must be quite expensive, and you may dock my salary until it's paid for…."

Paul shook his head. "No need for that. And no need to stay and repair the damage. I'll see to it that Mrs. Clairbourne—"

"Nay, I insist. 'Tis my fault. I should have kept Juliet under better control."

Mrs. Clairbourne entered the room. That good lady turned pale and made a noise like a wounded animal when she spied the spreading ink on the rug. Paul turned to her, assuming command of the situation as a general might on the field of battle.

"Mrs. C., I beg you to take Juliet upstairs to her nursery and watch her until Miss Siddons is able to join her," he began. "And send an army of maids up here to clean up this mess with whatever elixir you think might do the trick."

"Vinegar." The housekeeper shook her head, making a tsking sound as she led Juliet away. "A great deal of vinegar."

Paul watched them leave and then turned to Becky. "Come. Follow me to my study."

As Becky trailed behind Paul's broad back, her mouth went dry. Well, this was it. She was going to be dismissed. She was abysmally incompetent as a nursemaid, just as she had been with everything else. She was no practical use as a milliner and couldn't even entice a lonely soldier to ask for her hand.

How foolish to think that God had called her here. That she had a purpose in life. Her purpose must be entirely different. She was meant to cheerfully toil at cheap bonnets the rest of her life.

Tears welled in her eyes. In no time at all, she would be back at the millinery shop, begging Nan for her old position. Would she even be able to see Paul socially without being humiliated into the very dust? 'Twould be quite awkward to see him over at Susannah's home, and be expected to speak with him, even though she had failed him so completely.

He opened the door and ushered her in, the scar on his face making his visage leaner, more unreadable than ever before. As he closed the door behind them, her anxiety welled within. She couldn't take this. 'Twas too embarrassing.

"I'll go," she burst out. What a relief to say the words aloud. "I can leave here within just a few moments, and I shall find a way to repay you for the rug."

"Go?" He arched one eyebrow and gazed at her, his arms folded across his chest. "Go where?"

"Go back to the millinery shop." She couldn't bring herself to say home. It wasn't home any longer. The site of her many failures, perhaps, but it wasn't home.

"Why would you want to do that?" Paul leaned against his desk and grasped the edge. "Aren't you happy here?"

To her undying shame, she could no longer hold back the tears. They streamed out of her eyes and down her cheeks, lavish and unchecked. "Aren't you dismissing me?"

"No. Why would I?"

Her tears were flowing too fast for her to gauge his expression; indeed, he was shrouded in a mist.

"Because I am terrible at what I do." Now that the floodgates had opened, there was some comfort in owning the truth. "I can't manage Juliet. She throws temper tantrums at every opportunity. I try to get her to stop. I try to make her a little lady. I just haven't the gift for it."

"Well, Juliet is high-spirited. Just like her mother."

"A good nursemaid would be able to handle her." Becky sniffled and pulled her handkerchief out of her sleeve. "I don't understand why God called me here, if all I am going to do is fail." Her knees trembled violently. In a moment she might fall if she didn't gain better control over herself.

"I don't think God had much to do with it. I don't hold much with providential direction. I asked you because I needed your help. And I still do. And what's more, I want you to be Juliet's nursemaid." Paul's voice was crisp and decisive. He was slipping back into his role of lord of the manor. In a moment he would turn cold and precise and this wonderful warmth between them would dissipate.

"No. I believe God sent me here, even if you do not. I must have a purpose in life. If this isn't meant to be my role, what could it mean?" She gave vent to her sobs in earnest. It felt good to cry, after all. Releasing all the pent-up frustration and anger and despair of the past few weeks…giving in to the feelings of inadequacy and helplessness…why, it felt awfully good to just let them flow from her, like a swift-moving stream.

"Becky. Don't." His voice was different now, huskier and somehow more intimate. He was drawing her closer rather than freezing her out.

She lifted her head from the now-sodden handkerchief and looked at Paul. He stood before her, a step closer than before, his arms outstretched in a beseeching fashion. "I beg you, don't cry. Please don't. It's the one thing I can't bear, seeing a pretty girl weep."

This Paul was different, somehow. In the space of a few moments, he'd become warm and kind. He didn't laugh or tease her, nor did he shut her out with an air of condescension. And he called her by her name. He was reaching out to her at a moment when she hurt most dreadfully.

If only he would stay this way forever—why, she would work for him as long as he needed.

She must stop crying. Paul would promise Becky anything—he would double her pay, he would find another helper for her, he would buy her the prettiest frock in London—if only she would stop. Emotional displays of any kind were horrifying, but none so much as one in the grip of tears. Especially a young, pretty lass in the hold of a weeping fit. Juliana knew this about him and had used it to her full advantage. He would promise Juliana the world, even allow her to marry a rogue and bear his child only a few months thereafter.

This was a vulnerability of his. It was far better than giving full vent to emotion, which was weaker still.

No, better to give a girl anything she wanted in order to keep her from crying, and better to never give in to feelings oneself. That way madness lay.

"See here, what can I do to help you? What is it that causes the most trouble?" If they could stick to the facts at hand, he would come up with a solution. And everything would work out just fine.

Becky kept her eyes cast down as she searched for a dry spot on her handkerchief. "Oh, I don't know. I don't think there's anything wrong with her. I think it's me. I must be doing something wrong, for it seems like every time we make a little progress, she suddenly jumps backward."

"Well, what sort of progress are you making?" He leaned up against the desk, clasping the edge of it once more. His shoulders relaxed. He could solve this problem, if only they could get to the root of it.

"Her clothes, for one thing. They were entirely inappropriate for a child—why, she was dressed more as an adult. And she doesn't eat or sleep with any sort of regularity or schedule. So I spoke to Susannah about it, and she suggested implementing some sort of regimen—some regularity in Juliet's life." Becky paused for a moment, glancing up at him with the fire quenched in her watery eyes. "Whenever I try to tell Juliet what to do, or where to go, or to stop playing at a given time—"

"She throws a temper tantrum." Yes, that was her mother showing through. "Juliana was the same way. It would throw the house in uproar, you know."

"So what did your mother do? How did she manage

Juliana?" Becky sank into the nearby armchair with the air of one struggling against defeat.

"Well, she let the servants handle it, mostly. And when she died, which was when Juliana was only about three years old, Father let the servants continue handling it. When I took over, she was willful and stubborn. I had a plan to iron things out—to bring her more to heel, you might say—but then that plan went out the window." Actually, to own the precise truth, it was Ruth's plan. Once they wed, she would come be mistress of Kellridge, and together they would handle Juliana.

And then, when Ruth died, all thoughts of Kellridge having a mistress, or of creating a family, or of making Juliana behave, had died with her. In fact, no one had behaved well, least of all himself. Ruth's death was an excuse to go on an extravagant binge. After which he was so ashamed, so filled with pain and remorse, that he split his life into two distinct halves—care of Kellridge, and then a life of debauchery.

Becky looked at him in question. She must be wondering why he'd grown so silent.

"Sorry," he apologized. "Bitter memories."

"Bitter memories? Oh, Paul, I am sorry." She heaved a gusty sigh. "If I were doing my job well, then Kellridge would continue to run with clockwork precision. Here I was, railing against the particular way you manage things, hoping for a little disorder to break up the monotony of perfection, and I seem to have gotten more than my fair share." She gave a weary laugh, showing the charming dimple at the corner of her mouth.

What a relief to hear that sound. Becky was one of

those women whose laughs, even when tired, were nothing short of enchanting. In fact, were she in a ballroom in London, crowded with all the most sought-after debutantes of the season, her laugh alone would bring the swains running. Too bad she hadn't the advantages of money and good family connections, even if her parents had been well-off. She could have married quite well.

He gave her a ruthful grin. "I don't think you lack as a nursemaid. In truth, the fact that you care so much, and want to do so well, makes me certain I did the right thing in entrusting Juliet to your care. You must understand that we had an entire household of people who could not force Juliana to mind. So you, being alone, are at rather a disadvantage."

"I do like Juliet." She gave him a shy smile, and those remarkable eyes of hers began to glow. "I like her spirit. I don't want to crush that part of her. I must be able to manage her."

That sounded rather like what Ruth had told him, so many years ago. Manage her, but don't try to rub out her spirit. Together, they had planned to send Juliana to a prestigious music school in London. She had such prodigious talent—her voice, and her skill at the pianoforte. She could have been an astonishingly good musician, had she any kind of method to her madness. The idea was to immerse her in her talent, give her routines and gently mold her into a fiercely gifted musician.

Instead, he'd hired a music teacher to come to Kellridge after Ruth died. While he was in London on his bender…and that blackguard, here, under his own roof…

Better not to walk down that road. After all, Juliana loved him. Signor Martinelli professed to love her. Perhaps Juliana found happiness and peace once she moved with him to Italy. 'Twas his own weakness, his own selfish indulgence in leaving Kellridge at a critical time, that was to blame.

He pulled himself from the distant shores of memory. "Yes, you must be able to control her."

"You mentioned before that you had a plan for Juliana, but that it never came to fruition. Could we implement something like it for Juliet?"

He glanced down at Becky. She was so young and so determined—softer and warmer than Ruth, for Ruth never lost her sense of aristocratic aloofness, even in their most intimate moments together. But Becky shared the same sense of drive and purpose. As Ruth had wanted for Juliana, Becky wanted to make a good life for Juliet.

He shook his head. Why was he even comparing Becky to his former fiancée? She was his employee, a servant in his home. He had renounced any kind of lasting dalliance after Ruth died. There was no future to be had in thinking kindly upon Becky, or in cataloging her virtues. He had forsaken the marriage mart, and Becky, being a respectful girl from a family he called his friends, was certainly no candidate for a flirtation.

Why was he even thinking of flirtations and dalliances at all? They were discussing Juliet and her upbringing, and nothing else.

He gave his head a decisive shake. Time to clear the cobwebs from his mind.

"We do need a plan for Juliet. It sounds as though she has trouble with making changes. No surprise, given how much she's been through." He sat in the chair opposite Becky and drew closer. "What kind of changes were you trying to make?"

"Well, I tried putting her to bed on a timely schedule, and feeding her meals on time, too. I tried feeding her more wholesome foods—a nursery diet, you might say. And I tried getting her to go to Sunday school, though that was a total disaster."

"And you've been making new clothes for her," Paul added.

"I haven't even tried making her wear them yet." Becky sat back in her chair. "All of these changes are meant for the best. I haven't meant to make things worse."

"No, of course not. And indeed, you are doing your job. Given that Juliet is a miniature of her mother, perhaps I can give a little advice. I had some experience dealing with Juliana, you know. And though I failed her miserably, perhaps we can learn from my mistakes."

Becky made a sudden movement in her chair, swiveling to face him. She regarded him frankly, honesty shining out of her eyes. "Why do you feel that way?"

Paul hesitated. How much of the truth could he tell her? Not that he didn't trust her. In fact, he had hired her because, knowing her family and the sterling character each member of it possessed, she would never gossip or violate his privacy. Would she think ill of him? He couldn't bear to see disappointment reflected in her eyes.

More to the point, would he be able to speak the truth without breaking down entirely? For that would be completely unacceptable.

He cleared his throat. As Juliet's nursemaid, she did deserve to know something of the truth.

"Suffice it to say that Juliana loved as passionately as she lived. And the man whom she chose for her affections—Juliet's father—was unworthy of her." There. That should clear matters up without undue emotional tirades spewing forth.

"I don't understand. How did you fail her? Surely a woman has a right to fall in love with whomever she chooses. How was her choice of husband your mistake?" She was still looking at him—nay, looking through him—with that frank and uncanny glance of hers.

"I allowed the blackguard into my home. You see, the plan was for Juliana to go to London to study music at a conservatory. After…my fiancée…died, I left Juliana here and went to London myself. I needed to get away, you see. I was gone for four years, only a few return trips to see to matters. When Juliana grew older, rather than send her away, I thought it would be better for her to stay at Kellridge. So I hired Signor Martinelli to come teach her while I indulged my grief." He swallowed. This was growing to be more than he could bear. More than he had anticipated. She must stop asking questions, or he would lose face altogether.

She shook her head. "I still don't see why you hold yourself accountable, Paul. I think it's lovely that she fell in love with her music teacher. They had so much in common. It's really rather romantic—"

He cut her short with a curt wave of his hand. "There's nothing romantic about it. And there's certainly everything to blame me for. I should have been here, supervising matters. Watching everything with a closer eye." The truth rushed from him, unchecked. "And thanks to my excellent guardianship, Juliet was born only four months after her parents' wedding."

"Oh." Color rushed into Becky's cheeks and she gazed down at the floor.

He fell silent, as well. He had said too much. Becky was likely horrified by his frankness. One wasn't supposed to say things like that to young unmarried girls. What had come over him? This was what came of losing control, of failing to maintain his grip on the clockwork precision that governed his life. Had he simply stuck to the matter at hand, things would have been fine.

"I still don't think it's your fault."

Startled, he glanced over at Becky. Though her cheeks were still rosy, she was looking at him with that same candid look—tempered, perhaps, with a sort of sympathy. As he stared, she continued.

"Knowing Juliet as I do, she hates being told what to do. And that's why we are working with her now, trying to mold her in such a fashion that she can be taught not just right from wrong, but how to govern her impulses and emotions. If that were never checked by anyone, why, Juliet would be a force to be reckoned with as a grown woman. This, I assume, is what happened to Juliana. So, no matter what you said, had she chosen Juliet's father as her heart's desire, nothing you would have done could have prevented their relationship. In fact, you would have made matters worse."

Paul considered her words. 'Twas the first time he'd ever spoken to anyone about it. No one, not even George or his many sisters, knew the depth and breadth of his guilt in the matter. Was there some truth to what Becky said?

"So now, let us turn from whatever has gone by," she added in a gentle tone. "We must decide what to do with Juliet's future."

He was pulled from the past to Becky's side in the present, her soothing voice keeping his worries and troubles and failures at bay. She was right, of course. They must set a course of action for Juliet. She must have some rules, and some regulations and some schedules. He would not allow the same mistakes to happen again.

"We shall try to implement changes in her routine one at a time. Perhaps she gets overwhelmed if we try to change too much. Let's start by giving her a regular bed and nap time. If she finally has enough sleep, she might cease in some of these tantrums."

"I think that is an excellent idea. And then, after two weeks of that, perhaps we could add another change? Like her diet—making her try new foods?" Becky gave a little half smile of encouragement.

"Yes. Precisely. You won't work on this alone any longer. Though you are her primary caretaker, we shall work together, as a team. We shall draw on my experience with Juliana, and you shall introduce the changes as you see fit. And we can meet once a day to discuss how things have gone and how they are progressing."

"Oh, Paul, that is brilliant." Becky clapped her hands and grinned, showing the dimple in her cheek. "I know it will make all the difference in the world."

Paul smiled in return, his heart warming a little to her good cheer. She was back on first-name terms with him again—a relief indeed. And this was the first time since Ruth died that he had promised any kind of partnership—particularly in the running and management of Kellridge—with anyone besides his estate manager, Parker. It was strange and heartwarming and frightening, all at the same time.

He wasn't a praying man, of course. But for the first time in ages, he wished he could turn to a higher power for comfort and direction.

# Chapter Eleven

Once Paul had shown confidence in Becky's abilities, and had promised to help her make the necessary changes in Juliet's life, 'twas amazing how much easier her position in the household became. She was now an equal partner in the supervision of one very wild child's life, rather than the sole manager of her care. Funny how having someone else to turn to could make everything run so much smoother.

Of course, Becky mused as she tugged the cotton nightgown over Juliet's head, it did no good to become overly optimistic. They still had a great deal of changes to bring about in her charge's life. Tucking her into bed at a decent hour, and allowing for one nap at midday, had already—only three days in!—made some pleasant changes in Juliet's behavior.

"Time to say your prayers," she reminded the child. Another astonishing development—Juliet was quickly picking up the English language. Perhaps her resistance to change had more to do with her inability to understand a word anyone said, rather than a patent refusal to accept a transition of any kind.

Juliet nodded and slipped out of her little bed, kneeling beside Becky on the floor. Becky patted her back, and then began. "First, we thank God for the blessings in our lives. Thank You, Lord! And we pray for those we love—take care of them, Lord. And we pray to become a good little girl in God's eyes. Amen."

"'Men." Juliet gave a decisive nod of her head, her black braid swinging over one shoulder. The braid was yet another change Juliet was getting used to this week—bedtime and braids. Otherwise, Juliet's hair was nigh on unmanageable.

"Now, off to bed with you. If you behave yourself, we can try going to Sunday school again." With a deft hand, Becky tucked the covers all around Juliet, swathing her in luxurious warmth. "Good night, little one." She placed a gentle kiss on Juliet's forehead.

"Night," Juliet murmured in return, staring up at Becky with her luminous brown eyes. Then her gaze shifted to a point directly behind and to the right. "Night," she said again.

Becky turned. Paul lounged against the doorframe, his expression unreadable by the single candle that lit the nursery. He must be here to discuss the day's progress. Her heart gave a joyful leap in her breast. These visits with Paul were quickly becoming the best part of her day.

"Night," he replied laconically. "I hope you were good today." He took a few steps into the bedroom and grasped the candle from the table.

Becky blew a last kiss to her charge and followed the flickering candlelight out of the room to the little parlor where they held their nightly conference.

Paul stooped and placed the candle on the table beside Becky's chair. "How did things go?"

Becky settled into her chair and took out her workbasket. "Oh, better than usual. Of course, she threw a bit of a tantrum when she was asked to put away her toys and wash her hands before dinner. She seems to hate making these transitions from one activity to another." She withdrew the lavender gown she'd been working on and smoothed it out on her lap. "Truly, for three days we've had excellent progress. She no longer kicks and flails, and I find myself able to make it through the better part of the day without bursting into tears."

Paul chuckled. "Well, that is always good to hear."

His laughter brought a smile to her face. Paul was always such jolly company when he was like this— friendly and open, not jokey or distant. She picked up her needle and threaded it. "And how was your day?"

"Oh, I worked with my estate manager, Parker. Making a few improvements to the tools and machinery we have on hand before autumn hits and we become so deeply involved in the harvest." His mouth twisted in a rueful grin. "I really should bring something to work on when we have these discussions. You make me feel positively lazy."

"Oh, this is relaxing to me. You know that. A little sewing, especially on a pretty dress like this, is the most comforting thing at the close of the day." She darted a quick glance up at him. Was he bored? Surely he had better things to do than sit around and talk to her about his charge. In time, when she gained better control of Juliet, would he cease these meetings with her? That would be horrid. If she kept entertaining him, perhaps he would stay. "Tell me, what do you talk with Parker about?"

"Well, we discuss Kellridge, you know. What needs to be done, what improvements should be made. Today we spoke about some business that would take me to London." He sat in a nearby chair, stretching his booted feet out. "I suppose I should do it sooner rather than later."

Paul in London? She forced her disappointment back to a reasonable size. Of course Paul would go to London. He'd been threatening to do so ever since she started her position here. Only the carriage accident and her complete incompetence had forced him to stay. And already, the scars on his handsome face were fading, giving him a slightly rakish and even distinguished air. And of course, she was handling Juliet better than before, with his help. So there really would be little reason for him to stay if London beckoned.

That was the way of it. Funny how her throat tightened at the mere prospect of it.

Was this her romantic side creeping back out? Stuff and nonsense. She must gain better control over herself. She couldn't simply fall all over herself every time a handsome man showed her the slightest bit of interest.

"I am sorry that we were the cause of so many delays on your part." Her voice sounded strained, even to her own ears. How absurd. She gave a little cough and continued. "I know you have a great many important things tying you to London."

"Ah, well. London can wait a bit longer. Kellridge is always my first priority. So it has been since I was a mere stripling." He twitched his booted feet back and forth. "So no need for apologies."

He cast a warm smile her way once more and fell silent.

Becky concentrated on a difficult stitch to hide her ruffled feelings, which surely must be writ plain across her face. She never was any good at hiding her emotions, and Susannah could always tell if they'd been up to mischief as children simply by staring into her eyes. So she must keep her head down for a moment. What did it matter to her if Kellridge, and not his niece, was his first priority? And was he implying that she had brought chaos to Kellridge? For it was not so; his tiny little tyrant of a niece had done that herself.

"I think I shall try, once more, to take Juliet to Sunday school," she ventured after a pause. "She needs to meet other children, and as we discussed, as a proper young girl she must begin learning about the Lord even at her young age. My hope is that, since we are establishing some small changes in her life, I can start this anew as well."

Paul made an impatient movement in his chair— one completely out of keeping with his indolent pose and his carefree way of speaking. She glanced over at him. His handsome face had hardened somewhat, and something flickered in the depths of his brown eyes. He merely nodded. "Of course."

The door to the parlor creaked open and the distinct pitter-patter of bare feet broke the sudden awkward silence. "Juliet, why are you out of bed?" Becky fixed her charge with a stern glare.

Juliet sidled toward her uncle, keeping her large eyes fixed on Becky. Her rosy lips remained pursed tightly, as though she were keeping a secret all to herself.

"Do you need a drink of water?" That was the usual excuse for a bedtime visit.

Juliet shook her head and shuffled closer to Paul.

"Did you have a nightmare?" She had, once or twice, dreamed of her mama. Perhaps that happened again.

Juliet shook her head again, sending her braid swinging back and forth. Becky sighed. "Then why, pray tell, are you out of bed? You know it is past your bedtime."

Juliet placed her small hand on Paul's sleeve. Becky eyed them both, wariness building within her. What game was her charge playing at? Just because Paul had grown to tolerate them, and agreed to help manage her, didn't mean that he would encourage familiarity.

"You come, too." It wasn't a question, but a demand made with the kind of firmness that would serve Juliet well some day, when she had servants and a home to run.

Paul's forehead wrinkled and he shook his head. "Whatever are you talking about, child?"

Juliet remained fixed in her position, her hand resting on his sleeve. She swiveled her head toward Becky. "Sunday."

For a moment, 'twas rather akin to putting together an odd jumble of puzzle pieces, trying to sort out what went where. "Do you mean…are you asking…do you want your uncle to come with us to Sunday school?"

Juliet gave a decided nod of her head. "Yes."

"Oh." One could almost pity Paul, caught as he was between a child's demand and his own resolute and unchanging mind. Indeed, Becky fought back a chuckle at the astounded look on Paul's face. "Oh, well. I don't usually go to Sunday school. It's not my forte."

Juliet folded her arms across her chest and faced Becky squarely. Stubbornness and determination creased her brow. "Me, too."

"Oh, now, wait. You certainly shall go to Sunday school if Miss Becky decrees it. Once you are an adult, then you can make your own choices." Paul settled back in his chair as though the matter were finished. "Go back to bed then."

"No." Juliet stamped her foot. "Not my…fornay."

Well, in a matter of moments, there would be a conflagration. That would likely mean that it would take another hour for her to calm down and then fall to sleep—and then, her sleep schedule would be completely thrown off. "Now, Juliet," she pleaded in her most reasonable tone, "your uncle is master here. The decisions he makes are good for everyone. If he says you must go, then you must come with me. It will be fun, you'll see. Lots of other children to play with."

"No." Louder now, and more demanding.

Paul sat back in his chair. "Is this what you have been dealing with on a daily basis?"

Becky stifled a grin. Now Paul was getting a fairly

good taste of a truly Juliet-esque temper tantrum. "Oh, no, sir. I've witnessed much worse."

"To think I would be hounded by a female in my own home about my lack of religious dedication," he grumbled. "Fine. If it makes peace in Kellridge and means you'll go to bed on time, then I shall go, too."

Becky shook her head. Amazing. One small child had already convinced Paul to improve his life for the better. Something no adult had been able to do. "Off to bed, now. You heard your uncle."

Juliet gave Paul a winning grin and then skipped back to her little bed. The squeak of the mattress ropes announced that she had, indeed, flung herself down. Hopefully, she would fall asleep within a quarter of an hour.

Had the meticulous standards of Kellridge, and their own pressing needs to fit Juliet into a routine schedule, been preserved? Yes, but at what cost? She dared not look at Paul's face. In a way it was rather touching, and even a little funny.

She simply could not shake the feeling that something rather extraordinary had just occurred.

So he had given in to his ward's wishes. What of it? Paul sat back in his chair. He was the master of Kellridge, and if he chose to go to a simple Bible lesson to maintain peace in his home, so be it. There was no need to feel so ruffled in spirit.

He cast about for something to say. "So...your sister Susannah, these Bible studies are her idea?"

"Well, they came about after Daniel restored the chapel at Goodwin for her wedding present. You know how hard he had to work to bring Goodwin up to some kind of standards. Things were much, much worse than Kellridge could ever be. I believe the Bible studies keep them grounded and also contribute to a feeling of community in their home." Becky looked up from her sewing, a gentle, teasing light in her eyes. "You need not fear it."

"Don't be ridiculous. I don't fear Bible study." Nothing would change because of it. He was still his own man, and master at Kellridge. No, indeed. He could go and be present, and thus set Juliet's mind at peace. Of course he wouldn't have to listen to the sermon, or believe anything he read. And he had a few more days to prepare himself for it, to assume the mask of casual indifference that he wore whenever anything that meant passion, or love, or depth of feeling presented itself. "If it means that she will go and not throw another tantrum, then I shall go through with it. A good general knows which battles to fight. He sizes up the situation and chooses where he shall spend his energy. That is all I have done."

Becky smiled, that winsome smile that seemed to signify her secret delight. "You are a good master, and a better strategist. Indeed, I am most grateful that you have chosen to help me in this fight to make Juliet a proper little lady. Your sacrifice is duly noted."

The flattery warmed his heart a trifle, but who was she to mock him? Becky Siddons—that little milliner whom he'd always teased in days gone past. His old mischievousness rose to the fore. If she'd been wearing a hair ribbon, he would have pulled it.

"Watch your tongue, miss, or I shall depart for London straight away and leave you at the mercy of my niece," he chided. "Or I shall tell Susannah that you are a dreadful nursemaid and send you home."

All the color drained from Becky's cheeks. "Do you mean it?" Her voice had a strangled quality to it. "Am I so awful?"

"No, no. Of course not." There he'd gone again, teasing too hard. When would he learn to rein himself in? "As I said before, I trust you implicitly. That's why I told you the truth about Juliana and Signor Martinelli."

"It's my greatest fear, you know. Being a failure. That's why I fell apart the other day when Juliet spilled the ink. I'd like to know that I have a purpose. That I shan't just fade into the background, or be bossed around by my sisters forevermore." She sighed, pursing her trembling lips. "I do so want to have a calling. And to answer that calling."

Paul nodded, keeping silent for a moment. She took this position so seriously. She believed divine intervention had brought her here. He had no right to tease her so mercilessly when she was working so hard and with so few resources. All he'd done was offer her the kind of support anyone should have, when faced with a daunting challenge. And what he should do was follow that support with praise, no matter how much he wanted to tease her.

An old saying floated back into his mind, from years and years before. What had Father said to him?

"Once, my father said something that might be useful to you, Becky. He told me that God doesn't call those who have everything they need to serve Him. Instead, He bestows everything you need upon you when He calls you. So remember that. You will have all you need to find your place in this world, in due time." He hadn't said anything remotely spiritual like that since before Ruth died. In fact, they'd have little debates about faith and God together as they sat in the garden at Kellridge or read together in her father's library.

"That's an excellent thought. I like that. I may write it down, to remember it whenever I feel discouraged." Becky laid her sewing to one side and placed her chin on her hands, her dreamy large eyes lifted, as though she saw something grand and powerful just beyond him.

Paul rose. He had done enough. Promised enough, comforted enough. These interviews with Becky stirred feelings within him that he'd buried with Ruth long ago. Her conversation led him down paths he hadn't traversed in years. And these changes were difficult and painful.

He bid her good-night in a curt fashion and headed downstairs to his study. Usually, after any demanding day, he would assuage his feelings in liquor. Now, the brandy bottle didn't beckon. The cut-crystal decanter, lit by candlelight, didn't wink in the same alluring fashion.

He simply had no desire for anything tonight.

He crossed to the windows and flung them open, allowing the sweet evening breeze to flutter through the room. He leaned out on the windowsill, staring across the fields of Kellridge, fields that smelled fresh, like newly tilled earth.

His actions were noticed now. He could no longer

hide behind the facade of being master. A two-year-old detected his lack of faith and brought him to heel. A lovely young nursemaid questioned his long-established methods and practices. Between the two of them, they had upended his carefully ordered life, just as a mule would kick over an apple cart. He was no longer able to conceal his actions, and already, he was beginning to change his ways.

He would go to Bible study. Nothing would change. He hadn't listened to a single sermon after Ruth's funeral. He had no need of anything God would promise, since God had seen fit to take Ruth away. He would go, but he would close his ears and shutter his mind against anything that might be said—anything that purported to speak to his heart.

So, his stance on Bible study and the Sabbath would have to change. His outward appearances must change. Juliet watched him and his actions with those large brown eyes of hers, assessing everything he did. Had he been able to escape to London before she arrived, he might have gotten away with never changing his ways. She was here now, and she knew him, and he must behave more properly to set a good example for her. 'Twould be a mere extension of the discipline he exercised over Kellridge. He would simply have to separate those two worlds—the world of his debaucheries, and the world that was his home—with an even greater distance.

# Chapter Twelve

'Twas good indeed to be walking out in this fine weather. Becky clasped Juliet's hand more tightly in her own and pointed at a flock of birds, startled into flight by their approach. Paul strode along beside them, his head turned toward the ground. If he was upset by Juliet's insistence that he accompany them today to Bible study, he didn't say so. His silence was rather unsettling. They had eschewed the carriage in view of the fine weather and with an eye toward wearing Juliet out. Though it was nice to be out in the splendid weather, the silence of her companions was a trifle grating on her nerves.

She had learned so much about Paul over the past few days. So much about his past, and about life at Kellridge. It was strange how people with so much privilege had so many troubles. Once her parents died and they moved in with Uncle Arthur, her family's troubles were simple and clear-cut. Survival. Even as Uncle Arthur squandered their last pennies, even as their uncle and aunt tried to force Susannah into marriage to a man of their choosing, the Siddons girls' one thought as a singular family unit had always been trained on survival.

But the Holmes family? So much fodder for a romantic novel. Unsuitable swains, forbidden love, a baby born too quickly for decent society, a quick flit to Italy. And that was just Juliana's life. No telling what escapades Paul had been up to while all this was going on. He had always been regarded as the bad influence on her brother-in-law. In fact, Daniel had been reformed once he'd found faith and Susannah, but rather in spite of his good chum Paul.

She snuck a sidelong glance at Paul. Yes, those scars suited him well. What secrets did he hide behind that laconic mask of sarcasm, or his precise method of managing his existence? He was a romantic hero at heart, surely. If she were an authoress, she would pattern her hero on him—the same lurking darkness beneath the smooth surface.

Juliet tugged at her hand as they neared the gates of Goodwin Hall, bringing Becky crashing back to reality. No more epic poems, or novels, or windswept moments on the moor. She must not roam the fields of her imagination any longer. She was needed here and now by a child who required her full attention.

"Yes, Juliet. We are here, at Goodwin. For Bible study." She spoke in response to the little one's squeeze. Though it sounded rather inane to keep repeating every trifling thing and making grand announcements about the obvious, it did seem to be improving Juliet's comprehension of English. "Goodwin Hall is my sister's home. And the little chapel in the woods here is where we are bound."

"Daniel seems to be in the process of plowing the far field," Paul remarked. 'Twas the first thing he'd said in a quarter of an hour.

"Yes," she replied, for want of something intelligent to say.

"I wonder what he's planting so late in the year. I'll have to ask him. His estate manager has some rather interesting notions about crops and allowing fields to lie fallow. I may have to have a chat with him some time. Perhaps he could advise me on Kellridge, though Parker is a good man." Paul stuck his hands in his pockets and began to whistle.

"Hoot, hoot," Juliet hummed in imitation. "Hooo."

Paul glanced down at Juliet and smiled—a genuine, warm smile that made Becky catch her breath. He had, up until this moment, been only stern or slightly teasing with his ward. Was he softening at last? She would say nothing, of course. Better to let the moment pass without remark, for Paul might feel he was being called out or mocked if she remarked upon it. His smile was an excellent sign, surely.

They skirted the edge of Goodwin Hall and made their way to the chapel, the scene of so much distress a week ago. Juliet's steps slowed a trifle and she stuck her fingers in her mouth. That was her sign that she was nervous. 'Twas a bad habit and one that she would have to break in time, but for the moment, Becky allowed her to continue. After all, 'twas much more important that they reach the chapel without Juliet giving vent to her temper.

As before, a group of children played in the clearing beside the building, and people—mostly tenants and servants, judging by their clothing—milled about. Becky searched the crowd for Susannah. Ah, yes. There she was. Even a modest white cap couldn't conceal the bright glory of her sister's hair. "Susannah," she called, waving her free hand.

"Becky, my dear." Susannah caught her skirts and bustled over to them, her smile lighting her face. "And little Juliet. So glad to see you again, you pretty thing. Why, that lavender dress just suits you."

Juliet didn't shrink beside Becky as she had before, but smiled shyly up at Susannah.

"Yes, your sister's handiwork with her needle is quite remarkable." Paul gave a courtly bow. "Susannah. Good to see you."

Her elder sister bobbed a little curtsy. If she was surprised to see the rakish Paul at her Bible study meeting, she was too well-bred to let on. "Why don't you allow me to take Juliet to the children's study? Then you and Paul may find your seats in the chapel. Nan and Daniel are already inside." She stooped and picked Juliet up. "Why, you are as light as a feather. Are you a little bird?" She continued chattering away to Juliet as she carried her toward the clearing in the woods.

"Do you think she will be all right?" Paul asked as he watched Susannah walk away.

"Susannah knows what she is about. She's making much over Juliet and also giving us the chance to make a hasty exit. Less likelihood of a temper tantrum this way." Really, her sister was so good with children. She could have been a nursemaid herself, had she not found her place as a milliner. And she would make a wonderful mother some day.

Paul tilted his head a little. "If you are certain…"

"Yes, let us go now." Becky turned and found her way through the milling crowd. She gave one last glance to the children's gathering. Yes, Susannah was there, introducing Juliet to the teacher. Judging from their gestures, they were making much over Juliet's dress. No screaming or cries as of yet. They were safe.

She crossed the threshold of the chapel and scanned the few crowded pews for her family. Ah, there they were, Daniel sitting in the front row beside Nan. "Excuse me. Pardon me." She managed to jostle her way up the small aisle and sink into the pew beside Nan. "I vow, this is quite a crowd today."

"Becky!" Nan threw her arms around her sister. "You are here. We weren't sure you would ever be able to come back, given how dreadfully your charge behaved."

Becky made an inward groan. Trust Nan to say something like that when her charge's uncle stood beside them.

"Paul? Are you really here?" Daniel stood, clapping his friend on the back. "I never thought I would find you in this chapel of your own free will."

Paul shrugged. "One has to set a good example for one's niece." He gave a hearty laugh, and the two men settled down on the pew, joking and laughing together.

Becky was surprised at how disappointing Paul's

answer was. So jesting in nature. On the other hand, what did she expect him to say? Paul made no secret of the reason for his visit today. And he never spoke about why he'd avoided church in the past. So why did it matter now? Did she really expect him to change in the space of one morning?

Even so, 'twas rather discouraging.

Susannah bustled in, squeezing beside Becky in the pew and wrapping her arms around both sisters as far as they would go. "Ah, this is good. Seeing both of my sisters here again."

"Is Juliet all right?" Becky gasped out the words as Susannah tightened her embrace.

"Yes, she will be fine. The children's teacher, Miss Eugenia, has taken her under her wing. And there's a child there about her age—the daughter of one of our servants—who is quiet and well behaved. They're sitting together now. Hopefully little Mary will be a good influence on Juliet and not the other way 'round." Susannah released her hold on Nan and Becky and leaned over. "So how on earth is it that Paul is here at Bible study today?" she whispered.

"Juliet convinced him." Becky pitched her voice to match her sister's. "She refused to come today unless he accompanied us."

"And Paul gave in? How marvelous." Susannah sat back, flicking a quick, assessing glance over Paul. "Perhaps being an uncle will do him a world of good."

"Yes, perhaps." She didn't want to talk about Paul any longer with her sisters, nor did she enjoy discussing Juliet's faults. Somehow, it felt rather disloyal to discuss Paul's questionable past or to catalog Juliet's flaws with her family. Why, her sisters had no knowledge of the whole of Juliana's story. And without that crucial information, anything that was said seemed judgmental and even petty.

Growing up, especially after Mama and Papa passed away, she and her two sisters had been rather like Robinson Crusoe, shipwrecked on a strange island. Together they had weathered the storm that was life with Uncle Arthur. Although, in truth, Susannah had always been the leader and likely sheltered her two younger sisters from some of the more unpleasant aspects of their uncle's avaricious nature.

The balance of their relationship had subtly shifted over the past year. Of course her eldest sister's marriage meant that Susannah would focus more on her husband and his needs, and the running of his household. After Susannah left—yes, that was when their triumvirate collapsed. Her sisters were as dear to her as ever, but she couldn't deny that the three of them had drifted apart since Susannah had married, and there was an emptiness in her heart that was now being filled by Juliet and Paul.

She settled back in the pew, focusing on Daniel as he strode over to the altar. Good—Bible study and prayer meeting was about to begin. What a relief. Though she loved seeing both of her sisters, 'twas unsettling to dwell on this change in their connections. She loved her sisters fiercely still, but she was compelled to defend and explain Paul and Juliet as she would defend and explain Nan and Susannah to outsiders.

In the space of a few weeks, her employer and her charge were becoming, well, not precisely dear to her, but she felt a strong sense of loyalty to them both. And that, surely, was to be expected after spending so much time in their company. All nursemaids must feel that sensation of allegiance. It must signify nothing more than this—that she was becoming good at her job.

With a sigh, Becky turned her full attention to Daniel. This new and confounding development must be placed to one side, to be examined later. Much later.

In fact, perhaps she shouldn't examine it at all. If it was her romantic nature rearing its head again, 'twould be best if she never thought about allegiances and loyalties and family history, and simply focused on doing her job and doing it well.

'Twas what God called her to do, after all.

Paul found it disconcerting to see Daniel, of all people, leading a prayer meeting. Many times Paul had helped his friend out of gaming halls, or aided and abetted his life of decadence. Though Daniel had given up drinking even before marrying Susannah, when you knew a fellow your whole life and then saw him make an about-turn in morality, 'twas rather discombobulating, to say the very least.

What would a fellow do for love? Paul stifled a smirk. Well, Ruth had never asked him to give up drinking or to delve deeply into religion. No, she'd tolerated his dissolution as a lady of quality would, by merely looking the other way. He'd had but a few deep conversations with Ruth, centering mostly upon how they would manage Juliana once Ruth became mistress of Kellridge. Even knowing she would be there to help him as he undertook the management of his ancestral home had been a great comfort in the months after Papa had died.

Would he have given up those things, if Ruth had asked him? Paul twitched uncomfortably in the pew.

Well, it didn't signify what he would have done because she'd never asked. And she died before they were wed, so his penchant for drinking and for cards had never become an issue between them.

Paul switched his attention to Daniel. Now, there was a fellow to whom matrimony seemed a blessing. By all appearances, Daniel didn't miss his old corrupt life. If anything, he always was in a maddening good humor now, captivated by his pretty bride and fully immersed in his new life as master of Goodwin. Since their marriage, life at Daniel's estate looked as though it had improved dramatically. And his newfound faith gave the impression of sincerity.

So then by these calculations, marriage could indeed be a partnership, one that could make a fellow turn away from what some people would consider sinful activities.

Paul folded his arms over his chest and stretched his booted feet out a bit. Beside him, Becky flicked one of her quick, appraising glances at his person, and then turned away. He was fidgeting too much. He must calm his roiling thoughts, for his restlessness disturbed Becky. She would take him to task later, surely.

Better to focus on Daniel. He could pay attention to what his friend said without really absorbing any of it.

"We chose as our study today the Gospel according to John, fifteenth chapter, fifth verse. *'I am the vine, ye are the branches: He that abideth in me, and I in him, the same bringeth forth much fruit: for without me ye can do nothing.'* Let's discuss this then, shall we? What does the Lord want us to know, and how can this apply to our own lives, as we go about our daily round?"

The crowd in the little church began to buzz with murmurs, as people turned to each other in the pews to thrash out the verse.

"Let us talk among ourselves—gather in little groups if you wish—and in a quarter of an hour, we shall congregate again and have a full dialogue." Daniel closed the Bible and beckoned to Susannah, who joined him at the altar for the debate. Nan leaped up and trotted obediently after her elder sister.

That left just Becky sitting beside him in the pew. She gave a sudden, sharp movement, turning to him with something like desperation etched on her pretty face. "We don't have to discuss it together. Truly, we don't, if it makes you uncomfortable."

Paul shrugged. If he made too big of a matter out of this, it would indicate that he cared about it. He could converse a little with Becky and not be challenged in any way by this Bible study. "Nay, let us ponder these questions together. Why not?" He drew closer to her and placed his left arm across the top of the pew.

"Well, I don't have much that's clever to say about it," Becky admitted. "Only that I truly enjoy this passage from the book of John. *'Without me ye can do nothing.'* I find it comforting."

Paul bit back a bitter laugh that surged up out of nowhere. "To me it sounds like the Lord is rather taking too much upon Himself."

Becky sat back in her seat with a defeated air. "I knew you would find this offensive. Shall we discuss something else instead?"

This time Paul couldn't suppress the laugh, but it wasn't a bitter one. Becky could be genuinely amusing. The sound of his mirth brought quick, seeking glances from those gathered at the altar, but he merely gave them a little wave. No need to be startled, gentle folk.

"Hark now, Becky-girl, a debate occurs when two opposing parties have a good thrashing out. Would you prefer that I simper and tell you pretty little fibs, and agree with everything you say?"

"'Twould be a sight pleasanter if you did," Becky muttered.

Paul grinned. "That wouldn't be a debate. It would be flattering and almost coy, but not a debate. Now tell me, in truth, why you find this passage comforting."

"Well..."

"Go on. I promise not to laugh." It was no fun to offend Becky. He just wanted to engage her. She was such stimulating company when she connected to him. The only way he could forge that connection to her, it seemed, was through argument or teasing. There had to be another way.

"Very well." Becky turned in her seat, fixing her eyes on him in a manner that a lesser fellow might find exhilarating. "You see, when Papa and Mama died, we stayed with Uncle Arthur. His household was vastly unpleasant, I can assure you. Despite the hardships we endured, my sisters and I remained constant in our faith and took care of one another because we trusted that the Lord had a place for us, and a lesson to teach us."

Yes, he had heard rumors about their time with their uncle Arthur. In fact, he'd met their uncle, and fleeced him at cards, many a time. "May I ask what lessons you learned?"

"That a life of dissolution corrupts more than just oneself. Though my uncle was the one who drank and played cards, he did so with our money. And his actions brought shame and dishonesty to his entire house. We learned that everything we do touches another person. Our actions affect everyone. And that simple lesson had a profound influence on how we would order our lives." She sat back, as though abashed by all she said. "So there you have it."

Paul ruminated on her words in silence. There really wasn't much to say. She had been through a difficult time, and it had transformed her. That was a common enough experience, wasn't it? After all, Ruth's death had changed him.

He turned off his thoughts with a snap. "Well, that is a thoughtful response," he admitted. "I must say, though, that you haven't precisely tied it to the verse."

Becky turned back to him, the light of challenge showing in the tilt of her chin. "Well, then. Apart from Him, I can do nothing at Kellridge. All I do for Juliet— it's—it's a calling, you see." She stumbled over her last words and her cheeks turned a becoming shade of pink.

"By that measure, then I should consider that my

life at Kellridge is ordered by the Lord, too. That everything I do is because of Him." What a fantastic, and troubling, thought.

Becky gave a quick, decisive nod of her head. "Precisely so." Then she fell silent.

The crowd broke up, and Susannah and Nan returned to the pew. Daniel directed the discussion from the altar, a most lively debate that nearly everyone in the room took up.

Everyone save him and Becky.

If he were to believe the verse, then he must surrender control to a higher power. He must believe that he could do nothing without the Lord, which was an altogether new experience and manner of thinking. He'd never thought of God as a being that gave, only as one that took away. His faith had tottered for some time, to be sure, but after He took Ruth and Juliana, Paul had no more use for any such "higher power."

If God gave as well as took away, if everything done in life was done through Him…why, that was a revelation.

God had given him many things. Kellridge. Good friends. A large family of brothers and sisters who hardly visited but loved him just the same. Vast material wealth. And even good health. He touched the scar that zigzagged his cheek. He could have been hurt much, much worse in that carriage accident, yet it never occurred to him to be grateful ere now.

God had even given him Juliana back, in a way, in the form of his rebellious, troublesome, but altogether sweet niece. His charge. His responsibility.

God had sent him a loving, caring nursemaid who stood up to him and sought out the best for her charge, despite his hesitations.

This was hard. Paul shook his head to clear his thoughts. 'Twas rather like learning Latin and finally being able to read the *Aeneid* in Virgil's mother tongue. From gibberish to clarity.

An entirely new world, one filled with questions and discoveries and answers was opening to him, if he would only push through the threshold.

## Chapter Thirteen

"If you'll pardon me, sir," Parker interrupted with a polite cough. "We need to discuss your impending trip to town."

Paul jerked back to reality. The vistas of possibility still beckoned, even as one went about his daily routine. The strange feeling that had overcome him in the chapel the previous day still clung, like a dream that would not let him go once he awakened. Even so, he needed to pay heed to Parker. He must not get wrapped up in philosophical and religious questions to the point that he was absent from his duties.

"Yes. London." He heaved a sigh. Somehow, travel had lost all its glamour. "So we have a new buyer for my shipping shares, then? Not that fellow Jacob Gail, I hope. That parvenu spends his money like water even as he apes at being an ordinary chap in the House of Commons. George warned me of him. Rumor has it that Gail illegally traffics in slaves. You know how my father felt about that, and I uphold that standard as well."

"No, this is a different fellow, by the name of Smith." Parker straightened in his seat. "Willing to take all your shares and at the price you dictated."

"Well, I do think it better to sell. I've been overseeing things from afar for too long, and as you know, my family has remained steadfast in precisely managing our shares. Knowing each passenger, the cargo and so forth. I have too much to attend to here. Are you certain he's willing to meet my price? I won't sell it for a farthing less, you know." Paul rocked back in his chair and clasped his hands behind his head. Something about this business did not set him at ease. Gail had backed off too hurriedly when Paul had turned him away. The speed with which a new seller had appeared—and one willing to meet his terms, too—was rather uncanny.

"Indeed, Mr. Smith has agreed to your terms. I don't know much of him, but if you would prefer, I can travel to London in your stead to oversee matters."

"No, indeed. I shall deal with the matter myself." He wanted to see who this mysterious Mr. Smith might be.

"Shall I send the word then? Will you be in London soon?" Parker gave him an expectant glance over the top of his spectacles.

Paul hesitated for a brief moment. Going to London meant leaving Kellridge behind, and with it, Becky and Juliet. A week or so ago he would have leaped at this chance. In fact, he'd done his carriage—not to mention his face—a grave disservice by rushing off as he did to avoid the very beings who now beckoned him to stay. And yet, business was business. Assuming this offer was authentic, he could net the kind of profit that would allow him to do just as he pleased for the rest of his life.

Surely that was worth a quick jaunt to London. Becky could manage very well on her own, couldn't she?

"Yes. Send word to this Smith fellow at once. I shall leave on the morrow, for the carriage is finally repaired." Paul glanced over at the mantel clock. 'Twas seven o'clock. Becky would be upstairs, readying Juliet for bed. If he didn't end this interview, he would be late for his meeting with her. "Is that all?" He employed the brisk tone he used whenever he was ready to be done with any matter of business.

"Yes sir. I shall tell your solicitor to expect you in a few days' time. Godspeed." Parker gathered the sheets of foolscap and the ledger book he always brought to their meetings, and with a respectful bow, quit the room.

Paul ran his thumbnail over the blotter on his desk. Somehow, the prospect of telling Becky that he was leaving was rather daunting, yet this wasn't a task he could put off.

He wasn't afraid of telling her. Not really. Yet, somehow, the thought of seeing disappointment reflected in those lovely eyes of hers…and what if she grew overwhelmed with her charge while he was gone? Suppose she had enough and quit while he was in London? Any other servant would be replaceable. In the space of a few weeks, Becky Siddons had become indispensable to him and to Kellridge Hall.

Besides, he had given his word that he would help her. He couldn't very well go back on his word now.

There was nothing to do but to go through with it, unpleasant though it might be. Paul stood and stretched. He needed to give instructions to his man to have his trunks packed. Though he needn't worry about packing clothes for London. He had plenty enough at the townhome in Grosvenor Square.

He took the stairs two at a time and knocked gently at the nursery sitting-room door. Becky opened it, her finger to her lips. "She's already fallen asleep," she murmured.

"Excellent. So no more getting in and out of bed a dozen times before falling asleep." Paul entered the room and closed the door behind him. "That is progress."

"Well, it's progress for now. We shall see if it lasts." Becky settled into her familiar comfortable chair and pulled out her sewing. He'd rarely seen her without some bit of needlework in her hands, usually for the benefit of his niece. 'Twas nice to see Becky always working to improve things for his charge.

He could remark upon that at length, but while it was a cheerful topic of discussion, he really did need to tell her about London. And that strange, foggy feeling wouldn't leave him. 'Twas almost pulling him back, as it were, holding him fast. If one believed in God, what would Paul's purpose in this life be? Could he really do everything without a higher power overseeing his every movement?

He gave his head a decided shake. Enough.

"I am afraid I am bound for London on the morrow." There, out with it. Be as blunt as possible, and state the facts squarely. "There's a pressing matter of business I can no longer delay."

Becky looked up from her sewing, her eyes widened. "Of—of course." She paid elaborate attention to the needle she'd been threading. "How long will you be gone?"

"Originally I had intended to stay the entire season, but…" He lapsed into silence. Did Becky's hand usually tremble that much when she sewed? Surely not. She was so deft with a needle. She was upset, and rightly so. After all, he had given his word that he would help with Juliet, at least until she was well in hand.

"Well, I wish you a safe journey," she rejoined, her entire being focused on the little nightgown she was stitching. "You should travel a sight slower this time. Don't break yet another axle." Her tone was jesting, but the frown that creased her forehead spoke volumes. Becky was not pleased.

He gave an appreciative chuckle. "You'll be all right then? Juliet seems calmer now. You've made great strides with her this week. A proper nap time, a proper bedtime and Sunday school." Really, he was reassuring himself as much as he was praising her. It would be all right, this once, to break his word.

"Yes, she has improved a great deal." Becky said nothing more.

They sat in silence for a while. 'Twas rather unnerving. Usually they thrashed out their plans for Juliet for the next day, the next week. And they would talk and jest about the day's activities. He'd come to genuinely enjoy this time with Becky. Their chats were such a pleasant and stimulating way to end the day.

If he were in London, he would miss that, too.

The ticking of the clock on the mantel grew more annoying with every passing second. He had to do something, anything to make this trip to London right.

"I don't suppose…you'd like to come along?" He drummed his fingers on the arm of his chair to deafen the ticking of the clock. "You and Juliet, of course," he amended. Though it scarcely needed to be said, if one considered their situation.

"Come along? To London?" Becky clasped the nightgown to her chest and gave a tentative smile. "Are you certain?"

"Well, why not?" Now that he made the decision, it made jolly good sense. Why hadn't he thought of it before? "You can entertain Juliet with all the sights of London, and enjoy a few of them yourself. Have you ever been before?"

"No, never. Matlock Bath is as far as I have ever journeyed." Two bright spots of color appeared on her cheeks, a most becoming shade of pink. "Are you quite sure? Traveling, even just from Cleethorpes, with Juliet was rather an ordeal."

"It's an ordeal we shall suffer cheerfully together." He rubbed his hands together with a brisk gesture. He was in control of the situation once more, putting things in order just as he should. "Juliet will need to grow accustomed to travel, for when she gets older, she will need to be in town for the season. Better to start her young, you know."

"What a wonderful idea. If you are really certain that all will be well, then I think it a perfect plan." Becky folded the night dress and placed it back in her sewing box. "I must begin packing. Indeed, I don't know how I shall sleep, I am so excited."

"I shall leave you to it." Joy fairly sang through his body. He'd kept his word and made Becky happy, too. And the journey—though, of course, Juliet was sure to be trying—didn't seem half as arduous now. As a matter of fact, the prospect of showing off London to someone who hadn't seen it, who had never had the chance to grow jaded and blasé about it, held special appeal. "We shall leave shortly after breakfast tomorrow."

Becky gave him a luminous grin, one that showed the dimple in her cheek and caused his heart to flutter strangely in his chest. "We shall be ready, I promise," she vowed.

He rose from his chair and gave her a courtly bow. "Until the morning, then."

She nodded, her eyes shining like amethysts, as he quit the room. The cobwebby feeling dissipated the moment he left. This was the right choice, the perfect plan for keeping his word. Better still, it meant Becky would be with him in London all the time, with her charming smile and guileless manner.

Not that that mattered, of course. She was his niece's nursemaid, nothing more.

But it was pleasant indeed to think upon.

As soon as Paul closed the sitting room door, Becky danced around with glee. She was going to London! Never, not in all her life, had she dreamed she would travel so far. Certainly not after Papa and Mama passed away. Why, a whole new world had opened before her this very night. She would have the chance to take Juliet to all of the sights. Even a stroll along the streets would be a grand occasion.

She must get to work at once. There was so much to be done to ready herself before the morning.

She pulled the bell rope. Surely Juliet's trunks were still located somewhere in the many nooks and crannies at Kellridge. And her own modest trunk was tucked underneath her bed. She could pull that one out herself and set about packing right away.

She passed from the sitting room into her bedroom, and kneeling on the rug, found the handle of her trunk. With a mighty jerk, she pulled it out from beneath the bed.

"Oh, don't try to do that alone, miss." Her maid, Kate, spoke up from behind her.

"Oh, it's no bother, really. It's quite light." Becky blew a wayward strand of hair out of her eyes and sat upon the trunk. "I rang to see if you or anyone else knows where Miss Juliet's trunks ended up. I need them."

"I am sure they were placed in the attic. Mrs. C. usually stows the luggage up there." Kate stared at Becky, her forehead wrinkled with something like concern. "Why do you ask? Are you going anywhere?"

"Yes. Mr. Holmes wishes to take his niece with him to London on the morrow. I've only just learnt about it. And so I must pack our things in a hurry so we may be ready when he is in the morning." Becky shrugged. There was always the possibility that she might awaken

Juliet once she started packing, much less moving trunks around. How could she manage this quietly?

"If you could make arrangements to have Miss Juliet's trunk sent down in the morning, I will gather all her things tonight." That really was the best solution to the problem. "And that way, we shan't be late, and I won't run the risk of awakening her. Of course, I'll pack my own right now."

"Yes, miss," Kate murmured. Then, assuming a confidential air, she leaned forward. "Are you quite sure that Mr. Holmes wants you and Miss Juliet to stay with him in town? In his townhome in Grosvenor Square?"

"I don't know where his home in town is located, but yes. I am certain that he wants us both to be there with him." Funny, her giddiness only increased as she spoke those words. Staying with Paul rather than having Paul leave them behind was such a vastly superior change of plans. Not that she would miss him so much, of course, but just that his help had been so wonderful these past few days. If they were making strides with Juliet, it must be in good part because they worked so well together.

"I don't want to speak out of turn." Kate's stern tone made all her happiness evaporate into thin air. "You should know that the way in which Mr. Holmes conducts himself in London is different from the manner in which he behaves at home."

"Surely you're not gossiping, Kate." Becky arched one eyebrow. Coldness began to settle at the pit of her stomach.

"No, I am not a gossip. But as one who has been in

service longer than you, I think it wise to inform you." Kate knelt on the rug before Becky, twisting her hands in her lap. "Mr. Holmes is the best master Kellridge has ever possessed, to be sure. His life in London makes up for his sober attitude here at home. I only know this because one of my sisters works for him in London, and she told me the tales."

"Why are you telling me this? I am merely assisting him with his charge." The coldness spread to her hands, and she suppressed a shiver.

"Well, I think you should know for two reasons. First, you should make sure that Miss Juliet is not ever aware of the nature of the things Mr. Holmes does in London, particularly if you are making her into a fine young British girl."

"I highly doubt he would behave in such a fashion before his niece," Becky bit the words out. Of course Paul would never do anything untoward where his niece might be watching. She had only known him a brief time, to be sure, but he'd never impressed her as another Uncle Arthur. He was, perhaps, too much of a tease and could be too rigid in the rules he set, but he never behaved improperly before a lady, not to her knowledge.

"Please don't be offended, miss. It's just that you are so new to service, and being that your family has been friendly with the master for some time, perhaps you don't see things as another servant would." Kate tugged at a fraying bit of the rug, keeping her eyes cast down. "All I can tell you is that Mr. Holmes takes his responsibilities as master here quite seriously. He is one of the best masters in the county. When he goes to London, he has the chance to play, and he does play rather hard."

"Very well. I thank you for telling me." If she continued arguing the point with Kate, then there would be no end to this interview. And as it was, this conversation was having a decidedly dampening effect upon her excitement. "Was there anything else?"

"I know you are working closely with Mr. Holmes to govern Miss Juliet. He visits and consults with you often. We all know there is nothing untoward in these meetings, but—" Kate stammered and fell silent for a moment.

"But what? You have said yourself they are perfectly innocent calls, and they are. Without his help, managing Miss Juliet would be much more difficult, at least until she learns better English." A sense of nervous unease crept over Becky. What was Kate implying? And would she ever leave?

"Nothing. I seem to have spoken out of turn." Kate rose from her seat on the carpet, her face set in a blank expression.

"I assure you that, while I am in London, I shall be there solely to care for Miss Juliet in my position as her nursemaid. Nothing unseemly shall befall us." Becky swallowed hard. This entire conversation was ridiculous, and really, a bit beyond what Kate should be bringing up. "I thank you for your warnings. I know your intentions are good."

Kate bobbed a curtsy. "They are. Will there be anything else?"

"No." Becky fought the rising tide of agitation that

welled within her. "Just see to it that Miss Juliet's trunk is sent down here first thing in the morning, if you please."

Kate nodded and, curtsying again, quit the room.

Alone at last, Becky stared at the roughened surface of her trunk. Her excitement about London was dashed all to pieces, and in its stead remained only uneasiness. Why had Kate sought to issue such a dire warning about life with Paul in town?

Based on her limited understanding, society dictated that all young gentlemen must carouse a bit while they were in company with each other. And the season offered many opportunities for this kind of play. There was surely nothing sinister in the way Paul acted while he was in town. For one thing, Susannah would know. Daniel and Paul were the best of friends, and Susannah knew all about Daniel's past. If there were truly anything terrible about Paul's character, Susannah would never have let her come to service here.

And it was highly unlikely Daniel would continue to be Paul's friend, after all the changes wrought in his character by marriage, if Paul were a terrible blackguard.

None of this made any sense. And it was spoiling the one chance she had to enjoy herself thoroughly in the biggest and the best town in all of England.

Becky stood and opened her trunk. If she busied herself with folding and tucking her belongings away, perhaps that brief flash of anticipation would return. She hadn't felt such hope or exhilaration since her fleeting, albeit imaginary, courtship with Lieutenant Walker.

A life without any kind of expectation was flat indeed. And while she'd given up on any silly notions of romance that horrid day on the moor, she could allow herself a moment or two of enjoyment in the course of her duties.

Surely that wasn't too much to ask of life.

## Chapter Fourteen

This was, by far, the most interesting trip he'd ever undertaken to London. Paul stared out the carriage window as Juliet bounced and wriggled in the seat beside him. Of course, it was also one of the few where he hadn't imbibed any kind of liquor. He needed a clear head to help Becky as she tried to contain his charge, who hadn't grown any more used to being cooped up in a carriage as the days progressed.

On the other hand, 'twas a sight pleasanter to travel with someone as stimulating in conversation as Becky. During his past journeys, he might give thought only to the pleasures of a baser nature awaiting his arrival. Or he might bring along a traveling companion as dissolute as he. This was, though, the first time since he was a lad that he had someone with which to engage in interesting and frank discussions. Or to show off the sights as they trundled into town. 'Twas rather refreshing, actually. For though Becky had been strangely reserved since they started the trip, with no more of the ecstatic glee she'd displayed when he invited her, she was still looking at the journey with fresh and appreciative eyes.

A length of iron railing flashed into view. They were nearly home. He pointed out the window. "See here, Becky—we're passing Hyde Park. Of course, it isn't the fashionable hour to be seen, so no one of consequence is there. Come this afternoon, the park will be mobbed with throngs of the wealthy and elite."

Becky smiled and quirked her eyebrows. "Fashionable hour? Why would it matter what time of day it was, if all you were doing was walking in a park?"

He laughed. "Yes, indeed. It does sound rather odd, doesn't it? You would be amazed at how strictly society governs these things. The proper time to stroll in Hyde Park is from half-past four to about half-past five, if one is a lady. Gentlemen may tarry longer."

"Does the park have many fine views?" Becky craned her neck to get a glimpse outside the window.

"I am sure there are many lovely vistas, but when one strolls in Hyde Park, one does so to admire the splendid display of humanity rather than nature. Ah, here we are, turning on to Grosvenor Street." He turned to face her. "Would you like to go for a stroll this afternoon? I should be happy to take you. It might be amusing for you to see how people parade themselves like peacocks in Rotten Row."

"Rotten?" Becky gave him a weak smile. "Nay, it all sounds rather too much. Especially after such a long journey. I am certain my afternoon will be occupied with getting Juliet settled."

"Juliet may come, too. Would you like that, little

one?" He glanced down at his niece, who pushed past him to place her small hands on the windowpane. "Ah, she knows where she is already. I vow that by the time she reaches sixteen, she will be as much of a diamond as her mama was." Funny, it didn't hurt as much to think of Juliana and what a belle she had been during her season. Was being around her daughter helping to assuage his grief and his guilt?

"I think I would rather acquaint Juliet with her new surroundings," Becky interjected, a pleading note in her voice.

Well, perhaps Becky was correct. After all, they had been traveling for some time. 'Twas probably best to put off sightseeing for tomorrow. He gave her a brief nod, and she cast a tight smile his way in return.

The coachman pulled up in front his townhome—and it remained an impressive sight to behold. The servants had given the exterior of the home a fresh whitewash and had recently, per his implicit instructions, painted the shutters a deep, dark shade of green. The ornate pillars stretched the length of all three stories, giving the building an air of detached formality. Had Papa prevailed, their townhome would have been in Lincoln's Inn Fields, among wealthy tradespeople, the sort of people most like his family. Mama had insisted on a fine Mayfair residence.

To Paul's dismay, there, on the front portico, was a familiar disheveled sight. John Reed, who, with Daniel, would carouse with Paul until the wee hours of every morning. His heart sank. John was a decent enough chap, but not necessarily one he wanted to introduce to Becky or Juliet. Ignoring propriety, he bounded out of the carriage ahead of its female occupants. He must quell John's certain exuberance.

"Paul!" he called, clapping Paul on the shoulder as he mounted the steps. "Does me a power of good to see you. You look awful, my dear fellow. That carriage accident has rendered your formerly handsome face as much appeal as a jigsaw puzzle. I had quite despaired of you coming to town. Now that you are here, we must celebrate."

"John, so good of you to form a welcoming committee of one." Paul flicked an anxious glance over his shoulder to where Becky was just helping Juliet out of the carriage. "You remember my sister Juliana? She passed away a few months ago where she was living abroad, and her daughter is now my ward."

"Oh, so sorry to hear she's passed. My sympathies, and all that." John removed his hat with a deferential air and peered over at Juliet. "She really is the spitting image of her mother, isn't she?"

"Yes, she is." Paul stepped aside as Becky mounted the steps with Juliet. "Miss Siddons, the nursery will be on the second floor." As he spoke, the front door opened and Edmunds, the butler for his townhome staff, stepped out. "Edmunds, please show Miss Siddons to the nursery suite. I shall be in presently."

Edmunds bowed and motioned to Becky. Juliet followed her nursemaid, shadowing her so closely it was a wonder she didn't become entangled in Becky's skirts.

John watched their progress, his eyes narrowing in a predatory manner as he glanced over Becky. Paul's throat tightened. John shouldn't be looking at a lady in that fashion.

"Come, let's take a stroll. It will do me good to walk about, accustomed as I am to riding in the carriage." Paul caught John's shoulder and spun him around, setting him toward the street. "Tell me, did you hang about awaiting my arrival for the past few weeks?"

"Nay, not I. I have better things to do. More amusing things, at least." John stuck his hands inside his jacket pockets with a jaunty air. "I did hear from my valet that your valet said you would probably arrive today. And since the information you receive from a valet is as good as gold, I thought I might as well wait for you as not. Shall we head straight to Brook's?"

"I'd rather walk a bit longer." Already the narrow streets of London were pressing in on him. Funny, he'd never found it quite so oppressive before. At least the sun was shining. He'd had enough of rain for the time being.

John laughed. "You Holmes lot and your eccentricities. Walking rather than playing cards at Brook's. I do hope that accident of yours hasn't affected your brain."

"Not at all," Paul rejoined in a hearty manner. Better to sound convincing, perhaps, than to be convinced oneself.

"Well, as long as you are in your right mind, you might tell me about that delectable morsel I saw entering your home." John jabbed him with his elbow. "I vow, I have hardly ever seen a female with such striking eyes. Purple, are they?"

"Miss Siddons does have violet eyes, yes." Paul kept

his reply curt as he ducked around a couple holding court on the pavement. Perhaps he could send a subtle message to John just with the tone and inflection of his voice. "She is my niece's nursemaid."

"What a decorative ornament to keep around one's home," John rejoined, directing them onto Mount Street. "And is she from the country, then? I daresay I should go back to Derbyshire and spend some time there among the locals, if such lovely prizes are to be found."

Anger boiled within Paul. Becky was not the kind of girl his class of gentlemen usually remarked upon at length. And she was surely too fine a person for cheap and tawdry observation. He stopped walking, facing his friend squarely. "Now see here, Reed. Miss Siddons is a member of my household. And her sister is married to Daniel Hale. She's a good girl from an excellent family, and she agreed to help me during a most difficult time. I won't have you speak of her in such terms again."

"My apologies, old chap. I had no idea." John backed up a step, holding his hands out in a defensive gesture. "I shan't say anything like it again. Shall we go to Brook's now? Walking in no particular direction is wearing out the heels of my boots, and extraordinary boots they are, though I say it myself."

Brook's, redolent of tobacco smoke, crowded with dissolute men spending vast quantities of money—at one point, this had held great allure. Indeed, he'd dreamed of fleeing his responsibilities in the country for just such an adventure. Now that the opportunity finally presented itself, the thought of going inside set his stomach churning.

Whatever was coming over him? He must be hungry. He should go home and have a decent meal and a rest. Then he would be himself again.

"Some other time. Tomorrow, perhaps, after I finish a pressing matter of business." He offered John his hand. "Thanks for meeting us. I am glad to be back." Even though he wasn't. Not really.

John returned the handshake. "Of course." He tugged his hat back on. "You know where to find me. I'll be at the club or the opera or recuperating at home."

Paul watched as John strode off down the sidewalk, cutting a fashionable picture of the dissolute gentleman as he walked. At one point, carousing with John had been the best part of any trip to London. Why did it ring hollow now?

He turned back toward his townhome, making his way to Davies Street. Now 'twas almost like they were on completely different paths, heading in opposite directions.

Yes, he definitely needed to eat something. None of this made any sense.

Surely living in London should feel more impressive. This townhome, for instance. Becky stared around her at her vast bedroom, with its lovely sky-blue ceiling. No room she'd ever stayed in was this elegant or well-appointed. And yet… She sank onto the soft bed, steadying herself as she rolled backward slightly. She already longed for the cozy cheerfulness of Kellridge, with her tidy little sitting room, and Juliet's bedroom just beyond. Here, Juliet slept in a room just down the hall. It was close enough to reach her, but still. This house lacked intimacy.

In fact, thus far London had failed to impress her, though in truth she'd seen very little of it. Was she so affected by Kate's dire warnings? Or was it just that draining to try to keep Juliet to her prescribed bedtime as they traveled? Tonight it had taken no fewer than three attempts at putting her to sleep—nearly an hour. Becky's bones ached from fatigue, and if she closed her eyes, the room whirled around her. This was not the exciting new world she'd expected it would be.

There was a gentle rapping on her door. Oh, no. Not Juliet again.

No, Juliet never knocked. Just cried outside her door since she was too small to reach the latch.

"Come in?" She couldn't keep the weariness out of her voice.

The butler, Edmunds, popped his head round the door. "If you please, Miss Siddons. Mr. Holmes requests an interview with you in the library."

"Yes, of course." Becky stood. "He must want to know how Miss Juliet is doing."

Edmunds gave a respectful bow. "Follow me."

She followed the butler down the wide, curving staircase, bumping her hand against an ornamental cherub on the balustrade. "Ouch."

"Are you all right, Miss Siddons?" Edmunds called over his shoulder as he turned down the hallway.

"Yes, thank you." She rubbed her sore hand. There'd be a lovely little bruise there tomorrow.

Edmunds paused before a glossy white door and gave

a discreet rap. "Miss Siddons to see you, sir," he announced before opening the door wider and ushering her in. All this formality! It should be impressive, but instead, it was tiresome. Becky fought the urge to make a face as the butler closed the door behind her.

"Becky, do sit down." Paul was lounging in a large leather chair by the hearth. "I'm sorry I had to ask you to come down here—there's no sitting room on the second floor."

"Oh, that's all right." She sat in the chair opposite Paul and rubbed the top of her aching hand.

"You look exhausted," he pronounced.

"I am." In days past, she might have struck back at Paul with a witty rejoinder, or at least a caustic comment about his lack of chivalry. This was not the right time for clever rebuttals, and there was no need to beat about the bush. "It took an hour to get Juliet to sleep tonight."

"An hour? I thought we were down to fifteen minutes, sometimes not even that." Paul ran his hand through his thick, sandy hair. "Was she simply excited about the new arrangements?"

"Yes." She was so weary, even speaking was an effort.

"Do you want to talk about it?"

Becky forced herself to meet Paul's eyes. She'd avoided looking at him as much as possible since Kate had spoken to her. What if she had accidentally sent some kind of ridiculous signal to him? One that was interpreted in entirely the wrong manner? He gazed at her thoughtfully and rubbed the fading scar on his cheek.

"I am sure it will take just a few days to settle in."

She added a bright cheeriness to her tone. "We are just…overwhelmed."

"That is understandable." Paul's voice comforted her weary spirit. He could be such good company when he chose to be. "Tell me, what do you think of my house here?"

What could one say? That the house was lovely and yet cold? "I do declare it is the most elegant place I've ever set foot in." There. That was the truth, after all.

"This place is all my mother's doing." Paul lounged back in his chair. "My father wanted to live in a fashionable part of town, too, but more among our class of people. Mayfair always has been a bit beyond our reach. I'm the only surviving member of our family who cares for it."

"Why don't your other siblings enjoy it? Do they dislike it so much?" She'd never heard much about Paul's family—only Juliana and George, and precious little at that. 'Twould be interesting to hear more about them. Perhaps they could provide another piece to the puzzle that was Paul Holmes.

Paul smiled. "My brother calls it a 'horror of modern architecture.'"

"Oh, dear." Becky couldn't contain a laugh at that. "That sounds rather harsh."

"Well, George is a sea captain. He feels most alive when he's strolling the deck of his ship, not cooped up in a Mayfair townhome. And my sisters are deeply embarrassed by its grandeur. They all vastly prefer the simple life in the country. All of my siblings refuse to come to London unless they have pressing business and cannot find a way to cry off." He paused for a moment, staring at the hearth. "Juliana came here once for the season. She rather enjoyed its grand drawing room with its superior pianoforte."

The shuttered look that usually passed across his face when he spoke of Juliana was completely absent now. He stared pensively at a fixed place on the hearth, but his shoulders remained relaxed. The change in him made her catch her breath, as though for the first time, she was being allowed to look inside a walled garden.

She was not ready to have the gate closed. Not yet. She steered the conversation gently away, for just a moment, for who knew how long he would remain at ease? "How many sisters do you have?"

"Well, let's see. Five, save Juliana. Caroline is the eldest, then Elizabeth and Cassandra. The others were born after me—Sarah and Hannah. They are twins and look as alike as peas in a pod. George was born before the twins." He shifted his glance from the fireplace and looked at Becky, his brown eyes warm. "And all of them married, happy in their lives and secure in their persons."

"Five sisters—one set of twins?" Becky shook her head. "I don't envy you the task of managing all that. Certainly not when you were so young yourself."

"When Papa died, all the girls were either married or engaged to be so. They all married rather young. Juliana was the last of the lot. And George, off to find his fortune as the second son, was already at sea. So you see, managing Juliana became as crucial to me as managing Kellridge." He fell silent once more.

"Of course, that makes sense." Her heart ached for Paul. What an awful lot he'd had to shoulder, and at an age when most men were able to live fancy-free, thinking only of themselves and of pleasure. Small wonder he held so steadfastly to order and to precision. His methods were likely the only way he could maintain his home.

Of course, she had been through a great deal, too. And with Susannah and Nan, they had come through the worst of life. But they'd done so together. Juliana had been a storm unto herself, unlikely to have done anything to ease Paul's burden. He must have felt so terribly alone.

She couldn't bear for him to fall to brooding about Juliana once more. He had done so much for Juliana, and was continuing to do so in caring for her child. If only he would see the good he had done, rather than considering just what he deemed his greatest failure.

"So, your brother is a sea captain, and your sisters are happily married." She ticked all of them off on her fingers. "That is quite astonishing. Where do your sisters live?"

He gazed at her as though drifting back through a fog. "Caroline lives near Liverpool, Elizabeth near Dover and Cassandra near Norwich. They met their husbands in London, but never returned, for they love the country life so. Caroline paints, Elizabeth is an excellent judge of horseflesh and Cassandra writes poetry. So they indulge these pursuits while running their homes and their families."

Poets, painters, musicians. Paul's family fairly brimmed with artistic talent. "And the twins?"

"Sarah and Hannah married twin brothers, of all things. They live together on a huge joint estate in Scotland." He gave a little chuckle. "And yet none of them have had twins yet. Most extraordinary, don't you think?"

"Yes." Paul was not just the annoying young man who teased her, or the stern lord of the manor. "Paul, why did you take Juliet? If you have sisters who have children, why didn't one of them step up to care for their niece?"

Paul looked at her, frank astonishment showing on his handsome face. "Juliet is my responsibility. Not theirs."

Becky blinked. "Didn't any of your sisters feel obligated to take Juliet?"

"Not really. I am the master of the family, and I made it very clear, since Juliana's marriage, that her problems were mine. Not that I consider Juliet a problem, mind you. But she is my primary concern."

He still felt the deep and abiding guilt that he failed his sister. Becky's heart surged with warmth for him. He was not a failure, no matter how much he chastised himself for Juliet's downfall. No, he was a good brother who shouldered all the family responsibilities as his siblings scattered all over the globe. His siblings sounded happy. They were married, at least. They had moved to places that beckoned, and refused to visit places they disliked. Meanwhile, Paul continued running Kellridge, maintaining the London townhome and assuming responsibility for his sister's child.

He was a good man.

Was he a happy man?

She couldn't ask why he never married. That was too saucy, even for someone as well acquainted with him as she, and even within the context of the newfound warmth they shared. "It sounds like your siblings all had a taste of adventure," she admitted. "What of you? Did you desire to break free yourself?"

"Of course. And I indulged in some rather unsavory pursuits which I shan't discuss with a lady," he confessed. "I am the eldest son. It's my duty to take care of my father's legacy. This trip to London is to see if selling my shares in shipping will be for the best. They were my father's shares, but I don't have his attention to the business. George does—it's part of his job as a captain. As for me, I would rather let them go and focus on Kellridge." This last came out in a rush, as though Paul were unburdening himself of something that tugged at his conscience.

"I am certain you will make the right choice." She kept her voice soothing, as though she were talking to Juliet at the end of a difficult day. "As far as I am concerned, you have done an excellent job in everything. I would even go so far as to say you're not the teasing rogue I thought you."

"Or the hateful master?" He gave her a wry grin, and her heart caught in her throat.

She shook her head. Words seemed too difficult, too tender, at this moment.

"Well, I am glad you think so, Becky-girl. Your opinion means a great deal." Paul caught her glance for a moment and held it. She couldn't draw breath. She couldn't look away.

Then he averted his gaze back to the hearth, and the gate to the walled garden swung shut. She stood on the outside, cold and breathless.

That glimpse of the real Paul had left her wanting more. If only he would let her in.

## Chapter Fifteen

Better to be done with the business at hand. This was, after all, what brought him to London in the first place.

Paul strode along the crowded, bustling streets of town. Eschewing the carriage was the right decision. Walking gave him time to think, to resolve the matter in his head and to make peace with it. Father would not be angry he was selling his shares; after all, Paul had maintained the Holmes family legacy with aplomb since his father's passing. Even George understood, though he'd made it quite clear he would be maintaining his ship. So there was no need for this niggling feeling of unease. Yet it persisted.

Paul sidestepped a lady hawking vegetables on the street and, as he moved around her, came face to shoulder with a man alighting from his carriage. "Beg pardon," Paul remarked. The man, a rotund fellow with a shrewd look about him, merely nodded. As the fellow closed his carriage door, Paul caught a glimpse of the bold letter "G" painted on the side. Nay, bold wasn't

even the right word. This was a florid, glaring mono-
gram that declared to all and sundry that it belonged
to Mr. Gail. In fact, engravers found much fodder for
satire in Gail's pretensions, and his carriage was one of
the most laughed about objects in London.

This portly fellow wasn't Gail. Paul drew to one side,
feigning interest in a shop window.

The man darted a few quick glances around, then
made his way up the sidewalk, along the very path Paul
intended to take. What would Gail's carriage be doing
in this part of town? Surely the big man himself would
be expected at the House of Commons in no time at all.

Paul followed the portly fellow as he traversed the
pavement, homing in on him as he would a fox when
on the hunt. Sure enough, the fellow opened the door to
the chambers of Poole & Blackburn, Solicitors. Clench-
ing his jaw, Paul waited a moment. Let his quarry have
time to make himself at home. Why it could be that he,
too, had business with the solicitors, and had nothing
to do at all with Paul's transaction.

"Not likely," Paul muttered under his breath.

He let himself in and walked up the creaking staircase.

"Mr. Holmes, good to see you." James Blackburn
greeted him at the landing. "I am so pleased you came
in to London to handle this matter yourself. I was rather
expecting your man of affairs."

"As you know, Blackburn, I handle all things re-
lated to my shipping shares myself. My father took a
particular interest in every aspect of the business, and
I treat it with the same care as he would." Paul shook

his solicitor's hand but glanced about the room. "Shall we go in, then?"

"Yes, of course. Right this way." Blackburn beckoned him to a room just beyond the top of the stairs. "Mr. Smith only just arrived."

Yes, he certainly had just arrived. Only a few moments before Paul himself, as a matter of fact. As his solicitor opened the door, Paul saw the same portly fellow he'd been following since seeing him alight from Gail's carriage.

So the sly dog was using a proxy. Smart business move, that. Gail probably thought Paul would send his man of affairs and never know the difference. Then he would purchase all of the Holmes shipping shares and leverage his influence to continue the illegal slave trade.

Never. The vague uneasy feeling that had plagued him through this entire journey dissipated like mist evaporating before the sun.

"May I present Mr. John Smith? Mr. Smith, this is Mr. Paul Holmes." Blackburn made the introductions briskly.

Paul nodded to Mr. Smith and extended his hand. "My pleasure."

"Well, gentlemen, if you will wait just a moment, I have all the papers here," Blackburn began, spreading the documents out on the surface of the table.

"That won't be necessary, Blackburn. I've only come to inform Mr. Smith I changed my mind." Paul quirked his mouth in a rueful grin. "I didn't want to be rude and tell him by proxy."

Smith blinked rapidly. "What if I doubled my price?"

Paul fought the inclination to chuckle. Gail had likely told the fellow to pay any amount of coin, as long as he brought home those controlling shares. One could almost pity him, once Gail found he failed in his mission. Almost.

"I appreciate the offer, but my decision isn't based on money." Paul gave a lazy shrug of his shoulders. "The more I thought about it, the more I realized my father entrusted me with those shares. Selling them would be dishonoring his memory." Paul glanced over at his solicitor. "I am sure no one here would wish me to go against my father's legacy."

"Of course." Blackburn shot an apologetic look at Smith. "So, if I am to understand it, you are no longer willing to sell—not at any price?"

"Not at any price," Paul echoed, his heart beating strangely against his chest. "I shan't entertain any more offers, but I do appreciate Mr. Smith coming by today. And Smith—I do wish you the best." He held out his hand.

Smith rose, his face drained of all color. "Of course." His handshake was cold and limp.

"Blackburn, I apologize for putting you through the trouble of drawing up the papers," Paul added. "Do send the bill round for your time. I appreciate, as always, your kind attention to these matters."

"Naturally, Mr. Holmes." The solicitor gathered the papers up, stacking them to one side. "We'll throw these on the fire, then."

A jolly good blaze that would be. "Thank you." With a last nod at both gentlemen, Paul quit the room and pounded down the staircase to the street. Once outside, he took a gulp of fresh air—or, as fresh as London air could be at that time of year.

Exhilaration sang through his very being, and with it, a strange, abashed feeling. Double the money on an already ridiculously large sum, and he had turned it down. He'd turned the offer away because selling those shares would have, most certainly, meant that the ships would be used to traffic in slaves. No human misery was worth any amount of coin.

He had to tell someone. The desire to laugh, yell and throw his hat up in the air was overpowering. Why, he hadn't experienced emotions this strong since he was a lad. He didn't want to shut the door on them—nay, the joy was too strong. If he wrote to George, his stolid younger brother would simply say, "Hadn't I warned you?" No celebration to be had there.

He took off down the pavement, weaving through the teeming crowds toward Grosvenor Square.

Becky. He must tell Becky.

As he made his way through the throngs, he picked out Gail's gaudy carriage, still waiting, its occupant likely rubbing his greedy hands together in anticipation of those shipping shares. Paul suppressed the urge to make a cheeky face as he passed. Better to keep one's head down and never let on that he knew what had transpired. That instinct of his—

Was it really instinct? Or was it divine intervention?

*I am the vine, ye are the branches.* If he could really do nothing without God, was it God who had warned him—who had allowed him that glimpse of Gail's carriage in the street—who had provided him with that guarded intuition from the moment Parker mentioned the deal?

His joy turned a shade more thoughtful. If it was so, then how could he profess himself an unbeliever any longer?

He rounded the corner, and a familiar pair greeted him—Becky and Juliet, out for a morning stroll. Becky didn't spy him at first; her attention was turned toward her charge. She was smiling down at Juliet and offering her some words of encouragement or praise. The dimple in her left cheek made its appearance, and his heart warmed at the sight of it. If he were to believe more in the workings of Providence, he'd understand that God had sent Becky his way, and Juliet his way, and together they made his life all the richer.

Juliet saw him first; she broke free of Becky's hold and ran toward him, her bonnet nearly taking flight. She threw her little body at him with all her might, and he caught her in his arms, spinning her round and round. "Did you miss me, little one?" He squeezed her tightly, then set her down as Becky bustled up, a confused and hesitant expression on her pretty face.

"Is everything all right, Paul? I'm so sorry. I should have kept better hold of Juliet." She straightened Juliet's bonnet.

"All right? Everything is extraordinary, Becky-girl. Congratulate me. I just turned down an exorbitant amount of money to do God's will."

Was Paul teasing her again? If so, it wasn't the least bit funny, making light of her feelings about the Lord and her purpose in the world.

She searched his face. His brown eyes flashed, but not with mockery. No, they were lit from within by a deeper, warmer light.

"I don't understand," she replied slowly. Exorbitant amount of money? What's more, he'd embraced Juliet when the little imp broke free and ran up to him. He called her Becky-girl. Paul must be in a thoroughly good mood—but why?

"Come, walk with me." He scooped Juliet into his arms, shifting her over to his right side, and offered Becky his left elbow with a courtly air. "You're the only person in London who will fully appreciate this. I couldn't wait to share the tale with you. I fairly ran from the solicitor's office."

He steered them down the path toward Hyde Park. This was the closest she'd been to Paul in their entire acquaintance, not just because her hand was tucked securely into the crook of his arm, but because of his delightful, confidential manner and the genuine smile he offered her. As they made their way into the park, they surely presented an odd trio to the handful of gentlemen strolling past: Paul, impeccably dressed as always, except for the hat knocked slightly askew by Juliet, who was cooing one of her nameless, wordless songs, her bonnet now hanging by its strings and the bodice of her dress smeared with—oh dear—smeared with raspberry jam.

While she, strolling along on Paul's arm in her simple nursemaid's gown, tried to conceal the glow of her cheeks by tugging her bonnet forward. What a strange world she had entered the moment he'd approached them on the pavement. Everything had turned upside down, and this heady mixture of wonder and bewilderment would not abate.

"The entire purpose of my journey to London was to sell my father's shipping shares. These formed the basis of his fortune, but a time-consuming one, for Father was always very intent on knowing each passenger of each ship, what every cargo hold contained. Over the years, we've used our shares to ensure that none of our ships trade in slavery." Paul nodded to a nearby fellow but maintained the same swift pace.

"The slave trade? Wasn't that outlawed over a decade ago?" Becky looked up at Paul. "How could it possibly be allowed to continue?"

"Slavery was quite lawful when Father had his shares, but even so, he would never allow it on his ships. That is why he kept such a close eye on every passage, and why he amassed so many shares. He felt, most strongly, that slavery was a heinous enterprise. When I inherited his shares, I shared his belief and his close attention to each ship. Unfortunately, Becky, the slave trade continues, even to this day. Many captains smuggle slaves aboard each ship."

Becky gasped. "That is dreadful. I had no idea." She had no idea about so many things. Paul was opening her eyes, bit by bit, to the reality of the world. She'd taken it so for granted that she was an isolated individual, untouched by any other person's suffering. Indeed, because of Paul, she'd grown to care for a child who was not hers, and felt loyalty to a family to which she didn't even belong. She knew more of suffering, of pain and of the bonds of family now than she ever had that horrid day out on the moor.

"Most young, gently bred women would not. I don't fault you for that, Becky-girl. Over time, though, the demands of Kellridge, of my sister—and well, of my own frivolous pastimes—began to take their toll. I didn't think I could give the shares as much attention as they deserved, so I decided to sell."

Frivolous pastimes? An unreasonable spark of jealousy kindled within her breast. Was Paul referring to a lady? Or many ladies, as Kate had hinted at? She couldn't trust her voice, so she merely nodded.

"I set the price ridiculously high, for I didn't want to sell them to just anyone, nor did I particularly want to sell them quickly. You see, even then I was having qualms about it. A fellow by the name of Gail wanted to buy them—offered to pay handsomely for them—but George warned me that he had a reputation for being a smuggler. So I refused to sell."

"Oh, that was good," she breathed. "What happened today that makes you so joyful?"

As they neared a clearing, he set Juliet down. "Run and play, little one."

Juliet obliged by dancing a few feet down the path, but staying close enough that she could observe them both. How far she had come, too. No more clinging to Becky's skirts, or throwing a kicking and screaming fit. 'Twas good indeed to see her progress, and to feel a part of it.

"Gail sent a proxy, a fellow named Smith, to buy them. I discovered the ruse, quite by chance, this morning on my way to sign the papers. Do you know what I did? I told Smith I wouldn't sell, not even after he doubled his price. I knew from the beginning something was off about the deal." He gave a sudden turn and grasped both her elbows, holding her close. "At that moment, I knew why I'd felt so uneasy—that lesson from the chapel flashed to mind and I suddenly knew that I could do nothing without God. That keeping these shares was my way of doing His will. And that by doing so, I would be assisting in ending a trade that is an abomination before God."

"Oh, Paul. I am so proud of you." What a good man he was, he had always been! Now he could become the best man he could be. "I am so thankful you have finally discovered His plans for you."

"I wouldn't have done so without your help. As soon as I felt it for myself, I could hardly contain myself for joy. I wanted to fly home just so I could tell you." With one sudden, swift movement, he whirled her around in the air, laughing. "Becky-girl, I feel like a new man. I cannot thank Him enough for bringing you into my life."

Becky couldn't suppress a smile, but as he set her down, she caught a giddy glance of the passersby openly gawking at them. It wasn't the fashionable hour, and the park wasn't teeming with fine couples, but that hardly mattered. Even to the few people gathered here, they must be making quite a display, one that might be completely misunderstood and which could quickly cause scandal. She took a step back, glancing over her shoulder. "Juliet?" she called, keeping her face hidden. She must gain control of her blush.

"She's right here." Paul swung Juliet up into his arms again. "Now, where would you like to go? I shall take my ladies wherever they like this afternoon. To the museum? Or shopping? Name the activity, Becky-girl, and we shall celebrate."

"Well…" Paul could be such jolly company, and his mood now was so exhilarating, that it would be lovely to spend the afternoon with him and with Juliet. She cast a nervous glance around as they made their way down the path. More than one gentleman turned and frankly stared in their direction. They had caused a sensation, and surely accounts of their embrace would be bandied about town.

If she were going to make a career of being a nursemaid, she must develop and maintain a sterling reputation. In the country, free from the prying eyes of others, she could afford to be more free and even, in some respects, consider herself on the same level as Paul. Here, in London, the differences in their stations were manifest. She must place some distance between herself and Paul if she were truly going to follow her calling in life.

"I have a better idea." She cast about for something intelligent to say, something that wouldn't sound obviously made up. "Why don't you take your niece out, just the two of you? I shall work on her wardrobe some more while you are gone. I have the prettiest little mauve play dress cut out. If I had an afternoon to work, I could have it stitched together in no time at all."

Paul nodded. "That would be nice. Juliet, would you like to see the boats on the Thames?"

Juliet cooed in appreciation. Becky took a deep breath. That crisis was averted.

"Then that's what we shall do." Paul leaned closer to Becky and lowered his voice. "I promise you shall have a reward too, Becky-girl. It's the height of the season, after all. Balls, musicals, operas, plays—something to see or do every night. Would you like to accompany me to a ball this evening? There's a stack of invitations on my mantel that I've never even paid heed to."

Her heart leaped at his congenial tone and at the thought of dancing with Paul. He was likely a very good dancer and it had been ages since she'd had the opportunity to attend any kind of function. Surely there could be no harm. And after all, he wanted to celebrate.

No.

Those glances in the park—they were merely a portent of the scandal that could break if she started being seen with Paul at any kind of affair. She was here as his niece's nursemaid, and though they got on well, she was nothing more to Paul than that. She must stop spinning daydreams and keep both feet firmly on the ground if she didn't want to invite gossip.

"I thank you for the invitation, but who would watch over Juliet?" She kept her tone light and teasing. No need to let on how confused and conflicted she felt.

"Balls don't start until long past Juliet's bedtime, and I could have one of the other maids check in on her now and again until we return." Paul steered them down Grosvenor Street. "What say you, Becky-girl?

Don't tell me you aren't interested. You look as though you were born to be belle of a ball."

She must remember that Paul was a teasing rogue. A good man, but full of wit and banter—and his compliments meant nothing. Otherwise, her head might be completely turned by his flattery and his intimate manner. "Nay, sir. I would take no pleasure in a ball if I were supposed to be caring for my darling Juliet." She reached over and straightened Juliet's skirt. Though she kept her tone light, what she said was true. She was here to care for Juliet, and it would feel odd indeed to relegate her greatest task to someone else.

Paul heaved an exaggerated sigh. "Very well. I suppose I shall have to think of some other way to show my appreciation." He opened the garden gate to let them pass through.

"You need not show me any regard, Paul. I am so happy for you. So happy that you've found your purpose in life and opened your heart to God." She must leave it at that.

If she said more, well, she might make herself a spectacle.

# Chapter Sixteen

"Where on earth have you been, old chap?" John Reed made an elaborate show of rubbing his eyes, as though amazed by Paul's sudden appearance at Brook's. "You've been in town all this time and haven't stopped in once? You might as well be still buried out in the country."

Paul accepted the good-natured ribbing with patience. After all, he would have said the same sort of thing to John, had their situations been reversed. He was no longer the same man he was a day or so ago, much less a few weeks. "Ah, well. Business has kept me busy. You know that taking care of my interests always takes precedence over any kind of pleasure."

"So the business is now done, and Paul is ready to play. I say, there are ample delights awaiting you here. Where shall we begin? Do you fancy a game?" John rubbed his thin hands together with glee.

"No, thank you." Paul glanced around the club. Nothing seemed fun or even remotely interesting. Just the same men doing the same reckless things they did season after season. None of it had any deeper purpose or meaning. How empty these pursuits had become.

"Perhaps a drink, then, to start the evening off proper?" John grabbed the bottle sitting before him. "A toast to being done with duty and commencing play?"

Drink? What was the purpose in that? He drank to forget, to ease the pain of losing Ruth and Juliana. That pain had ebbed. He'd accepted their deaths as tragic, but now that he was gaining in faith, his comfort grew. Neither one of them felt pain any longer. They did not suffer. Now their memories would be with him forever. Juliet was Juliana all over again, and his delight in his niece increased—not in the least because of Becky's expert care in making her into a little lady.

Becky. What a treasure she was.

"No drink." He tossed the phrase off with a casual air. He didn't need to drink any longer because he didn't need to forget. He must now focus on the present.

"No drink!" John goggled at him. "Are you in your right mind? Are you ill?" His brows drew together with concern. "You must be, for I have never heard you turn aside an opportunity to imbibe."

"I am in my right mind, and I am not ill. I thank you for your concern." Why had he even come here tonight? He didn't desire to be at Brook's. He'd much rather be at home, since he couldn't entice Becky to accompany him to a ball. Now, if she were here, instead of John, he could be talking to her—telling her of his plans for Kellridge in the autumn, discussing how best to care for Juliet, and showing her the few wholesome pleasures of town life. Ever since yesterday, and that walk in Hyde Park, 'twas almost as if she were avoiding him. Could he have done something to displease her?

"How do you know for certain if a gal doesn't like you?" The words burst forth before he could contain them. He closed his eyes. What a ridiculous mistake. Talking about Becky with a rogue like John. This would certainly lead to disaster.

"Oh, ho, so the lad is lovesick," John chortled. "No wonder you forsake drink. Are you still eating, or are you wasting away from love, like a Byronic hero?"

"Now, see here. Sometimes I question why I even bother to hang about with a chap like you," Paul began, and then paused. Well, he had always stayed with John and Daniel because they were good drinking friends, though Daniel was always rather more of a good friend than just someone to imbibe with. John was a good enough sort of fellow, just—now that the haze of too much liquor had long since lifted—rather shallow.

"There, there. No need to get all up in arms. I may be a rogue, but I can honestly say I understand the workings of the heart and its nobler emotions," John replied easily, holding up his hands. "I haven't heard you breathe a word about another woman—not in all seriousness, of course—since Miss Barclay died. You must admit that I had reason to be surprised."

"Yes, that's true." Paul passed a weary hand over his brow. "When I was engaged to Ruth, our affection was mutual and almost predictable. She came of a noble family, and I had wealth. We met at a ball here in town. Our courting followed its usual course. Not that

I loved her any less, but our romance was the stuff of primers—precise and conventional. This situation in which I find myself now is trickier."

"Why so?" John put his elbow on the table and rested his chin in his hand. "The lady isn't married, is she?"

"No, of course not." Paul rolled his eyes. Why on earth was he even bothering with John? Because John was here, and Daniel was in Tansley, and since the female in question was Daniel's sister-in-law, things could get thorny if he weren't careful. "To some, it might seem that she is of a different background than mine, though she is as much of a lady—if not more so—than any debutante in any season."

"Ah. This girl—she doesn't have purple eyes, does she? Excuse me, I should say violet." A smile hovered around John's lips.

"How on earth did you know?" Paul hissed. He himself only began to feel it yesterday, in the park.

"You defended her so vehemently against my dubious compliments and affections that I thought it quite obvious," John rejoined, breaking out into a grin. "She is a lovely creature, Paul. Quite unlike any lass I've seen in town."

"She is, indeed." Paul sighed. He might as well spill the whole story, since 'twas obvious that his emotions were on display. Who knew? Perhaps John could help him. Not likely, but one could always hope. "The problem is, of course, that she works in my household. I don't want to impose upon her or expose her to any kind of untoward advance. But I genuinely like her company.

I don't think I am in love with her, but I crave her company beyond anyone else's."

"I assume you want the chance to get to know her better, but to what end? Do you honestly think you would marry her, should the opportunity arise?"

Marry Becky? Paul could list a dozen arguments to put that idea from his mind. "I have only ever known her as a friend of the family, or a servant in my household." Yes, 'twas all true. Even so…

Paul sighed. "I admire her immensely. I do want to know her better, but it feels she's suddenly begun to avoid me and I can't fathom why." He sat back, looking at his friend expectantly. Surely John would come up with a volley of jests, and then tease him once more.

"You haven't answered my question," John prodded. "Why do you want to know her better?"

"I don't know about marriage or anything else at this moment." He just wanted to be more in Becky's company. When he was with her—well, it was hard to say, but her very presence was welcoming and warm. She eased the loneliness in his life, made him yearn to be a better man. "I just want to spend more time with her. To be friends, if nothing else. I invited her to a ball, and she wouldn't go. Said she needed to attend to Juliet, though I promised to have a maid check in on the child and be with her at all times."

"Well, you can hardly blame her for refusing a ball." John shrugged. "You must see matters from her side. She may worry that she is being preyed upon, or that she will open herself to censure if she spends too much time in your company. Or she may not be certain that you are seeking her out. A ball would put her before all the eyes of society and would invite talk. Why not try for something a little less grand?"

Paul nodded. Perhaps there was something in what John said. At least his friend was taking this conversation seriously and not merely joking about. He hadn't considered how Becky might feel about going to a ball, or that accepting his invitation might place her in a tenuous position. He had only wanted to celebrate—to give Becky the chance to wear a pretty dress, to dance with her, to show her the artificial elegance of a London ballroom and to hear what she had to say about it.

On the other hand, what if he offered to bring her to something more mundane? "Lady Cheswick is offering a musicale on Monday afternoon. Perhaps I could invite Becky to that. A musicale is more sedate than a ball—perhaps she would accept?" In the past he had always avoided musicales—boring, stuffy affairs they could be, with predatory mothers practically flinging their daughters in his general direction.

"Well, that's better than a ball, but it still has a slight hitch. It's a society event, and at the thought of any society event, she might cry off to avoid inciting any kind of talk." John rubbed his thumbnail back and forth over the tablecloth. "What if...what if you invited her not because you want to spend time in her company, but because you think it might be an improvement for Juliet?"

Paul nodded, as John's meaning dawned upon him. "You mean...tell her that the musicale might be an opportunity for her to learn more about music, and thus instruct Juliet as she grows up?"

John sat back in his chair with a self-satisfied smile. "You've said that Juliana was musically inclined. It stands to reason her daughter might be, too. Why not allow Becky the chance to see what a London musicale is like, so that she may start bringing up your ward to take her place in society as a talented and accomplished young lady? My mother always told me that 'tis never too early to begin. I believe my sister Jane first held a bow at two years of age."

This was an excellent idea, for what John said was true. If Juliet were truly to grow up and display artistic talents, then her nursemaid and later her governess would have to instruct her. Becky, being a country girl, would have no knowledge or expertise in this, at least as far as how a young lady would display this talent in society. Did Becky even play an instrument, or sing? He had no inkling of her talents beyond her obvious beauty and charm, her penchant for drama, and of course, her deep affection for his niece.

He must get to know her better. And Lady Cheswick's musicale was the perfect opportunity to do so.

"Upon my word, you give sound advice." Paul beamed at his companion. "I daresay I never thought you capable of stringing two sensible words together, my good fellow."

"Well, I shan't do it often, I assure you. This was rather a special case. Now, may we please turn our attention to the delights this evening promises? I rather fancy a game of faro."

Paul shook his head, pushing his chair away from the table. London night life had decidedly palled. His usual heady rush of excitement when contemplating cards, drink or any other licentious behavior was simply no more. "I'm an uncle now, and a guardian. The desire to indulge in dissolution has completely fled me. I think I'll go home." He would discuss the possibility of his feelings for Becky with John, but nothing more. The newness of his acceptance of Christ was still too tender to share, particularly with an unbeliever like John. He would wait and talk it over with Becky and Daniel—people who could prop him up in faith, and not attempt to tear it down.

John shrugged and stifled a yawn. "Well, I say, have a ripping good time at home. I'm off to find a game." Then he was off, winding his way through the crowd toward the back rooms.

Paul watched John's progress, allowing himself a small, wry grin. Thanks to his dissolute friend, he now had the means to court Becky Siddons.

It only remained to convince the lady in question that she should accompany him to the musicale. Given how neatly she had evaded him thus far, this would not be an easy task.

'Twas only an embrace given in the excitement of the moment. She must not read too much into it.

Becky rolled over on her bed and jammed her pillow over her head. Paul hadn't met with her that evening—not because he forgot, but because she requested they forego their usual nightly discussion about Juliet. She could still feel his hands holding her upper arms, no matter how often she rubbed them, or how tightly she wrapped her shawl about her. And she couldn't sit down with him face to face when her emotions were still swirling about—just as he had twirled her about the day before.

The Becky Siddons of a few months ago would have already been planning her trousseau, based on that one moment in the park. She had progressed so far since those days. Surely she wasn't some simpering ninny still believing that every man who passed her way was expiring for love of her.

His invitation to the ball was kindly meant as a gesture—merely that, and nothing more—to celebrate his victories. He had, after all, saved his father's legacy from becoming forever stained with the blot of slavery. He had found his way to Christ. Surely those were a heady combination of triumphs, and he should rejoice in them.

After all, what he had done that day caused her to glow with pride. How many men, faced with the chance to make an enormous fortune, would turn away because of a moral objection?

Not that it mattered to her. But it was good to know that Juliet's guardian was such an upright man.

Her head throbbed, and a slight tickle in her throat made her cough. She hadn't felt herself since they arrived. If only she would feel well, perhaps she could handle her emotions better.

Until she could rein in her emotions and ensure that she wasn't going to make a cake of herself over one quick embrace in the park, she would have to continue avoiding Paul. She must keep encouraging him to enjoy the time spent with his little niece, but she must absent herself whenever possible.

She was not marriageable material. So she had decreed when Lieutenant Walker wrote and announced, oh so casually, that he'd married another. Thus she must put her blinders to anything—or anyone—that might cause her to swerve from her path. Entertaining ridiculous notions about a man as important and—well, if she were perfectly frank—handsome as Paul Holmes was nothing more than a silly distraction.

She must go to church in the morning and pray for help in overcoming her ridiculous feelings. She could pray now, but the formality of a church appealed to her sensibilities. In church, everything would become more concrete.

London had churches, surely. She must find one and go to services—she could even bring Juliet along.

There was nothing for it. She couldn't sleep. She might as well cease trying. The headache simply wouldn't abate, and perhaps if she rose for a while, it would finally go away.

She groped in the dark for her wrapper, which was draped across the foot of her bed. Then she tied it around her securely and rose. She could check on Juliet. Not having Juliet's room close to hers was so strange; she didn't like it. In those few weeks at Kellridge, she had grown so accustomed to hearing Juliet's deep, even breathing, and to being able to peep in on her at any time of the night.

She fumbled with the tinderbox on her bedside table until she struck a light and lit her candle. The guttering flame drove all the panic from her mind. She was just tired, that was all. A quick check on Juliet, and she would calm down enough to sleep.

She tiptoed across the floor and eased her door open. No telling if anyone was still awake. It was well past midnight according to the long-case clock at the end of the hall.

Outside Juliet's door, she paused. A flickering light shone underneath. Surely one of the other servants hadn't left a candle lit inside her room? That was dangerous— a sure way to start a fire. She wrenched the door open and gasped. A man—a large man—hovered over Juliet's bed.

A scream caught in Becky's throat and her heart pounded in her breast. Surely this man was trying to kidnap her darling girl! She put her candle aside and crossed the room in two large strides, casting her glance about for anything that she might hurl at the scoundrel.

The hovering figure straightened, and in his flickering candlelight she caught a glimpse of his face as he raised his finger to his lips. Her sudden strength dissipated, leaving her knees wobbly.

'Twas Paul, and not some footpad.

Paul quirked an eyebrow at her and motioned her out into the hallway. Becky followed, grasping her candle as she quit the room. The heady combination of relief and mortification at being caught in her wrapper made her head spin.

"I thought…I thought you were a footpad, bent on kidnapping Juliet," she gasped as he closed the door behind them with a quiet click. "I am so sorry."

"Nay, I am the one who should apologize. I never meant to frighten you. When I got home, I decided I would check on Juliet and make certain she was sleeping well." He patted her shoulder. "Are you quite all right? You look rather pale."

Was she all right? Well, she was embarrassed beyond measure, and weak as a kitten as her potent intensity fled. She nodded. Words were not even possible at the moment, not the way her teeth chattered.

"I've never really checked on Juliet before, so I can well understand your worry. 'Tis my fault, and I cannot apologize enough. It's just—when I got home from the club, I needed to reassure myself she was all right." He shrugged, shaking his head with a rueful gesture. "I know that sounds strange."

"Not at all." His concern was heartening. In fact, his entire manner toward his niece had changed so dramatically over the past few weeks that it warmed her heart. He treated her as a father should—concerned for her safety, involved in her upbringing, enjoying her company. That was as it should be. "I was worried about her, too. I don't like being this far from her. I am used to having her so close by at Kellridge. So I came to check on her."

"Everything is better at Kellridge, isn't it?" He cast a reassuring grin her way. "Not to disparage my mother's taste in houses, but this townhome simply isn't as comfortable as home. It's no matter. We will leave in a matter of months anyway."

Months in London? Perish the thought. At Kellridge they had their own wing of the house, and she could come and go as she pleased. She could see her sisters again. Back in Tansley, Susannah could talk some plain sense to her—Nan most certainly would—and help her to overcome her runaway emotions.

"I am planning to take Juliet to church on the morrow," she ventured. Might as well make her intentions known. Perhaps Paul could direct her to the closest place of worship.

"Excellent idea. May I join you? It's been far too long since I darkened the doorstep of St. George's."

Of course his newfound faith would lead him to a desire to attend services. She had hoped for an escape for just a few moments—a place of quiet contemplation in which to ask her Father for strength—but it was not to be. The very man she was running from wanted to join them.

Of course, she must welcome him, for what he was asking was both good and honorable.

"Yes, certainly you may. In fact, I should need your help in finding St. George's, since I am wholly unfamiliar with town." Her head gave another painful throb. "Shall we walk together in the morning?"

"That sounds capital." Paul took her hand in the crook of his elbow and escorted her to her doorway. "Until then. And I do apologize for scaring you so much." He gave her a courtly bow.

"Not at all. I am sorry I was looking for something with which to strike you," she rejoined.

Paul laughed quietly and, with a small wave, walked down the corridor. As she let herself into her room, she leaned against the closed door and took a deep breath.

Headache, sore throat, sleeplessness and terror. Really, she was acting more and more like a Gothic heroine.

She must grab hold of herself if she were to persevere through the next few months—not to mention the rest of her life in her chosen profession.

# Chapter Seventeen

Walking to church with Becky and his niece—why, this was a natural and good feeling. For someone who had only recently found his way to Christ, this was an event that could best be described as exhilarating. Both of them had, in their different ways, brought him closer to God. He was prepared to give thanks for that, to begin his life anew as one who knew he could do nothing without Him. He desired to ask for guidance, as well—some sort of direction in his feelings for Becky Siddons. His conversation with John had awakened his sensibilities. Was he, in fact, developing some sort of *tendresse* for her?

His regard for her had certainly deepened over time. Last night, when she'd burst into Juliet's room, determined to strike anyone who dared to lay a finger on his niece—well, 'twas a terrifying moment, to be sure, but a heartening one. No one had ever cared for Juliet as fiercely as Becky did, save perhaps Juliana. Even so, 'twas unlikely that Juliana would burst into her daughter's room and threaten someone with bodily harm. No—his sister would have screamed and gone into hysterics. He loved his sister, but her foibles were always all too apparent.

Becky cared for Juliet the way a mother should. She was concerned about his niece's safety and the quality of her sleep. She dressed Juliet in simple frocks made by her own hand—a style of dress that gave Juliet freedom of movement. She ensured Juliet ate a proper diet. She had cared for Juliet's spiritual development. All of this, coupled with her determination to slay a robber last night, cast her in an entirely new light. Becky Siddons was no longer a pretty, vexing little thing that he enjoyed teasing. No—she was more. A young woman, beautiful in face and in her person, but also beautiful in soul and in spirit.

But what to make of all this? The answer must come to him. Perhaps the church service would speak to him, or at the least, open his mind to more possibilities.

An early morning shower had left streaks of mud in their path. As they neared a particularly large puddle, Juliet cooed in glee. Paul quirked his mouth with ruthful delight. Juliet would still be Juliet, even though they might endeavor to iron out her more rambunctious tendencies. He swung Juliet up in the air with a quick flex of his arm, and Becky, on Juliet's opposite side, did the same. Juliet flew through the air, crowing in delight, and Paul glanced over at Becky. She, too, was smiling—a thoughtful, absorbed smile. But she did not meet his eyes, even though their movements were in perfect harmony.

"What are you thinking of, Becky-girl?" He kept his tone light. If only she would speak to him squarely, as she had done in times past. With a Siddons gal who spoke her mind, a fellow knew where he stood. This new Becky was withdrawn and silent, and frequently absent. He missed her sweetness and impulsive nature. He missed seeing the dimple in the left corner of her cheek. What had effected this transformation?

"Oh, nothing. Just this awful headache. It persists no matter what I do." She gave him a wan smile, and then focused her attention on the church as they drew closer. "What a lovely place it is! I confess I have never seen a church this fine."

Paul turned his attention back to the matter at hand. St. George's was an impressive place, with its six imposing columns marching along its facade. "Wait until you see inside. The galleries are particularly nice."

Carriages of all shapes and descriptions pulled up to the front steps, and fashionable ladies and gentlemen milled about outside, greeting each other with languid waves, or bows and curtsies. St. George's was the most popular place of worship in Mayfair and attracted the more spiritually inclined of the *haut ton*. The excitement and wide-eyed wonder he'd felt at his conversion was completely lacking in this congregation.

Becky halted, her brows drawn together. "Is it quite all right to bring children in? I don't see many here."

"Oh, Juliet can come along. I am certain the smaller children are already inside. The early morning rain, you know. Staying outdoors too long is an invitation to muddy their fine clothes." He eased her forward again by tugging at Juliet.

"Perhaps I should sit in back." Becky halted once more. "This place…'tis finer than any church I've attended."

"Nay, we shall all sit together in the family pew." Paul gave her a reassuring smile. "No need to fret, Becky. You look as pretty as a picture today. Indeed, none of these women can hold a candle to you."

What he said was true and not mere flattery. Even as silent and withdrawn as she was, Becky still cut an elegant figure. Her dress was plainer than the other gowns on opulent display this morning. Her bonnet was trimmed with a ribbon in a dark purple shade that highlighted the shadows of her eyes. Yet, for all her simplicity, she had more style about her than any other lady. Some women just possessed that gift of refinement. Others couldn't buy it, not with all the gold in their coffers.

His graceful compliment merely deepened Becky's frown. "If you're sure," she replied distantly, and then turned her attention to Juliet, fussing over her bonnet and dress before they entered the sanctuary.

He fell silent and gave himself over to the task of finding their family pew and settling Becky and Juliet beside him. In a moment he would give all his attention to the service—to singing hymns, to listening to scripture, to paying heed to the sermon. As he gazed at the altar, one thought grew fixed in his mind. He needed guidance. Now that he had opened his life to Him, he needed to know his next steps. As

a man of business, his path was sure and set, but as a
guardian—as a man—he needed more.

St. George's was quite beautiful, Becky reflected as
they left the church. Not at all like the cozy Bible study
she'd grown used to at home. The sermon was good
enough, but never touched a deep chord within her, as
discussing the scripture was wont to do. All the same,
she had given it a go, and Juliet had behaved passably
well. Her little charge had swung her booted feet, and
curled up on the pew as though to sleep, but finally settled down when Becky tugged her into her lap.

Now, as they strolled home, Paul gathered Juliet into
his arms and drew closer to Becky's side. This physical proximity to him was wreaking havoc on her sensibilities. She resisted the urge to reach up and touch
the scar on his cheek with her gloved finger. She must
be running a fever—no decent nursemaid would ever
entertain such thoughts about her employer.

Becky switched her thoughts to practical matters.
Lunch would be served soon, and she could put her
charge down for a nap afterward. Perhaps she might
take one as well. Her head still ached, and despite her
best, most unobtrusive efforts with her handkerchief,
her nose still had a tendency to run. If only she could
shake free of this physical malaise, perhaps everything
would fall into place. She would stop making such a
fuss about Paul and shoulder her duties as Juliet's caretaker with good cheer, and cease any and all foolishness.

Foolishness? Aye, that was what it was. So many
women, elegant, well-bred and beautifully gowned,

had been sending discreet looks at her employer while they were supposed to be paying attention to the sermon. Becky wasn't so naive as to misunderstand their glances. Her employer was a most eligible bachelor. He was wealthy, handsome and charming. The wonder of it was that he hadn't chosen a wife yet. Perhaps that was his design in returning to London with his charge? To find her a proper mother?

That certainly made more sense than bringing Becky to London for a change of scene and a chance to broaden her horizons.

"You know, I was invited to an event and I think it would be beneficial for you to come along." He leaned toward her with a confidential air. "Lady Cheswick is having a musicale tomorrow afternoon and, while I will be going, I think you should come as well."

"A musicale?" Becky shot him an uncertain glance. A musicale was likely more sedate than a ball, but could she afford to place herself at any kind of risk? If the musicale were being hosted by a member of the *ton,* wouldn't her presence be cause for some question among Paul's friends and acquaintances?

"Yes. As Juliet's nursemaid, I want you to see how young women present themselves and their musical talents in society. As the daughter of two musicians, I suspect my little niece will, in time, show some aptitude for music as well. I'd like for you to help me shape her gift at an early age, and Lady Cheswick is providing the perfect opportunity for an introduction. What do you say?" He looked down at her, an intent glance in his brown eyes that made her heart give a strange leap in her chest.

"Well…" If this were to be a part of her responsibilities as she raised Juliet, she could not well cry off. But would she invite comment by appearing? "Are you certain it would be all right? I do not want to provoke any kind of interest among the *ton*. Since I am merely a nursemaid in your household, I worry that people would think it untoward if I came along with you." There. She was being forthright, explaining her hesitation. Perhaps now he would see her side of the matter.

"I appreciate your concern." He ducked as Juliet grasped an outstretched twig on a low-hanging branch, popping the brim of his hat as she let go. "But Lady Cheswick has known my family for years. She and my mother were old friends. She'll think nothing of it if you come along. And if she doesn't, then no one will—for all of society follows her lead. At least as far as matters of protocol are concerned."

If that were indeed the case, there was nothing to stop her from going. In fact, if she continued to object, she might attract more attention from him than if she simply went along with it. After all, 'twas her duty to bring Juliet up as a proper English lady. Moreover, Paul was right. As the daughter of musicians, Juliet would likely have prodigious musical talent. And as Juliet's earliest influence, it would be Becky's responsibility to guide and shape that talent.

That settled the matter. She would accept his invitation.

"As long as you think it beneficial for Juliet," she conceded.

He grinned down at her, an expression so frank and joyful that she caught her breath and turned away. She was so awfully susceptible to romance. If she were a heroine in a novel, her romanticism would be her greatest flaw. Her head had been so turned by Lieutenant Walker's brief attention that she'd fully expected a proposal by penny post. Frustration mounted within her, boiling in its intensity. She hadn't changed as much as she wished to, for here she was, once more, finding herself entranced by a handsome man who merely desired her to do one thing. In fact, he wanted her to do one thing only—care for his niece as he paid her to do.

Her persistent desire to read flirtation into every friendly thing a man did was most ridiculous. She had overcome this before, and she would again. She must. Otherwise, she would become a desperately silly old maid, reading a romantic insinuation into every sideways glance.

"Come, Juliet," she sang out as they neared the town house gate. "Let us see what the cook has prepared for your lunch. What do you think? Perhaps some eggs?"

Paul swung Juliet down from his shoulder and opened the gate. "Have you gotten her to try eggs yet?"

Juliet scurried over to the garden and picked up a stick. Becky gave an inward sigh. Not that she minded Juliet's appreciation of nature, but the way the child picked up rocks and twigs, or splashed in mud, certainly made it more difficult to keep her tidy.

"Nasty." Juliet enunciated the word clearly, punctuating it with a whack of her stick against the garden path.

"What? They're delicious. And so good for a growing girl." She bustled over to her charge and took her free hand. "Come on, now."

"No." All at once, Juliet grew as heavy as a sack of lead and as boneless as a jellyfish. She sank to the ground, still grasping Becky's hand. "No, no, no!"

"Now, Juliet, be reasonable." The child must be tired and in need of a nap. Her sleep schedule had been completely thrown off with travel. "You must eat. Otherwise the insides of your tum will stick together." Sometimes silliness worked where reason failed. Becky bent down to scoop Juliet up, and her forehead gave a painful throb.

"No. I. WON'T!" Juliet was shrieking now, a piercing wail that cut through Becky's headache like a knife. She tossed her stick aside and flopped back to the ground, kicking and flailing, her lovely lavender dress now thoroughly streaked with mud.

"Has she always been this awful?" Paul rumbled, glancing down at his niece with a quizzical air. "I thought she'd been improving."

"She has." Becky gave up the struggle. Perhaps, as she and Nan had discovered that one morning before Sunday school, Juliet would calm down without an audience. She moved a few paces away across the garden path and Paul followed. "I think that, given the rigors of travel, and adjusting to a new home, our methods of curbing her temper have frayed a bit. She's not sleeping as well or as timely as she did at home, and she's not eating as she should."

Paul nodded. "The excitement of London is beginning to pall, is it not?"

Becky pressed her hand to her forehead. "I am afraid so."

"What should we do?" Paul, usually so self-assured, so controlled, so exacting in his response to any emotional situation, looked all at sea. He regarded Juliet, still rolling about on the garden path, as one would look at a particularly rare and interesting specimen of plant or animal.

"Aren't you the expert?" Becky retorted. "Is she not just like your little sister?" The moment she said the words, she wished them back. It wasn't Paul's fault Juliet was too tired and too hungry to behave. Or that Becky's head was being pounded from the inside with a large mallet.

"I confess that she reminds me more of my sister in this moment than ever before." A sheepish look stole over Paul's face. "But when Juliana was in the throes of temper, my mother had the servants care for her. I never really had to intervene in a display like this."

"Well, I am the servant now." Becky paused. She was sounding shrewish and snappish, when really she was just overwhelmed. London was supposed to be such a lovely change of pace, such a thrilling voyage to a new world, but it had utterly failed her. She'd gone all mawkish and fancied herself developing a *tendresse* for Paul Holmes. She'd failed at making Juliet into a little lady. Here she was, barking at her employer like a Pekingese while her charge lay thrashing in the garden, refusing to eat a simple lunch of scrambled eggs.

How ridiculous to think she'd been called here by Him.

Or worse, had she been called by Him and found lacking?

Hot tears filled her eyes and she turned away, blinking rapidly. She must gain control of herself. And the best way to gain control, as she learned from the master of all self-control, was to absent oneself from the situation entirely. She must return to Kellridge, and once home, she must rein in her galloping emotions. She was still well within the three months' trial she'd promised Paul and Susannah. He could apply to an agency here in London and find a perfectly suitable nursemaid to bring home.

In the meantime, she would just have to quash her own silly notion of romance, especially as it applied to Paul Holmes.

"I think we must go home." The tears dried the moment she began to speak. "I think this trip to London was a mistake."

A wounded look flashed across Paul's face, deepening the scar on his cheek. "But—I thought—I mean, I think it's been successful."

Becky waved her gloved hand at Juliet, who had ceased her thrashing and was now making mud pies and sniffing loudly. "Do you call this an improvement?"

Paul shrugged. "Ah…"

"Paul, let us be honest. We are still well within the three months I agreed to, and I am failing miserably. I request that Juliet and I be allowed to return to Kellridge as soon as possible. While you are here, you have the ability to make inquiries for a suitable nursemaid."

There. Now it was out. Her heart gave a painful tug. 'Twas so hard to say it out loud. One could think of it privately and ruminate on it without feeling so horrid. Even so, the mere thought of leaving Juliet...and Paul... forever? This was the hardest decision she'd ever made.

Paul scowled, his brows drawing together. "I will not seek out a new nursemaid. You will stay with Juliet, for I desire you to do so. As her uncle, I find you the best match for caring for her."

She hadn't expected outright refusal. "But, Paul—"

"Absolutely not." The door to his emotions, that inner door that allowed her to gain closer access to his feelings and thoughts, must have swung shut, for he looked at her with the same calm reserve as he had the first day she argued with him at Kellridge. "I will hear no more on the matter."

"I am very sorry to defy you, sir, but I must tender my resignation." Her head throbbed atrociously. "I am entirely unsuited to the position and will return to my sister's millinery shop as soon as I may." She raised her head, forcing herself to look him in the eyes.

Paul glared at her for what seemed like an eternity. Becky's heart hammered an uneven tattoo in her chest. Would he ever answer?

"Very well." Paul's words fell like leaden weights. He glared at her, icy disdain writ plain across his handsome face. His expression tightened so that the muscle along his jawline leaped. "How quickly would you want to go?"

"As soon as ever possible. Tomorrow, if I may." She glanced away from him. She could no longer meet his contemptuous gaze. If she did, her expression might show her struggles, and worse, her silly infatuation with him. She was supposed to have grown in maturity and wisdom, doing the work the Lord sent her to do. Instead, she'd grown overly sentimental. What a stunning disappointment.

"But…if you leave tomorrow…then you will miss the musicale. Surely you can wait a little longer." His voice was hesitant at first, as though he were unsure of what to say. But then, in true Paul fashion, he finished as a declaration. "You will, as her nursemaid, do as I say. At least until I can find a replacement for you."

"It is most important for me, as her nursemaid, to provide an environment in which she can flourish," she spat. "I have utterly failed at this so far. Of course a musical education is lovely, and should be attended to in due time, but someone more skilled than I must provide her with the very bread and water of care. Proper rest, wholesome food, fresh air, comfortable dress. Since coming to London, the fragile schedule I set for her has come tumbling about my ears. I cannot help but see the results in the way she's behaving today—especially when I thought we had come so far." She paused, breathing deeply. This was the kind of argument they'd had in the early days of her engagement, not at all like the peaceful discussions they'd established over time.

She missed those calm deliberations. She'd set herself away from them so as not to reveal her feelings for him.

"Very well."

She shifted her glance to Paul. He was staring down

at the garden path, his hands clenched at his side. Did he mean it? A sensation both wonderful and horrible filled her being. Wonderful that she was going home. Horrible that she was leaving Paul behind.

"Thank you." Now that she'd won the battle, she must be gracious in victory. "Then it is all right if we leave on the morrow? May we have the carriage?"

"Do what you desire," he replied evenly, through clenched teeth. "I'll make inquiries of a new nursemaid and return to Kellridge as soon as possible. Until then, I ask that you remain in your position. I do not want the other servants burdened with caring for my niece."

Becky gave a brief nod, and then bustled over to her charge, now coated in mud and humming to herself. "That's enough playing, Miss Juliet. You will come with me now," she asserted, and helped Juliet rise from her place on the garden path. Paul led the way into the house, opening the door for both of them, and waiting patiently as they passed by.

Becky didn't dare to look at him. If she did, she might fling herself at his feet weeping, or do something outrageous.

Funny that a skirmish so hard-won could leave such a sour taste in her mouth.

## Chapter Eighteen

She should be happy.

They were headed home, after all. Three days on their journey now. In another few days, she would be home—no, not home.

Kellridge.

She must stop thinking that Kellridge was her home. It was merely her place of employment until Paul found a new nanny. She leaned her head against the cool glass of the carriage window and tightened her hold on Juliet. Her throat burned as it had for the length of the trip. If only she could press a button or speak a single word that would make them arrive immediately. They were all so travel-weary.

Juliet rested against her, a dead weight. Becky's arms ached from the strain of holding her, but she didn't dare change her position. Her charge was sleeping, and that was all that mattered. Becky glanced down at Juliet's tired little face, her pale complexion and the bags under her eyes. Poor dear thing. She needed rest and a lot of it. They all did, in fact.

She should be happy it was all over, that she'd gotten her way in the end, that she didn't even have to say goodbye to Paul. Yes, happy—or at least satisfied. But she was neither of these things. She was troubled, and tired, and heartsick over the whole affair.

"If you please, miss, we should be nearing Hinckley soon," her traveling companion, a maid named Sally, murmured from across the seat. "It'll be time to change the horses."

Becky glanced up at the maid. Paul had insisted on sending her along as a helper on the journey, and Becky had acquiesced, afraid of any more scenes. Sally had been quite helpful in pointing out the scenery as they passed, or in estimating their arrivals, but Becky's throat hurt too much for conversation. "Yes, thank you. I shall awaken Miss Juliet only when we pull into the yard."

"I daren't say this, Miss Becky, but you look rather peaked." Sally quirked her brows in concern. "Are you quite all right?"

"I feel…dreadful." What a relief to finally say it out loud. "Honestly, I cannot wait to reach Kellridge. How far are we from our final destination?"

"Two days, perhaps less if the roads stay fine." Sally made a tsking sound under her breath. "I knew you didn't look well, not from the moment we left town."

"How do you know so much about the journey?" Becky gazed at Sally in frank curiosity. "It seems like you can gauge every stop along the way."

"I grew up at Kellridge," Sally replied. "My sister is still in service there."

"Oh, is she really? What is her name?" Becky adjusted Juliet just a trifle—perhaps it would make waking her up easier if she tried the process in slow increments.

"Kate. She was Miss Juliana's maid for ever so long."

Becky suppressed a start. So Sally was Kate's confidante, the one who informed her of all her master's doings in London? Then, of course, Kate had used that information to warn Becky against the one thing she'd done—become a fool over Paul. Her cheeks burned with shame.

"How nice." She said it because she had to say something. The silence was dragging on far too long.

"You look feverish now." Sally closed the gap between them and laid her ungloved hand on Becky's forehead. "I knew it. You've got a fever. Well, there's nothing for it—we shall have to send for a doctor."

"No, indeed." Becky jostled Juliet gently. "I can make it to Kellridge, if we've really only a few more days to go."

"Mr. Holmes wouldn't like it." Sally pursed her lips. "His orders are that he is to be kept informed of all the goings-on of the households and their servants. If you are ill, we need to send word to him. When we stop at the inn, I shall send a runner back to London."

"No. Don't." Becky's heart hammered in her chest. She must be able to do something right, even if it just meant making it back to Tansley without further disaster. "There's no need, for I will be quite well enough to stick to my duties until he finds a new nursemaid. It would only cause undue concern."

"Your devotion to Miss Juliet is most pleasing," Sally replied in a gentle tone. "Even so, you must take care of yourself. You'll be no good to her at all if you allow yourself to sink further and further into illness."

"I don't want Mr. Holmes to think I cannot handle this one simple journey," she admitted. "Please don't tell him. I beg you—I already feel so inadequate to this task." To her horror, tears sprang to her eyes. If only Susannah were here to advise her. Her eldest sister would know what to do, and would do it briskly and decisively, with no shilly-shallying.

"I understand." Sally patted her shoulder with a comforting gesture. "Truly, Mr. Holmes will not think ill of you. He is a kind and generous master—the best in Derbyshire, we all believe."

There it was again—that divide between the public master and the private man. Wasn't Sally the one who'd gossiped about all his activities—had warned her own sister about him? "I heard once that he was profligate— the kind of man who might take advantage of a lady."

"Mr. Holmes? I presume my sister told you a thing or two about him. Nay, she always allows her imagination to get the better of her. He enjoys some of the more reckless pursuits that all the young bucks in his group run with, but he would never do anything truly immoral. He was so changed this time. Perhaps having his niece with him has finally lain to rest that instinct to run wild." Sally shook her head. "Now, we must come up with a solution."

"Mr. Holmes wants me to take care of Juliet until he returns with someone to take my place," Becky admitted. "I am trying to be strong, but in truth, I am not sure I can even manage that. Can you help me? Would you be willing to split the duties with me until I feel better and he comes home?" Becky turned as much as her charge's weight would allow her, facing Sally squarely. "We can still send word to Mr. Holmes, but we can ask if it would be all right for you to help me with Juliet at Kellridge until I recover. He is so very particular about each servant's duties—I know he would want to know if we changed things about. Do you think we can do that?"

"Yes, that sounds like a good plan." Sally gave her an encouraging smile. "I've watched you with Miss Juliet and will try to duplicate your efforts. I can send word from the inn to Mr. Holmes about our change in duties until you recover. Are you truly up to two more days' travel?"

Becky rolled her head back against the seat. Now that she had a plan, something to focus upon beyond her own failures and ill feelings, fresh determination filled her soul. Once she was at Kellridge, and able to get over her sickness, she would find a way to extricate herself from her tangled emotions. Until then, she would only care about one thing—making it home in one piece.

"Yes, I shall persevere."

"None of these nannies will do." Paul lounged back in his chair and regarded the employment agent frankly. "These women are decades too old to keep up with my niece."

"Well, Mr. Holmes, we have only a few young women looking for positions as nursemaids at the moment." The man rifled through the papers on his desk. "This girl Flora might do. She's eighteen, and has been in service before, serving as a nanny in another gentleman's family. I can give you a reference. Here, you may read through her recommendations yourself." The employment agent handed the scrap of foolscap to Paul.

Paul pretended to pore over the document. "Yes, well, she looks fine. I'll take her. Can she be ready to leave for Derbyshire within a week or so?"

"I'll have to ask, but I am sure Flora will be most happy to accommodate." The employment agent held out his hand. "I'll inform the girl at once, and we shall be in touch."

"Excellent." Paul left his card and made his goodbyes, with a distinct sinking feeling in his stomach. Surely this Flora would do as well for him as Becky had. She had more experience, at least with one other family. Perhaps life could ease back into its routine of carefully portioned existence now. He could stay in London for long periods of time again, without worrying about having to help raise his own niece.

Paul strolled along Fleet Street, his head still in the fog in which it had persisted since Becky's departure half a dozen days before. Row upon row of shops stretched before him, their windows beckoning alluringly in the morning light, yet nothing interested him.

Her words still rang in his ears. "A suitable nursemaid," she'd pronounced. Very well. Then Flora would fill her place in Juliet's life. Surely Flora would be willing to work with his niece's foibles, or to care for her as a mother should. Would Becky even say goodbye? At least Becky was with Juliet for the time being. For a few more days, his niece had the comfort of her presence, the soft music of her voice, the gentle way she had of tilting her head to one side as she listened—

He gave his head a brief shake. Whatever was the matter with him?

He strolled over to a shop window. A cunning little paper theater, complete with paper dolls in colorful costume, lay in opulent display. What a clever plaything for someone as creative as his niece. He would buy it for her and bring it home. She would love it.

He ducked into the shop and purchased the theater, along with a china doll arrayed in a splendid walking costume, and a few jigsaw puzzles. It was high time his niece had some proper toys, he reflected as the shopkeeper's assistant wrapped his purchases in brown paper and tied them with gold twine. Becky had seen to that too, just like she had everything else since his niece came into his life—making over old toys from the attic so she would have playthings when she arrived.

That was Becky's way. Such a warm and generous female, so attuned to the needs of everyone around her. Trying so hard to follow the path God had set in her life.

He gave his address to the shopkeeper and quit the store. The packages would be delivered later. In the meanwhile—

In the meanwhile, he would buy Becky a gift.

A parting gift. A thank-you for enduring a difficult

few weeks. Why not? Didn't most employers give a kind of bonus to servants who did well?

He hadn't bought a gift for a respectable female in years, unless a fellow could count his sisters. What would Becky desire? If he gave her anything consumable, like a gift of a length of cloth, she would turn it into a gown for his niece. Even after she quit his employ, he could see her toiling over a gown for Juliet. That was just her way.

No, he must find something special, and it must be for Becky alone. Something that would show the esteem in which he held her.

He ducked into a jewelry shop. Surely he could find something worthy of Rebecca Siddons in here.

The shopkeeper snapped to attention at his approach. "May I help you, sir?"

"Yes. I need a gift for a young lady. An extraordinary young lady." Paul drummed his fingertips on the counter. "Something truly fine, and unlike what you would see most women wearing about town."

The shopkeeper beetled his brows. "Well, we do have some very nice bracelets, or perhaps some earrings?"

Paul shook his head. "No. Nothing like that. She's not showy in that way. I want something she can wear that is both dazzling and modest, for that's what she is."

The shopkeeper's mouth quirked. "Dazzling and modest? That's rather a singular combination."

"Yes, she is truly a rare creature. With violet eyes." Paul heaved a sigh.

"Violet, you say? Well then, might I suggest amethysts?" The shopkeeper laid a piece of velvet upon the counter, and then draped a necklace over it. "This is a pendant necklace, the kind a lady wears in the evening. Three large amethysts surrounded by diamonds, and a smaller, rounder amethyst pendant beneath each, also surrounded by diamonds."

Paul gazed at the necklace as it winked in the light. Becky did have a very graceful neck, and these stones would set off the color of her eyes to perfection. This was a proper thank-you. This was the kind of gift a woman could wear with pride and hand down to her daughter someday. That thought was almost as pleasing as the necklace itself. "Yes. This will do nicely."

"If I may say so, sir, your wife will love it. These jewels were mined in Russia and are quite the finest of their type," the shopkeeper announced.

"Wife?" Paul echoed. "She's not—"

"Beg pardon, sir. I had no idea." Rapid color filled the shopkeeper's face. "Most men don't buy things this fine for women who aren't their wives."

Paul suppressed a groan. "This particular lady merits these jewels."

The shopkeeper merely gave a circumspect nod. "Of course, sir. Shall I have it sent round to your residence?"

Paul shook his head. For some reason, he needed to have that necklace with him. "No, I am going home now. I'll just take it with me."

The shopkeeper bustled about, tucking the necklace into a leather box and wrapping the parcel. The vague, uneasy feeling that had hovered about Paul this entire morning simply would not abate. Even purchasing these gifts, fun though it was, did nothing to alleviate his discomfort. When would he see Becky again? When would he hear Juliet's burbling little laugh? London was deadly dull without them.

He tucked the parcel into his jacket pocket and strode home in the grips of preoccupation. Why even stay in London if it was no longer amusing? Once he had tried to flee Kellridge and the very company he now craved, for the dubious delights of town. Now those indulgences were an anathema to him. He missed Becky's stimulating conversation, her kindness—and if a fellow were to own it, she was downright decorative. Yes—the sunshine of her company and the beauty of her person was what he longed for, and now he would be denied them the rest of his days. Becky was leaving him, and the certainty of it made his stomach drop like a stone. He desired Kellridge, Tansley Village and Becky's fair companionship, and not another day in the stuffy old townhome in Mayfair.

As he opened the garden gate, Edmunds strode out onto the portico. "If you please, sir, a message just came by runner. From Sally, as she was traveling back to Kellridge."

"Sally?" He quickened his pace and snatched the missive from Edmunds's gloved hands.

*Dear Mr. Holmes—*
*Miss Siddons is quite unwell. She is aware that she promised to stay on as Miss Juliet's nurse-maid, but she is too ill to continue in her position. I am quite happy to help care for Miss Juliet until*

*Miss Siddons has recovered, or until you return
with a new nursemaid.
Your servant,
Sally Baker*

Paul read the letter three times through. Perhaps he
could squeeze more meaning from the letter if he read
it again and again. But no. All he knew was that Becky
was ill and unable to continue caring for Juliet.

Becky would never cease caring for Juliet unless she
was terribly sick.

Stark terror seized hold of Paul as he crumpled the
letter in his hands. Becky was dying. She had to be. She
would never shirk her duties as long as she was well.
That headache she had complained of—why hadn't he
called for a doctor? Why had he let her return to Tansley alone? This was his fault entirely.

"I am leaving for home at once," he pronounced
firmly, his voice sounding quite unlike his own. "I'm
going to ride out. Have a horse ready for me in less than
a quarter of an hour."

"Sir—" Edmunds sputtered. "Surely a carriage—"

"I haven't time for a carriage." His heart hammered
against his rib cage. He must see Becky again.

Edmunds nodded, rubbing his hands together briskly.
"An emergency, I suspect."

"Of the worst kind." A fellow couldn't stand still at
a moment like this. He paced up and down the portico.
"I will send word as soon as I am home. Never mind
giving orders to the stable—I'll ready things myself.
There's an employment agency sending round a new

girl to take care of Miss Juliet. Tell them that I have no need for her services any longer."

"Of course," Edmunds replied. "I shall handle the matter, sir. There was a parcel dropped off earlier from a toy shop. Shall I…?"

"Bring that over to the stable. Those are gifts for Miss Juliet. I'll carry them in a saddlebag." Paul jumped off the portico and strode back round toward the stables. "Hurry!" he called.

Never had he quit London in such haste. Within a quarter of an hour, heart still pounding, his hands sweating inside their gloves, he was saddled and on the road, going the breakneck pace of a runner. By carriage, a fellow could make it to Tansley in a week. He was not ceasing, unless it was to change horses, until he reached Becky.

No sleep. No inns. Meals quickly gobbled while he changed horses. The burning desire to see Becky once more overcame all physical discomfort.

Once before, he'd lost someone dear to him, but was he ever in love with her? His mind fell into the rhythm of the road and he gave himself to think. When he and Ruth became engaged, they'd agreed to a yearlong engagement. Long enough for Paul to come out of mourning for his father so they could enjoy a proper wedding. That was what Ruth had wanted. What he didn't realize at the time was how much could happen—not just in the space of a year, but in the space of a few months. Within just weeks of their formal engagement, Ruth contracted a fever and died.

When she died, Ruth took all that had been good in

him with her. She'd given elegance to his rough edges. Offered wise counsel. She'd been his helpmeet. When she passed, he had nothing left. After a most unseemly display of grief, he had merely existed, chasing pleasures when duty was done, never feeling particularly enthusiastic—

Until Becky Siddons entered his life.

Because of Becky, he had learned to accept and acknowledge his failings. He had become a good uncle. He'd even found his way to God. All within a matter of weeks. His life would never be the same again. He must tell her so, now, while he still could.

His courtship of Ruth had been dispassionate. 'Twas almost a foregone conclusion that they would marry, the moment they met. That was why her death was such a jolt. 'Twas not the proper ending to the tale.

Becky—she was different. She was tender, and gentle, and kind, and warm—

He loved her.

"Oh God," he called out as he galloped over the main road. "God, I love her. Please don't take her. Not yet. Please, I beg You. I must tell her so."

The road stretched before him, undulating like a ribbon across the countryside. The pounding of the horse's hooves merely echoed the beating of his heart. He would reach her in time. He would not let her go without telling her how much she meant to him. He would beg her to have him.

The neat, tidily divided compartments of his emotions broke open. He could no longer be a master in some months and a man in others. Nor could he be a different person at home than he was in town. He would never be jaded again. No, life was too precious for cynicism. Thanks to Becky, he was whole once more. Paul Holmes was a master, a brother and an uncle.

And if Becky would have him—if he reached her in time—a husband.

# Chapter Nineteen

"Well, Miss Siddons, I don't think you need worry overmuch." The doctor placed her wrist back on her bed and glanced over at Mrs. Clairbourne and Susannah, who stood wringing their hands. "I think she just has a cold. Not uncommon when one has been traveling. The air in London is bad, especially for one not used to it. Coming home was the correct choice."

Becky nodded. "My headache started when I arrived in town." Along with her burning eyes, and her heartache too, for that matter.

"Bed rest is the best option for now. I recommend a brew of weak tea with honey, hot broth, foods that strengthen. Now that she's home in the fresh air of Tansley, she will perk up in a matter of a week or so. I shall check back in within a few days." The doctor straightened, scribbling some notes on a piece of foolscap. "Mind you, young lady, don't get up the moment you feel a little relief. Find something quiet to occupy your mind until the week has passed."

Becky gave him a wan smile. Her mind was hardly quiet. In fact, it was treading the well-worn path of what-might-have-been with Paul, sometimes veering down the trail of embarrassment—had he seen or suspected how much she cared?—then detouring along a pathway of bitter despair. If she could break the cycle of her thoughts, she might lie peacefully in bed, planning how to extricate herself from the mess in which she was tangled. As it was, she could only close her eyes and see Paul, the stern set of his jaw and the disappointed look in his eyes as he gave her permission to go. Her heart heaved painfully against her chest.

"I'll see to it the young lady follows your orders to the letter," Mrs. Clairbourne responded briskly. "Come, Doctor. I'll see you out."

The doctor gave Becky's arm a final pat and smiled in a kindly manner. "Be good," he admonished. Then he followed the housekeeper out of the room.

Susannah sank against the foot of her bed. "Shall we move you to Goodwin?"

Becky rolled her head back against her pillow. "I suppose so. I can't continue on here. Anyway, Paul—Mr. Holmes—is bringing a new nursemaid to replace me."

"Do you want to talk about it?" Susannah regarded her evenly.

Becky's cheeks burned, but not just with fever. "Does it show?"

"Only to someone who knows you well." Susannah laid a cool hand on her brow. "I shan't make you talk about it if you feel too ill."

"There's nothing much to discuss." Becky turned

away, embarrassment flooding her being. "I just fell in love with a man who didn't care a fig for me. Again."

Susannah patted her arm. "Becky, do not be so hard on yourself. We'll bring you to Goodwin, and you can forget all this nonsense."

A patter of footsteps sounded on the floor, and Becky glanced over. Juliet tiptoed into the room, her eyes opened wide, her doll tucked firmly under one arm. She paused, regarding Becky with a solemn air. Then she leaped onto the bed, snuggling close to Becky's side. Becky tucked her arm around Juliet, drawing her closer.

"No need to worry, chicken," she cooed. "Just a bad cold. The doctor says I'll be fit as a fiddle in just a few days." She stroked the top of Juliet's head. The child had retreated to some place within herself on the journey home, clinging to Becky as she would a piece of driftwood. Poor thing. She must be frightened. How long had Juliana suffered before she died? Did her daughter witness it?

No matter how dreadful Becky felt, she must keep her spirits high before Juliet. The little girl had already endured so much. And—sudden hot tears filled Becky's eyes—she must leave her darling. "Oh, Susannah," she whispered. "I know you are right. It is time for me to go. Even so, my heart is breaking. How can I leave them?"

Becky blinked rapidly. Juliet mustn't see her cry. Not when she was trying to reassure her charge that everything would be fine. "It's just—so unfair. I never meant to fall in love with everyone at Kellridge, from my charge to my master."

"If you've given notice, then there isn't much that

can be done," Susannah responded softly. "I'll take you home with me. Once you are well, perhaps you can think on this again. But until then, Becky, you must simply let the matter go."

"I must bury my feelings. Unrequited love is the very essence of poetry, is it not?"

Becky sniffed.

Being a heroine was horrid.

Susannah rolled her eyes. "Now you're getting maudlin. I'll have to see to the arrangements. You are in no state to do so yourself."

Her door creaked open and Mrs. Clairbourne entered. A smile softened the corners of her mouth when she spied Juliet sitting with Becky on the bed. "See there, missy?" she sang out. "I told you Miss Becky was going to be just fine. No need for worries."

Juliet ducked her head and burrowed closer to Becky.

"We're brewing some weak tea for you now, my dear." Mrs. Clairbourne went about the business of fluffing up Becky's pillows and smoothing her counterpane with brisk good cheer. "And we'll have you settled and comfortable in no time at all. Is there anything else I can bring you? A book from the library, perhaps?"

"I'll have to take my sister home with me," Susannah interjected. "While we appreciate your hospitality, she will be more comfortable at Goodwin. Can someone care for Juliet until Mr. Holmes returns?"

Mrs. C. nodded. "Sally is caring for her already. But the little lamb is so taken with Miss Becky. It will be difficult indeed to pry her away."

"Well, I am afraid we must." Susannah employed the

brisk, cheerful tone she always used when faced with a challenge. "Of course, Miss Juliet may come to visit."

"Has Mr. Holmes found a replacement for me yet?" Becky twirled her hair nervously. "Perhaps he is already coming home."

"He hasn't sent word, which is rather unusual." Mrs. Clairbourne's normally placid brow furrowed a bit. "But we shall press on as we always do. Sally will assist with Miss Juliet. If you really want to go to Goodwin, we can start moving you there this afternoon."

Becky fought a rising tide of panic. "Could Juliet stay with me at Goodwin? We can bring her toys there, and she can play quietly with me. Indeed, I should prefer that to any other arrangement, at least until Mr. Holmes sends word from London." Becky patted Juliet's back with a comforting gesture. 'Twould do her heart good to have her charge about. The child's company would help keep her mind from running on endlessly about Paul.

Susannah shook her head. "Becky—"

"I cannot say goodbye just yet," Becky retorted firmly.

"We cannot remove Mr. Holmes's niece from his house without his express permission," Susannah admonished. "Really, I think the fever is affecting your brain, Becky."

"Your sister is right." Mrs. Clairbourne gave her a kindly smile. "Of course we could bring Miss Juliet to visit. After all, the point of the bed rest is to get you well and on your feet again quickly. If you shirk the doctor's orders, you will likely set yourself up for twice the amount of time in recovery."

"I promise I wouldn't overtax myself." Once again, her heart gave a painful, poignant tug at the thought of leaving Kellridge. "I know how seriously you take your duties here, and I know your dedication is pleasing to Mr. Holmes." Mrs. Clairbourne clasped her hands together and tilted her head, her spectacles winking in the late-morning sunshine. "Listen to your sister, for she has your best interests at heart."

"Thank you, Mrs. Clairbourne. Now, we should begin planning Becky's departure." Susannah gave Becky a brisk smile and rose from the bed.

The housekeeper nodded. "Yes, let's go downstairs. I am certain we will need help in getting her things packed."

Mrs. Clairbourne and her sister turned to go, but both halted as the door slammed open.

Paul stood on the threshold. Wait, could that man be Paul? 'Twas like him, to be sure, but this man was so much scruffier than Paul's usual sophisticated self. The growth of a beard darkened his jaw and chin, and dust clouded his attire. His brown eyes, completely bereft of their usual mocking light, burned into hers. A saddlebag was draped across his shoulder.

She could not swallow. She could scarce draw breath.

"Mr. Holmes—" Mrs. Clairbourne began, but Paul cut her short with a wave of his gloved hand.

"Leave us," he announced curtly.

"This is most unseemly." Susannah drew herself up to her full height. "I will certainly not leave you here with my sister."

Paul spared her a glance, his jaw tightening. "What I have to say, I must say to Becky alone. Again, I say, leave us."

Becky was there. She was alive.

She regarded him with eyes that were startlingly wide in her pale face, but she wasn't gone yet. He still had time.

Something stirred under the counterpane beside Becky. As he watched, his niece emerged from under the blanket, a smile lighting her little face.

"Uncle," she declared. Then she scrambled out of bed and ran to him, her arms outstretched.

He gathered Juliet close and kissed the top of her head, breathing a silent prayer of gratitude. How he'd missed her. Life was a dreary desert without Juliet and Becky. Lord willing, he would never part from either of them again.

"Go with Mrs. Clairbourne and see if there's a cookie for you in the kitchen." He patted her back, directing her toward the housekeeper. Mrs. Clairbourne obliged by taking Juliet's hand, and led her from the room. Susannah looked as if she would speak again, but merely shook her head and left, closing the door with a quiet click.

He dropped his saddlebag on the floor and crossed the room in two quick steps. Becky still said nothing, though her complexion seemed a shade whiter. He paused at her bedside. He couldn't turn away from her. So often on the nightmarish trip home, he'd been certain he'd lost her, or that he would be too late—and the certainty of those thoughts was a knife twist in his gut each time.

"I've spent too much of my life in regret for my own failings." His voice sounded rough, almost angry. Becky blinked, as though his words struck her. He must soften his tone. In his haste, he was making a hash of things. He cleared his throat, ducking his head. "Forgive me. I should start anew."

"Won't you sit down?" Becky asked in a gentle tone. "You look rather...tired."

"I've been riding straight through for days after getting your message," he admitted, sinking onto the edge of her bed. Of course, 'twas highly improper to talk to Becky alone in her bedroom, much less sit on her bed, but he was done with propriety for the time being. "What I have to say cannot wait a moment longer. Rebecca Siddons, I love you. With every fiber of my being, I desire you to be my wife."

He took her hand, so cold and so small, in his. "I am a fool and a coward," he rambled on. The contemplations that had occupied his mind over the past few days—the meditations that kept him awake and riding on down the miles of road—spilled forth. They could not be contained. "You are the heart and the soul of Kellridge. The mother my niece never had. The helpmeet I always needed. You are the most charming, the loveliest girl I've ever encountered, and I must ask you to please, please be mine. I know you are ill—even now you are sick, my poor darling, but I'll take care of you—" He was babbling like a madman.

"Paul." Becky tried to free her hand but he refused

to let go. "You mustn't worry. The doctor says it's only a cold. I'll be right as rain in a few days."

He raised his head, searching her face. "Are you certain? The doctor said you'll recover?" A sudden glad rush poured through his very soul. God was good—and Becky was going to live—

"Yes, Paul. I am so sorry we worried you—"

Paul cradled her close. "Thank You, God," he breathed against her temple. "I cannot thank You enough."

Becky placed her hands against his chest and sat away from him, keeping her chin tucked down. "So now that you know the truth…"

"It doesn't change my sentiments a bit." He finished, smiling down at her in relief. "The question is—how do you feel? You haven't answered me yet."

She raised her chin and gazed at him as though she were seeing him for the first time. Being regarded so intently by one so lovely was rather breathtaking for a fellow, actually. "Everything is different than I thought. When we were in London, I realized I would have to find a new position somewhere else. I couldn't go on making a ninny of myself, the way I had before. But as soon as I returned to Kellridge, I came to the realization that I love you—and Juliet—more than anyone I've ever known. I can conceal my affection for you no longer."

"No more concealment. No more containment." He brushed a lock of wavy dark hair off her forehead. "When you left London I was a miserable excuse for a human being. And when I heard you were ill, I just— I couldn't bear it. I couldn't lose you. You've made me whole again, Becky-girl. Do you see all you have done? But for you being here, I would still be walling myself up inside tidy little boxes. I would continue living an unfulfilled life. I would not have found my way back to God. My life now is so rich and so full of hope—and I must share it with you. I implore you to say yes. Please say you'll be mine."

Becky ran her finger along his jawline, focusing on the path of her fingertip as though uncertain that he was really there. "Yes—if this is real, and not a dream, I'll marry you."

"Becky-girl." He gave full vent and kissed her with all the tenderness and raw, aching fear that had plagued him for the past several days. He was home now, and Becky would be his for the rest of his life, and he need never go without her for another day. How good life was! At length, Becky pressed her hands against his chest, setting herself away from him.

"I cannot be certain this is not some fever-induced dream," she whispered, her eyelashes fanning out over her cheeks, which had turned a most becoming shade of pink.

"I know. I have been reminding myself from the moment I laid eyes on you that everything was going to be fine," he admitted. "You have no idea how afraid I was. I thought for sure I would be too late, and that you would be so ill that I couldn't see you—or worse."

"Why were you so afraid? The note we sent just said that I might need help with my duties until I recovered. I didn't even want to send anything, but Sally, the maid you sent with me, was most insistent. She said that you'd want to know everything about Kellridge, especially if there were a change in the servants' roles, even just temporarily." Becky gave him a small smile. "Why were you so certain that I was on my deathbed?"

Her question was an acute one. Becky was no fool, and his reaction to the message from Kellridge had been extreme. Yet he could not apologize for it, because now he had finally overcome the emotional quagmire that held him prisoner for so long.

Would Becky care to hear the truth behind his mad flight to see her? That he had thought he was losing her, as he had lost Ruth Barclay?

He didn't know much about women, but even so, it was unlikely that Becky would want to hear about another woman while he was holding her in his arms. He must tread carefully indeed. For he was done with walling off his feelings and his past. They were a part of him, and dividing his life up once more between the master and the man, or the private and the public, was something he was no longer willing to do. If Becky was to share in his life, she must know the truth.

"A long time ago, around the time that Father died, I was engaged to a young lady. Her name was Ruth Barclay." He swallowed. Saying her name aloud would never be easy. Some part of him would always grieve her. "Ruth was going to help me run Kellridge. She and I had plans on reining in Juliana. She was a fine woman, and was going to be a good wife."

Becky said nothing, but she didn't pull away from him. That was an encouraging sign.

"Ruth passed away of a fever before we had a chance

to wed. When she died, I don't know what came over me. I was already grieving the loss of my father—indeed, we had postponed our wedding until after I was to come out of mourning—but when Ruth passed, I lost all control." He gathered his strength, for this would be the hardest part of his confession. "When Juliana found herself with child, I vowed to remain fully in control of Kellridge and everything in it forever. I hated for anything to dominate me the way that grief had controlled my life."

"Paul, darling. You take too much upon yourself." She stroked his cheek with a tender gesture. "So much anger. You were a young lad too, you know, and grieving the loss of two very important people in your life. You must forgive yourself. Juliana would have done just as she pleased whether you were at Kellridge or not. Surely you know that now."

"Yes, I suppose that is true," he confessed. "But I could have been a better brother, a better master. I felt so inadequate to both tasks, you see. When I fancied you were dying—I couldn't lose you the way I'd lost Ruth. I ran from London like a madman, Becky. I loved Ruth, I admit. But life without you would be intolerable. I had to tell you before 'twas too late." He couldn't help it. The futile fear and grief he'd been prisoner to for the past few days welled anew, and he kissed her once more. 'Twas too good to be true that Becky was still alive, and would be fine, and loved him despite his many failings.

"Oh, my," Becky breathed, setting herself away from him once more. "I am quite overcome."

For the first time in days, Paul laughed. Becky reddened as he chuckled, turning her face against his chest. "Don't mock me," she ordered, her voice muffled by his jacket.

"Indeed, I do not mock you," he rejoined. "I am just as overcome, myself. I have been given such incredible gifts, Becky-girl. You have helped to open my eyes to them. I love you."

"You love me?" Her question was hesitant, breathless even. As though she could not believe the truth that lay before them.

"More than I ever thought possible." More than he'd felt for Ruth. What he felt for Becky was deeper and purer than anything he had experienced in his life. This was a bond he would nurture and protect for the rest of his days. He had been given a second chance at life, and he would never let it slip through his fingers again. "With you by my side, Becky-girl, I have all I need."

"I love you, too. I was so certain I was just being a ninny once more. I thought I had fallen in love with a man who would never feel the same about me. I vowed to be sensible, to find a new position and forget about you both. Once I returned, I realized how difficult it would be to let you both go." She sniffed, rubbing her face against his lapel. "I am so glad I don't have to leave. While it might make a very romantic poem, 'twould be an awful existence."

He couldn't suppress a chuckle as he kissed the top of her head. "Darling Becky-girl. Our romance has just begun." He paused for a moment. It had been too long since he had fun with Becky. She was jolly company and for too long, matters had drifted between life and death for them. "I have something else for you. Can you guess what it is?"

She furrowed her brow. "Is it something…about the new nursemaid?"

"Flora? Poor girl. I sent word that I no longer needed her once I heard from you. Guess again." A grin broke out across his face.

"Do you mean…arrangements for Juliet? I plan to persuade my sister that she's coming with me until the wedding." Becky folded the top of her coverlet down and smoothed it with her hands. "I shan't be without my darling girl. I would miss her too much."

"No. It's not about Juliet. Though I will miss you both terribly, I will honor your wish." He leaned against the footboard. "I know better than to cross swords with you when it comes to Juliet's care."

"Good. I am glad you learned your lesson." She gave a decisive nod.

He couldn't suppress a laugh. "What of me, then, Becky-girl? Shall I waste away from loneliness while my two best girls are away? How shall I spend my time?"

"By doing what you do best," she pronounced. "Being master of Kellridge and managing everything to a nicety until our return."

"Somehow, the thought of being master of Kellridge loses its glamour when I think of being here alone," he admitted. How had he ever existed before Becky and Juliet entered his life? How empty his existence had been. How terribly vast and blank. He gave a quick shudder. How good God was to bring love and warmth to him.

"You'll survive." She pressed her hand over his, smiling. "I have given two good guesses. May I know the truth now?"

"No. Give it one more go." He would savor this moment a bit longer.

Becky pouted, twirling her hair about her finger with that gesture he adored. "Very well. I say that you forgot to tell me that you're really a prince from a foreign land and that I shall be elevated to princess when we are married. There. Is that it?"

Paul roared with laughter. Trust his romantic bride-to-be to come up with such an outlandish scenario. "No, indeed. In a family of staunch Whigs? My father would be appalled."

"I've given my three guesses. Time for you to unveil the truth."

"Only this." Paul reached into his jacket pocket and withdrew the necklace he'd purchased in London. He handed her the leather-bound box. "Go on. Open it."

Becky took the box from him with an almost hesitant gesture. "Oh, Paul." She snapped open the lid. "Oh, upon my word," she breathed.

The amethysts sparkled brilliantly in the morning sunlight. He couldn't have arranged a more breathtaking manner to show off his gift to her, not if he had tried. "Here. Let me help you clasp it."

"What? No. I cannot." She lifted the necklace out of the box, holding the pendants as gently as she would Juliet. "I cannot accept this, Paul. 'Tis far too fine."

"Indeed you can, and you will." He took the necklace from her palm and draped it around her neck, pulling her luxurious waves of dark hair aside so he could properly fasten it. "After you left, I wandered around London in a daze. I purchased an entire boatload of toys for Juliet, but I wanted something special for you. As soon as I saw these jewels, I knew they would be perfect. They just match your eyes." He stood back, admiring his handiwork. "I was right, you know. You look lovely. I mean, you would look lovely anyway, even without the necklace. A fellow feels a certain satisfaction when he buys his fiancée something truly elegant."

"I can't accept it though, Paul." Becky's pretty face reflected true distress. "I have nothing to give you in return. I mean, I could make you some lace or some such, but I need time to prepare."

He sank down beside her on the bed, wrapping his arms about her shoulders. "You have no idea what you've given me. Before you came into my life, I was a wastrel and an idiot. I looked only to dubious sources of what I thought would bring me pleasure. Of course, I had no inkling of a spiritual life. But you changed all of that. And I am infinitely richer because of your presence in my life."

"Somehow it doesn't seem enough." She rolled her head against his shoulder.

"Your love is more than enough. You are downright generous." He squeezed her gently. "No more nonsense about not accepting my gift. For one thing, it brought me great pleasure to buy it for you. I like the idea that I shall have a wife to whom I can give pretty and stylish gifts. Moreover, it is I who worries about it not being adequate. If you continue to protest, then I shall have no other recourse than to go out and buy something truly outrageous and ostentatious. So be forewarned."

She chuckled, burrowing her head closer. "I know you far too well to accept that challenge, Paul. So, I merely say, thank you for the necklace. It's exquisite and I shall treasure it always."

He tightened his hold on her, resting his chin against the crown of her head. "Just as I shall treasure you."

## Chapter Twenty

This was his wedding day. Even though Paul had antic-ipated this event for what seemed like forever, the feel-ing of disbelief still clung as the carriage rolled toward Goodwin Hall. He shook his head. At any moment he might awaken, only to find that this was all a dream. That Becky had never accepted his hand, or that Juliet had never come to live with him. He shuddered. What a nightmare that would be.

The carriage pulled to a halt in front of the hall and he leaped out without waiting for the coachman. Shield-ing his eyes from the sun, he glanced up at the second-story windows. Perhaps he could catch just a glimpse of Becky. Seeing her so seldom, when he was used to seeing her throughout every day, was dispiriting. And rather depressing, if a fellow admitted it.

The front door opened, and Daniel stepped out onto the portico. "It's no use searching for Becky, old man," he said with a laugh. "She's in the back of the house and under the strict supervision of her sisters. There's no way you'll see her before the wedding."

"That's too bad." He shoved his disappointment to one side. He would see Becky soon, and by the end of the morning, she would be his wife. He could wait a tiny bit longer. But…just a tiny bit. "Is Juliet with them?"

"Yes, of course. Juliet cannot bear to be apart from Becky, you know that. Besides, she, too, is getting dressed up. I vow the Siddons sisters have made her a veritable doll." Daniel clapped him on the shoulder, turning him away from the house. "Come, we'll see to the arrangements in the chapel. Not that there's much to do, mind you. Everyone at Goodwin has been busy perfecting every last detail. But it might keep you occupied and calm your nerves."

"I'm not nervous." Paul shrugged. "Just impatient. I've missed both my girls."

"Not nervous?" Daniel crowed. "I don't believe it. Why, I was beside myself with anxiety by the time my wedding day rolled around."

"I know," Paul responded dryly. "I was there, offering you a drink which you declined. Susannah's good influence had quite overtaken you by that point."

"And I can tell that you haven't touched a drop yourself." Daniel slashed at a bit of shrubbery with his walking stick as they passed. "How long have you been abstaining?"

"Weeks now. I had a conversion of sorts when we were in London." Paul sighed. There hadn't been much time to talk to Daniel about the transformation he had undergone. First and foremost in his mind, he had been concerned about getting Daniel's permission to wed Becky. And once he had that, there had been a license to procure and a wedding to plan. "Once you told me that the Siddons girls work on a man like a tonic. Do you remember saying that?"

Daniel chuckled. "I do. It was after my wedding, when you were looking so downcast and, at the same time, so arrogant. I wanted you to find the same happiness I did. Susannah, Becky and even Nan are each extraordinary in their own way."

"Well, Becky worked on me like a tonic. With her help and encouragement, I opened my heart to God's love. And all at once, the driving need for drinking and other dark pastimes lost its hold on me. And now, I feel I can truly be a good husband and a caring father. I want you to know that I will take care of Becky always." Paul fought a rising lump in his throat. He wasn't going to go all weepy and soft now, of course not. He was still in control of himself. He was still a man. But he couldn't deny this strangely humble feeling and this desire to explain his transformation to his good friend.

"I knew you would, old chap. Even before I knew that you had completely opened yourself to God. When you returned from London, I could see you had utterly changed. And I told myself it was just a matter of time before Becky helped you find your way to Christ as well." Daniel paused, turning to look him in the eye. "I am mighty pleased to hear that it has already happened, though."

"I wouldn't have asked for her hand if it hadn't," Paul admitted. And that was the truth. Until he had become a whole man, body and spirit, he would never have dreamed he could ask Becky to be his.

Daniel nodded, a kindly light in his eyes. They continued on to the little clearing in the woods where the family chapel at Goodwin beckoned, drawing him on to the next, and the best, episode of his life. "You'll have the chance to see Reverend Kirk," Daniel remarked as he opened the door. "He married Susannah and me, you remember. A fine man of the cloth who has helped me quite a bit on my spiritual journey. He's conducting the ceremony—we wouldn't have a wedding at Goodwin without him."

"I look forward to seeing him again." His memories of Susannah and Daniel's wedding were hazy—wrapped in the layers of mockery and cynicism in which he used to find comfort. It would be good to meet the reverend, as a man made new. He followed Daniel into the chapel, and Reverend Kirk was sitting on the front pew. The older man rose, a smile spreading across his wrinkled face.

"Mr. Holmes, how good to see you again." Reverend Kirk extended his hand. "Especially on such a blessed occasion."

"Reverend Kirk, thank you for coming here today." Paul clasped his hand warmly. "I am so glad you are officiating."

Behind them, a gentle buzz ensued as his tenants and servants, as well as those of Goodwin Hall, began to file into the pews. The ceremony would begin in just a few moments if people were already beginning to arrive. And in less than an hour, Becky would be his wife.

He had thought of this moment often throughout the interminable wait for the license. What would he feel like? What would his thoughts be? And now he knew. All his old conceit melted away, warmed by Becky's love. He was utterly humbled. Becky knew all about him and yet she had agreed to be his despite his many flaws.

"My son, I look forward to seeing you over at St. Mary's any time you and your wife can attend," Reverend Kirk said.

Paul turned back toward the reverend. Wife. How good that sounded. "Thank you, Reverend. I confess it's been far too long since I drove to Crich and attended services at your church. We look forward to it. In fact, I would think of it as a way to mark my new life."

"New life?" The older man smiled. "As a married man, I presume?"

"As a married man, yes, but also as one who has found faith," Paul admitted. He wanted everyone to know it—he who had concealed and boxed in his feelings for so long.

"I am so glad to hear it." A warm light glowed in Reverend Kirk's eyes.

"Listen to Reverend Kirk and lean on him often," Daniel piped up from beside them. "He has been a rock on my journey of faith."

"I shall." Paul nodded at both of them. He had so much more than he ever dreamed. Reverend Kirk and Daniel would both be there to help him if his courage flagged. Becky would be by his side. And Juliet would grow up under his care, a living reminder of his dear, maddening Juliana.

These people, all of them, were integral to his existence, when he had spent years feeling so very alone in the world. Like the jigsaw puzzle he'd brought Juliet from London, he was incomplete without all these pieces.

He was a whole man now, full in spirit, and his bride was the one who had guided him to the Lord. If he could, he would climb onto the chapel roof and shout it to the world. He had so much to atone for, and yet, he was excited beyond measure to begin the process.

"Oh, Becky, do hold still. I cannot tie your bonnet with any degree of success if you keep wriggling," Nan moaned, tugging the brim of Becky's straw bonnet down.

"I can't help it. Where is Juliet?" Becky glanced around the room she'd occupied since coming to Goodwin. "I don't see her anywhere." It wasn't like Juliet to just disappear, and not being able to see her caused Becky's already jumpy nerves to fray.

"She is with one of the servants, don't fret." Susannah knelt beside her, fluffing out her skirt. "Now, I think you are ready." She stepped back a pace and considered Becky from head to toe. "You look lovely."

"Do I?" Becky turned to the looking glass and studied her reflection. The bonnet Nan made especially for the occasion was nothing at all like the practical, sensible creations she sold in the shop. No, this was a delightful confection, with froths of lace lining the brim and pretty ribbon roses clustered around the sides. A broad pink ribbon held the bonnet in place under her chin, and Susannah had tied it in a particularly fetching bow. The overall effect, when paired with her white silk gown and her amethyst necklace, was breathtaking. "I've never owned anything as beautiful as this ensemble," she gasped, touching the neckline of her gown with a tentative hand. "I feel like a princess."

Nan kissed her cheek. "You look absolutely wonderful."

"Come now, girls. Let us all embrace before we walk over to the chapel." Susannah held out her arms, and Becky and Nan drew close as she hugged them tightly. It was a sweet gesture, one that brought tears to Becky's eyes, but their relationship would never be the same again. Her life and her purpose was now inextricably bound to Paul and to Juliet, and the mere thought of being able to go home to Kellridge caused her heart to leap in her chest.

The triumvirate had, as she suspected before, collapsed. But she would always love her sisters, no matter what.

"I love you all." She sighed. "Thank you for making my wedding day so perfect. A bride could not ask for more."

Susannah grabbed a posy of sweet pea and violets and handed them to her. "Your bouquet, my dear. We love you, too. I am so happy to see you happy, Becky."

"I love you, too," Nan added, but her voice was a little reserved and her eyes downcast. Poor Nan. Was she feeling left out? Becky placed her hand on her sister's arm as her bedroom door flew open.

"Becky!" Juliet flew into the room and hugged her around the waist. Becky reached down to pat her darling's shoulder, and gasped in horror. Juliet's fine lawn dress was streaked with mud. Her curls, so neatly arranged by Susannah only an hour ago, were now a mass of tangles down her back.

"What on earth have you been into?" Becky extricated herself from Juliet's embrace and set her posy aside. Then she glanced down in growing dismay. Even Juliet's slippers were caked with mire.

"Mud pies," Juliet proclaimed happily. She squeezed Becky around her waist once more, burrowing her cheek into her white silk skirts.

"Upon my word, she is filthy! Where is the servant who was supposed to be watching her?" Susannah strode out into the hallway. "No one is here," she said. "They must have been called away for the ceremony." She came back into the room. "Child, you are a sight."

Juliet nestled closer to Becky and hid her face.

"She's ruined your gown," Nan piped up. "Oh, dear. You are smudged from head to toe."

Becky patted Juliet's back tenderly, staring down at her damaged dress. "Well, I did look rather fine. For a few moments." She couldn't suppress a chuckle. "This is absolutely perfect." For so it was. They had managed to smooth the rough edges from Juliet, but she would always be herself. She would never become a docile little lady, and that was all right. In fact, it was brilliant.

"But your storybook wedding! Whatever are we going to do?" Nan began pacing, as was her habit.

"You're needed at the chapel in just a few moments. Everyone will be waiting."

"I'll go and ask them to delay the ceremony," Susannah pronounced. "In the meantime, Nan, help Becky and Juliet to clean up. If their gowns are too spoiled, well, they will simply have to put on something else. It's not ideal, but at least they will be clean."

Becky shook her head firmly. "No, indeed. We'll go as we are now."

Her sisters let forth a chorus of distressed cries.

"You cannot be serious!"

"Don't be absurd!"

"I am serious, and I am not absurd," she rejoined. "Once I had dreamed of a life where everything was just so. In my romantic fantasy, I married a handsome, faultless man, lived in a small and cozy house, and in time, I would have a beautiful, bouncing baby to call my own. It was a pretty little flight of fancy, but rather empty. I wouldn't wish any of it back. My storybook wedding needs nothing more than this mite here." She gave Juliet's cheek a gentle pinch. "Along with Paul, scars and flaws and all."

"But…you're a mess." Susannah shook her head.

"Nay, we're authentic." Becky gave her sisters a satisfied smile. "This is the wedding and the life I want. It's better than anything I could have imagined."

Susannah cast her arms up in the air and heaved a gusty sigh. "Very well."

"It's bizarre, but if it's your wish…" Nan shrugged her shoulders.

"It is." Becky took Juliet's grubby hand in hers and grabbed her posy. "Let us go to the chapel."

Her sisters followed her through the back corridors of Goodwin and out to the garden. The chapel wasn't far, just a short walk to the clearing in the woods. But every step was an eternity. Would she ever get there? Her eagerness to see Paul was overwhelming, causing her breath to come in short bursts.

At last they reached the chapel door. "Here. Let us go in first," Susannah muttered, tugging Nan into place in front of Becky. "We'll save the best for last."

Becky smiled, choking down a laugh at Susannah's sarcastic tone. Trust her sisters to only care about appearances. She may not be a romantic any longer, but she would never lose her artistic touch. And this was art. Between them, she and Paul had created a beautiful life at Kellridge, one that she was impatient to continue.

The little church was packed with people. She picked out familiar faces in each pew as they walked in up the aisle, mostly tenants and servants from both houses. Becky smiled broadly at Mrs. Clairbourne as they passed. The housekeeper's eyebrows shot up to her hairline when she spied Becky's dress and Juliet's mud-caked attire. They would certainly hear from that good lady after the ceremony.

All that must wait, and it didn't matter now, for her sisters marched over to their pew and she spied her husband-to-be for the first time in too long.

At first, his eyes glowed with an intensity that made her heart pound in her chest. But then, an incredulous look spread across his face. "Are you quite all right?" he muttered as she drew close to his side.

"Of course," she whispered in return. "One has to make mud pies on one's wedding day." She tugged at Juliet's hand. "Right, little one?"

Juliet gave a vigorous nod.

Paul quirked his eyebrow. "I see. I gather my niece was being rather naughty."

"Not at all," Becky assured him. "She was merely being herself, and I could not ask for a better niece."

Paul placed his arm around her shoulder and drew her closer. "Are you certain this is what you want?"

She rested her head on him for just a moment, savoring his strength. "I couldn't dream of anything else," she replied.

Reverend Kirk began the ceremony, and while she paid heed to his words, her mind drifted a bit—back to the moor, on the day that she found Lieutenant Walker had jilted her. What if he hadn't? What if she had gotten her heart's desire then? She suppressed a shudder. Nay, the Lord knew what He was about. He knew that she needed Paul and Juliet, and He had found a way to bring them all together.

They would never part again.

She glanced out from under her bonnet brim at her soon-to-be husband's scarred cheek and clasped Juliet's dirty hand more tightly in hers. What she'd told her sisters was true. Once she had dreamed of a perfect life, filled with romance and mystery. But life with Paul and Juliet was infinitely more satisfying.

As Reverend Kirk asked her to repeat her vows, she

did so with nary a tremble in her voice. Then she smiled at her husband.

True romance did not come to her on a windswept moor. No, it came to her in the hundreds of tender glances, the camaraderie of conversation at the end of the day, at the shared concern over a tiny human being. Romance was in the daily round of setting out a routine for a headstrong child, in caring for a man with a wounded cheek and in helping that man find a path into spirituality.

As her husband folded her into a tender embrace to seal their troth, Becky melted into his hold.

Truly, a heroine could not ask for a happier ending.

\* \* \* \* \*

Dear Reader,

I confess that children were very much on my mind as I wrote Becky's story. In fact, my own daughter Olivia and one of her friends, Taylor, were the inspirations for Juliet's character. Olivia is now seven, but when she was two, she and Taylor ruled their tiny classroom at our church's Mothers' Day Out. They were the smallest of the group, but both had iron wills and it was astonishing to see the other children defer to them in every little thing. I had fun recalling those memories as I wrote about Juliet.

Children are also on my mind for a different, and sadder, reason. My daughter's friend Maddie passed away from brain cancer just a month ago. Maddie battled against that terrible disease with everything she had. Her parents were her staunch and unyielding advocates. Watching her battle taught me a lot about strength and bravery. Her battle also enlightened me about pediatric cancer. I had no idea how underfunded the studies are for cancer in children, and how few options are open to pediatric cancer patients and their families.

To that end, I am donating ten percent of my royalties on this book to CURE Childhood Cancer, a nonprofit cancer research foundation dedicated to finding cures for childhood cancer. It's not much, but it's a step in the right direction. If you want to learn more about Maddie's story, simply search #fightformaddie on Google or any other internet search engine.

If pediatric cancer has touched your life in some way,

I would like to hear your story. You may email me at lilygeorgeauthor@gmail.com. I am also on Twitter as @lilygeorge2, and on Facebook as LilyGeorgeAuthor.

Thank you for allowing me to share this story.
Blessings,
*Lily*

## Questions for Discussion

1. In the beginning of the book, Becky has a rather fixed view of what her life should be. By the end of the book, her entire view of the world has changed. Have you ever been frustrated when you thought life should go a certain way, and then it changes on you?

2. Paul loses his faith when his fiancée, Ruth Barclay, passes away. Is this a normal reaction? Can grief take away your faith? Can it enrich your faith?

3. Becky is secretly jealous of Susannah's marriage. What is the most effective way to deal with jealousy?

4. Paul divides his life neatly between debauchery and responsibility. Is this a good way to live?

5. Paul allows his siblings to follow their own paths while he shoulders all of the family's burdens and responsibilities. Why would an eldest brother do this? What effect does this responsibility have on Paul?

6. Nan and Becky have gone from being very close to very distant because of the responsibilities of

running the millinery shop. Why would running a business put increased pressure on family relationships?

7. Becky and Paul work together to try to bring routine and order to Juliet's life. Do children really need routine?

8. Paul blames himself for Juliana's downfall. But was it really his fault? Have you ever accepted the blame for something you could not control?

9. Becky feels that she is called by God to be Juliet's nursemaid. Do you feel that your career is a calling? How does this affect your daily life?

10. Becky also questions her calling as a nursemaid. Have you ever felt uncertain of the plans God has for you? What did you do about your uncertainty?

11. Both Becky and Paul come to the realization that, had they married other people, their lives would not have been as wonderful as they imagined. Have you ever imagined your life should be one way and then found out later something better was around the corner?

12. Discuss Paul's notion of the whole man—one who blends spirituality and responsibility. Does this coincide with your idea of being whole?

13. Becky feels that she must leave Kellridge because she is afraid she cannot mask her feelings for Paul. Then she realizes that she cannot leave Juliet behind. Have you ever felt like you had to stay in an uncomfortable situation because of a child?

14. Paul's conversion to faith starts with John 15:5. Is there a Bible verse that resonates with you?

15. By the end of the book, Juliet has changed a little but still remains true to who she really is. Do you have kids in your life who resist change? How do you work with this challenge?

# REQUEST YOUR FREE BOOKS!

## 2 FREE INSPIRATIONAL NOVELS
## PLUS 2
## FREE
## MYSTERY GIFTS

*Love Inspired*

### HISTORICAL
INSPIRATIONAL HISTORICAL ROMANCE

---

**YES!** Please send me 2 FREE Love Inspired® Historical novels and my 2 FREE mystery gifts (gifts are worth about \$10). After receiving them, if I don't wish to receive any more books, I can return the shipping statement marked "cancel." If I don't cancel, I will receive 4 brand-new novels every month and be billed just \$4.74 per book in the U.S. or \$5.24 per book in Canada. That's a saving of at least 21% off the cover price. It's quite a bargain! Shipping and handling is just 50¢ per book in the U.S. and 75¢ per book in Canada.* I understand that accepting the 2 free books and gifts places me under no obligation to buy anything. I can always return a shipment and cancel at any time. Even if I never buy another book, the two free books and gifts are mine to keep forever.

102/302 IDN F5CN

---

Name _____ (PLEASE PRINT)

Address _____ Apt. #

City _____ State/Prov. _____ Zip/Postal Code

Signature (if under 18, a parent or guardian must sign)

### Mail to the Harlequin® Reader Service:
**IN U.S.A.:** P.O. Box 1867, Buffalo, NY 14240-1867
**IN CANADA:** P.O. Box 609, Fort Erie, Ontario L2A 5X3

**Want to try two free books from another series?**
Call 1-800-873-8635 or visit www.ReaderService.com.

\* Terms and prices subject to change without notice. Prices do not include applicable taxes. Sales tax applicable in N.Y. Canadian residents will be charged applicable taxes. Offer not valid in Quebec. This offer is limited to one order per household. Not valid for current subscribers to Love Inspired Historical books. All orders subject to credit approval. Credit or debit balances in a customer's account(s) may be offset by any other outstanding balance owed by or to the customer. Please allow 4 to 6 weeks for delivery. Offer available while quantities last.

---

**Your Privacy**—The Harlequin® Reader Service is committed to protecting your privacy. Our Privacy Policy is available online at www.ReaderService.com or upon request from the Harlequin Reader Service.

We make a portion of our mailing list available to reputable third parties that offer products we believe may interest you. If you prefer that we not exchange your name with third parties, or if you wish to clarify or modify your communication preferences, please visit us at www.ReaderService.com/consumerchoice or write to us at Harlequin Reader Service Preference Service, P.O. Box 9062, Buffalo, NY 14269. Include your complete name and address.

LIH13R

"What do you do besides work, talk and text on your cell phone, Dale Massey? What do you do for fun?" Faith stepped closer.

Simple fun? He couldn't remember. Every activity had a purpose. Entertaining clients, entertaining women, entertaining his next move as heir to Massey International. "I play tennis, remember?"

Faith shook her head. "The way you play doesn't sound fun at all."

"I play to win. Winning is fun."

She stared at him.

He stared back.

The overhead light bathed Faith in its glow, caressing her hair with shine where it wasn't covered by the knitted hat she wore. Dressed in yoga pants and bulky boots, she looked young.

Too young for someone like him.

"How old are you?"

Faith laughed. "Slick guy like you should know that's no question to ask a woman."

Her hesitation hinted that she might be older than he

thought. She'd graduated college, but when? He raised his eyebrow.

"I'm twenty-seven, how old are you?"

"Thirty."

Faith clicked her tongue. "Old enough to know that all work and no play makes Dale a dull boy."

"You think I'm dull?"

She'd be the only woman to think so. His daily schedule made most people's head spin. Yet this slip of a girl made him feel incomplete. Like something was missing.

Her gaze softened. "You don't really want to know what I think."

He stepped toward her. "I do."

She gripped her mittened hands in front of her. Was that to keep from touching him?

They were close enough that one more step would bring them together. Dale slammed his hands in his pockets to keep from touching her. No way would he repeat today's kiss.

"Honestly, you seem a little lost to me."

He searched her eyes. What made her think that? Lost? He knew exactly where he was going. His future was laid out nice and clear in front of him. But that road suddenly looked cold and lonely.

*Will city boy Dale Massey find a new kind of home in Jasper Gulch, Montana, with the pretty Faith Shaw?*
*Find out in*
*HIS MONTANA HOMECOMING*
*by Jenna Mindel,*
*available November 2014 from Love Inspired.*

# *Her Holiday Family*

by

# WINNIE GRIGGS

### An unexpected gift

Reserved widow Eileen Pierce never considered herself the kind of woman who was cut out to be a mother. She wouldn't know what to do with one child, much less ten. But when handyman Simon Tucker is stranded in Turnabout, Texas, with a group of young orphans at Christmas, she can't turn them away.

Simon knows there's more to Eileen than meets the eye. Though his easygoing demeanor immediately clashes with her buttoned-up propriety, Simon's kindness soon threatens to melt Eileen's stern facade. Simon and the children already upended Eileen's quiet, orderly life; will they do the same to her guarded heart?

*Available November 2014 wherever*
*Love Inspired books and ebooks are sold.*